THE SHEPHERD'S LOVER

Hannah-Alison Cragg

W0309790

First Published in 2021 by Blossom Spring Publishing
The Shepherd's Lover Copyright © 2021 Hannah-Alison Cragg

ISBN 978-1-8382421-6-9

E: admin@blossomspringpublishing.com

W: www.blossomspringpublishing.com

Published in the United Kingdom. All rights reserved under International Copyright Law.

Contents and/or cover may not be reproduced in whole or in part without the express written consent of the publisher.

Names, characters, places and incidents are either products of the author's imagination or are used fictitiously.

Acknowledgments

To my maternal grandparents, thank you for your love, and for introducing me to the English countryside, stately homes and culinary delights.
To my paternal grandparents, for your faith and encouragements.
To my siblings, your daily life has given me an abundant source of material.
To my dad, for your invaluable advice, support and input. Without you this book would have contained a definite overuse of the words 'rushed', 'suddenly' and 'slightly'.
To my mum, for passing your love of books on to me from a young age. Thank you for teaching me the value of words.
And to my shepherd lover, the true inspiration for this book.

To my shepherd lover, this is all for you.

CHAPTER ONE

A Wedding

'Make haste, make haste or else we'll be late! Not today of all days!' the lady cried out whilst straightening one child's hair and hurriedly buttoning up the collar of another. 'Eleanor, Eleanor! Where are you? Why is no one ever here when I need them?'

The lady's husband appeared out of one of the nearby rooms.

'Ah, there you are John!' she exclaimed. 'Please take these jackets and place them in the carriage, in case the weather turns.' She thrust an armful of fabric into the man's arms and ushered him out of the door. Her husband looked first at the bright blue sky, from which a glaring sun was already verging on being too warm, and then back at the jackets.

'Do you really think these are *necessary*?' he asked, but she was gone and with a sigh he passed the jackets to Francis to load into the carriage.

Inside the manor house another door opened and a medium-sized, fair-haired boy appeared. The lady lunged and seized hold of his arm, turning her effervescence towards him.

'Charles, come here at once and sort your hair out. It would not do for you to arrive looking like that and disgrace the whole family, to say nothing of the bride and groom! Now don't raise a breeze,' she scolded as the boy yelped in protest as his mother viciously attacked his hair with a comb she had produced from her personage. 'Eleanor, where *are* you?' his mother called forcefully and the boy winced sharply.

The young lady in question, whom her parents had

christened ‘Eleanor’, was at that moment standing in her room as far away from her mother's agitated acclamations as possible. Stood in front of a full-length mirror, she was slowly and painstakingly turning around, examining her appearance from every obtainable angle to assure herself that there was nothing in her figure that was displeasing or undesirable. And indeed, she could find nothing unsought for which she was extremely thankful, for she had spent the better part of an hour in her bedroom, preparing herself. And there was no question about it, Eleanor looked undoubtedly pretty. On this certain special day she was dressed in a cerulean blue gown of light taffeta which enhanced her slender figure. Her feet were shod with dainty white and gold slippers, which only just peaked out from underneath the hem of her gown. She had hung a plain gold chain around her otherwise bare neck and she wore a gold bracelet around her very petite wrist to match. Eleanor's hair, which she had curled and styled so that it hung lightly in waves around her narrow shoulders, was ash blonde and fell halfway down her back. Her facial features were, like her figure, very pleasing to the eye. Her complexion was pale but with a healthy tint of red in her cheeks, giving her a pleasant look of youthfulness and bloom, and her lips were lush and full. But her eyes were the primary attraction of her face. Several young men had lost their hearts while staring into those sparkling eyes. They were round with long, sweeping eyelashes and their soft ocean blue colour, with just a shimmer of silver, put even the calmest of lagoons to shame.

Content with her appearance Eleanor turned to grasp her satin reticule from where she had abandoned it on her bed. Her eyes flicked briefly around the room to ensure that everything was as it ought to be. Her room was one of her most favourite places in the house; whenever she entered her room it always felt like a breath of fresh air, so she liked to make sure everything was uncluttered and in place. The silk curtains, which were a delicate shade of palest lilac, were drawn back from a sash window, framing the view of verdant ash trees, which were clearly visible from all the windows on the front side of the house. To the right of this window stood a polished desk of rosewood, upon which stood a crystal vase of flowers, a wad of writing paper, an inkwell and a selection of quills. The only other furniture in the room were a rosewood dressing table, a petite chest of drawers, and the full-length mirror, which was bordered by a simple gilded gold frame, enriched with tiny leaves and rosebuds at the corners. The fabric of the covers on Eleanor's bed and that of the headboard were palest lilac to match the curtains and the overall appearance of her bed, with its upholstered headboard, crisp bed linen and array of neatly arranged cushions, looked both welcoming and pretty. The cream panelling of the walls and expansive window guaranteed that the room was always flooded with light during the day. Lavender pouches, which were discreetly stuffed into pillowcases and drawers all around the room, ensured that a subtle, yet sweet fragrance greeted one as soon as one entered the room.

Satisfied, Eleanor ventured out of her room and began to descend the staircase, only to instantaneously be set upon by her flustered mother, who was by now close to hysterics.

'There you are at long last Eleanor! Where have you been all this time? I have sorely been in need of assistance.'

Only when she had finished her wrathful tirade did she observe her daughter's appearance and was immediately appeased.

'Oh Eleanor, you look very elegant and becoming!

Indeed, I am sure you shall shine everyone else down!'

'I'm afraid you're biased mama,' replied Eleanor and she smiled at her mother's abrupt mood changes. Just then her younger siblings Abigail and Ethan stampeded into the hallway, breaking the fragile peace with a deafening squabble.

'Mama, tell Abigail that it is my turn to ride in the front of the carriage. She rode in the front last time!'

'Ooh, you liar! It is most definitely my turn this week. Undeniably! Unquestionably!'

'No it isn't! Mama, tell her!'

Their mother ushered them along the hallway and towards the main door, her active mind running mentally through a list of things she had yet to accomplish in the next few minutes.

'Abigail and Ethan, cease your foolish prattling or else we shall be late. Neither of you will sit in the front, now get going!' she commanded. 'Hurry!'

And with that the busy mother rushed them off towards the carriage, before scurrying off in the opposite direction, calling to her husband as she went. Eleanor smiled. She was accustomed to the hectic and lively household with its equally hectic and lively occupants, and she had grown to love it, even if her chaotic family could at times be acutely exasperating.

The front door opened and her father appeared in the doorway, having seen to his wife's bidding. He was adorned in a white shirt, olive waistcoat, cravat and trousers, and a hat was tucked under his arm. Eleanor's father, Mr John Ashmore, was a thoughtful, passionate and intelligent man, eminently successful in his profession and very considerate, composed and enduring when it came to his family. Eleanor and her father were very alike in numerous ways - they understood each other well and their relationship was admirable.

Mr Ashmore smiled and winked at his eldest daughter before striding composedly after his wife's rapidly receding voice, whistling a jovial tune as he went, quite the contrast to his spouse. A grandfather clock chimed the tenth hour, a cry sounded and not a full ten seconds later Mrs Ashmore rushed back up the corridor with her husband in tow. A bag was swinging from her right arm and in her left hand she clutched a hat, scarf and stray stocking. Eleanor’s dog Rumpus, a small furry thing, was yapping excitedly at the lady’s heels.

'Come Eleanor, we’re leaving!' her mother called to her in passing and Eleanor hurriedly rushed down the last few steps, grasped her shawl and, with a last fleeting glance in the hallway mirror, she hastened to join the assembling family outside.

Amidst shouts of 'Must I wear this tie?' ‘Where did I put my hat?’ ‘The dog has just stolen my glove!' and 'Hurry up, we're already late!' the family piled into the carriage. Eleanor was the last to leave the house. Francis was waiting for her, the carriage door held obligingly open and she smiled her thanks to him as she slid into her seat, just as her mother was on the brink of tears, convinced that they would arrive too late. Francis assumed his position as driver and with a light jolt the carriage started. Francis was their coachman on special occasions, gardener and shepherd most days, man servant when needed and groomsman all week.

'Do not trouble yourself Mama,' said Eleanor in a pacifying sort of voice. 'For it is less than half an hour to Faymor Hall and we are departing in very good time.'

Her mother thrashed about for a minute with the pile of jackets, scarves and bags which she had positioned on her knee, before settling down.

'Yes, we have left in plenty of time! And even if we are late, it would not greatly matter. The ceremony was held this morning I hear, attended only by the very closest members of the family. We are simply invited to the celebration, a much more fluid affair, where we may come and go as we please.'

Eleanor's youngest brother interrupted.

'But I thought it took a really long time to travel so far.'

As the carriage turned out of the driveway of their estate, Eleanor's elder brother, Charles, leaned in eagerly to explain.

'You see Ethan, it all depends on the direction of the wind and the structure of the wheels. If, for example, we should be voyaging into the north, against the wind, we would be noticeably slower than if we were travelling south. And then of course, you've got the conglomerate wheel classifications, which can also impede the optimum speed.'

'Ah!' said Ethan and nodded understandingly. Fortunately, Charles failed to notice the acutely confused look on his younger brother's face.

Charles was a very well-read and intelligent boy who was also blessed with an almost accidental handsomeness. However, his deep musings and near-constant internal calculations gave him a slightly absent and glazed look. Before Charles could expand on the complex science of carriage wheels, Abigail chimed in.

'I wonder what colour the bridal flowers will be? And will she have pretty shoes, do you think? And is the groom handsome? I find it most disappointing that we have not met him yet, but he must be exceedingly rich! I hope she wears a gown with lots of lace. They are quite the most attractive dresses for a wedding, don't you think Eleanor?'

Abigail was a couple of years younger than Charles and a couple of years older than Ethan. Her hair, which she had inherited from her mother, was thick, wavy and auburn. Her doe-eyes, which were almond shaped and chestnut brown, she had inherited from her father. A light smattering of freckles were scattered across her nose and cheeks and her mouth was invariably open, either talking about something or apologizing for something.

'Hmhmm,' Eleanor answered distractedly, as she watched the scenery pass by out of the window of the landau. Abigail looked at her sister in exasperation.

'Mama, Papa, Eleanor wasn't listening to a word I said!' she protested.

'Hardly surprising considering the amount you talk,' Charles murmured. He had little patience with his sister's chatter. Abigail gave her brother a deeply hurt look, but said nothing more, instead choosing to follow her older sister's example and observe the passing countryside of Mayhaven.

Mayhaven, the county in which they lived, was known far and wide for its vitality and life. The people who lived there were, on the whole, healthy and thriving, with open hearts, sharp minds and strong bodies. The countryside of Mayhaven embodied the very best nature had to offer: from rolling hills, to sparkling brooks, to fast-flowing streams, densely pined forests, rich orchards, meadows of wildflowers, luxurious estates, homely cottages and the finest food and flowers the country possessed - this was surely the place to live. The soil in Mayhaven was exported to other counties who hoped they too might be able to produce such deliciously sweet fruits and magnificent blooms if they could but obtain the same quality of rich, dark soil which abounded here. But it would seem that there was some magic in the air for nowhere else outside of Mayhaven could come close with their efforts, whether they used the same exported soil or not.

The water in Mayhaven was also a marvel and a mystery to many. Every well dug in Mayhaven, be it in Felowspring, Wenerfield, Talisbrook or Denersdath, consistently provided the clearest, purest imaginable water, which always tasted as cold and refreshing as if one had dipped one's hands into a mountain stream gushing directly out of the rock face itself, while elsewhere water was considered a risky substance for consumption, being so often polluted in one way or another.

Mayhaven was surely not perfect; it was said that some more potentially unsavoury characters lived in the densely wooded Wenerfield and in every seemingly perfect place there are sure to still exist disagreements and more ugly aspects, which one would rather not mention. But, taken as a whole, it was surely one of the nicest places to live.

With Abigail happily and *silently* occupied and Ethan too excited to talk, a peaceful calm fell on the carriage. The silence, however, was short-lived, for it was not long before they sighted Faymor Hall. This was the cue for a renewed outburst of excited chatter and fantastical speculations from the younger members of the family, most of which were either entirely unrealistic or utterly nonsensical.

Faymor Hall was a handsome and impressive looking building, constructed from sizeable grey slabs of rock. However, very little of the original material of the structure could be distinguished due to the vibrant array of ivy, climbing roses and other such vines. These plants stretched far across the stonework of the house, almost exclusively concealing the grey stone beneath. It was said that Faymor Hall had once, many years ago, belonged to royalty, which accounted for the extensive grounds attached to the building. The fields and hills to the south and east of Faymor Hall had been left wild and untamed, whereas the west side had been cultivated and preserved exquisitely. A stately garden, fastidiously maintained, stretched out, complete with moss green lawns, tidy flower beds and a graceful water feature at its centre. When standing at the entrance to Faymor Hall one could just make out a little gate in the far corner of this garden, set in a tall brick wall, leading to the orchards. Although the season of blossom had all but ended elsewhere, not so in Mayhaven. A glimpse of high-reaching trees, some laden heavily with fruit, others adorned with cherry blossom, could be caught over the brick wall.

Situated on the summit of one of the lower hills in Mayhaven, Faymor Hall could only be reached by means of a winding, cobbled path, laid centuries ago and quite worn down by feet, hooves and wheels. The Ashmore carriage had now reached the foot of this path. And so it was that the carriage began its jerky ascent, not at all helped on its way by the inquisitive heads precariously poking out of its windows, causing the carriage to rock dangerously. Ignoring their parents' wise, sensible (and in their view, boringly safe) counsel, the children craned their necks out of the carriage as far as their spines would allow, each of them anxious to be the first to spot anything of interest.

Eventually, after what seemed like an eternity to the youngest members of the family, the carriage drew to a halt in front of a staircase leading to the main entrance of Faymor Hall. The wheels had barely stopped turning when Ethan and Abigail simultaneously flung open the doors of the carriage and fell over themselves to run up the stairs. Charles was slightly delayed for he wanted to conclude his interrogation of their obliging coachman Francis (the topic of Charles' questioning was the intermediate speed of a conventional carriage and the possible benefits of developing rectangular carriage wheels), though he also shortly followed his younger siblings, leaping down from the front of the carriage where he had been questioning Francis and up the stairs two at a time, his combed hair becoming tangled in the wind and his once smart attire becoming rumpled and dishevelled. Eleanor, despite her eagerness to make the acquaintance of the other guests and explore the palatial house, remembered her age and manners and respectfully waited until Francis was prepared for them to disembark. Then, however, her curiosity overcame her and, leaving her parents to follow at their own leisurely pace, she hurried up the steps and through the open doors into Faymor Hall.

Looking around, Eleanor found herself in a spacious, grand and well-lit entryway which was, to her surprise, already crowded with guests. Searching the multitude of people, she could just make out her brothers and sister ploughing their way through the crowd, blissfully oblivious to the guests they shoved or stood on in the process. Eleanor was soon joined in the doorway by her parents and the three of them entered the room together. Almost immediately they were set upon by a vivacious and somewhat overly enthusiastic distant aunt on her mother's side, who insisted on engaging them in a lengthy conversation about the joys of such a happy occasion. It did not take long for Mrs Ashmore to also energetically participate in the discussion. This involved many frenzied hand gesticulations and loud exclamations, which drew a certain amount of, for Eleanor and her father, unwanted attention to their little group.

Tactfully excusing herself, Eleanor withdrew to explore alone. First, however, she thought she ought to seek out the bride and groom, so as to pay her respects and add her good wishes to the ever-growing pile surrounding the couple. Finding them was not a strenuous task, for more than half the guests had gathered in a tight circle around the newlyweds. Reaching them however, proved to be more involved. Eleanor managed to press through the compact ring of people into the inner circle, thanks to her slender build, and was able to examine the bride for the first time. She was wearing an ivory white dress with a plunging neckline, short puffed sleeves and a lace ruffle around the hem. She wore a petite lace veil in her hair. Her facial features were pretty, in a harsh, striking way, and were framed by beautiful chocolate brown hair which was pinned in curls to the back of her head. Laila, the bride, had been a close friend of Olivia and John Ashmore, her mother and father, for as long as Eleanor could remember. Laila exclaimed in delight as she saw Eleanor standing by her and embraced her warmly.

'Look, Kiran,' she said, tugging at the arm of her husband's sleeve and lightly pushing Eleanor forward. 'This is the young lady I was telling you about.'

Kiran turned round and gazed at Eleanor eagerly. Then he bowed, took Eleanor's hand and lightly kissed the surface.

'A pleasure to make your acquaintance, Miss,' Kiran said sincerely, straightening up and placing an arm around his bride's waist. They both smiled at Eleanor warmly.

'How are you Eleanor?' Laila inquired.

'I am well,' Eleanor replied cheerily.

'And your family? Are they also all in good health?' Laila asked.

'Yes,' Eleanor smiled. 'They are all in good health and high spirits to be here.'

Laila laughed: 'I can imagine!'

A voice from somewhere in the crowd called for the

bride and groom and, with apologetic glances, Laila and Kiran excused themselves in order to greet the next well-wisher. Eleanor did not mind, for she could hear faint strains of music floating in from one of the rooms, indicating that the dancing would soon begin.

Sidling her way out, she sought the source of the music, bumping into Abigail and Ethan as she did so. Abigail immediately seized Eleanor by the arm with an urgency in her voice as she exclaimed dramatically:

'There you are! At long last! We have been searching for you for hours!'

Eleanor sensibly refrained from pointing out that this was not possible, as they had arrived less than half an hour ago. Ethan, however, was not so tactful.

'No we haven't Abby!' he corrected his sister matter-of-factly. 'We only started searching a few minutes ago.'

Eleanor fought to hide a smile at her brother's outright truthfulness, but Abigail merely brushed her brother's comment aside with a wave of her hand.

'Details aren't of any significance now,' she said haughtily. 'What I was going to say, before I was rudely interrupted...' here she turned to glare at her brother whose attention was by now solely focused on the source of his next meal.

Ethan had spotted out of the corner of his eye an adjoining room where he could see a long table, laden with food. He didn’t know exactly what the food was but even his inexperienced eyes could recognise that it looked good. Had he perhaps been a little more knowledgeable in cuisine and had he drawn a little closer to the feast table, he might have recognized a towering pyramid of marzipan sweets, skilfully sculpted to perfection, standing next to a large tray of jam tartlets and dessert biscuits, behind which roughly one hundred footed parfait glasses stood, filled with whipped syllabub, in the flavours lemon and peach. Alongside these was a vast bowl of fruit trifle, several smaller bowls with cranberry and orange jellies, and of course, the wedding cake. Abigail however had not noticed.

'What I was going to say is, that the dancing will be starting any minute now and they have specifically requested for you to be in attendance! You are to dance at the top of the line of dancers, beside Kiran and Laila, and they are going to be opening the dancing any minute. Hurry, hurry!'

She turned to leave, but a sudden afterthought came to her. 'Oh, and Laila said they've got *iced creams*!'

And with that Abigail released her hold on her sister's arm and leapt off to find another victim to vent her boundless energy and chatter upon. Eleanor followed Ethan into a spacious ballroom, where the floor was gleaming like a mirror and the musicians were, in one corner, preparing to play. Kiran and Laila were gliding onto the polished dance floor where they were to open the first set with a quadrille; other guests had gathered around tables and chairs at the edge to observe and converse. Seeing her parents seated at a table on the other side of the room with her aunt and uncle, Eleanor made her way towards them, Ethan drifting distractedly behind her.

'Ah, there you are!' Mrs Ashmore proclaimed. 'I was hoping you would not miss the beginning of the dancing.' She turned to Eleanor's aunt and uncle, her own sister and her brother-in-law. 'Eleanor is a very gifted dancer, so graceful.'

Eleanor blushed and quickly hushed her mother.

'What is the matter? I was simply telling the truth,' Mrs Ashmore replied indignantly. Eleanor was about to retort but was saved at that moment by the musicians striking up their instruments and commencing to play. It was a lively tune which set Eleanor’s foot tapping the rhythm as she watched Laila's skirts twirl and Kiran's shoes tap.

Whilst she watched, Eleanor felt the curious sensation of a pair of eyes resting on her, scrutinising her, observing her, studying her - and the feeling unsettled her. Eleanor shook her head slightly and laughed inwardly at herself, determined not to let her vivid and on occasion exaggerated imagination run away with her and distract her from being present. However, she could not thoroughly shake off this feeling that she was being watched. Her mind was quickly diverted to more pleasant things when her cousin, Taylor, who was a few years her senior, energetically sauntered up to her and asked her to dance.

'Would you do me the honour, M'lady?' Taylor asked with an elaborate bow and dramatic flourishing of the arms.

'Gladly,' Eleanor replied, matching his grin, and she meant it. She allowed him to lead her out to the centre of the ballroom and they assumed their starting positions, beside Laila and Kiran. Other couples were now joining the bride and groom for the next set of dancing in the centre of the ballroom.

Taylor was moderately tall for his age, with a shock of jet-black hair and correspondingly dark brown eyes to match. His rather oversized feet and melodramatic mannerisms gave the inclination of a hopeless dancer, however Taylor was very light on his feet and full of energy, making him a very entertaining, yet fully capable dance partner. As they now curtsied and bowed and began to dance an energetic polka, Taylor led Eleanor faultlessly through the steps, even finding the breath to fill her in on the condition of his dog, Jeffrey. A few years ago, Taylor had found a little orphaned whelp by the side of a road and had adopted him. The 'whelp' had now grown thrice the size and had extremely long reddish fur, a big wet nose and a mouth which constantly slobbered. Taylor, who liked to travel, had had to find someone to look after his pet while he was away. An elderly man by the name of Donald had kindly offered to assist, except Taylor worried now that Jeffrey was getting too big for Donald to manage, for he already reached the old man's waist and Taylor was of the opinion that Donald required supervision just as much as his dog Jeffrey did! Eleanor listened with interest to all he said but could not respond; she was far too out-of-breath from the dance to waste precious oxygen by talking. Taylor didn't mind though, he unceasingly had enough words circling round in his brain to last them both.

However graceful Taylor was while dancing, that elegance was not far-reaching, for the minute he stepped off the floor he became a walking liability. As the dance ended Taylor proceeded to escort Eleanor to her parents, but in the short distance between their current position and the table Taylor managed to collide spectacularly with a servant bearing a tray of wine glasses, sending them and the unfortunate servant sprawling on the ground. Taylor apologetically assisted the man to his feet but, while enthusiastically brushing the man down, managed to tear his cravat. The servant looked close to tears and Eleanor tactfully intervened, pulling Taylor away by the arm and forcefully leading him to a seat next to her parents.

As the celebrations wore on Eleanor danced with various other partners. Some of these dances were very enjoyable, for many of the gentlemen could dance well and were amiable and interesting to talk to. Nevertheless, a few were a painful test of patience and endurance for poor Eleanor after she had been stood on, bumped into and jerked around by some less rhythmically gifted gentlemen. She bore it all stoically nevertheless and even managed to smile and thank them at the end.

Meanwhile Abigail, who occasionally suffered from delusions of grandeur and liked to think she was just as grown up as Eleanor, tried to remember and put into practice the steps to a few of the dances, but only proceeded in tripping up everyone around her. After this had happened recurringly, she was cordially yet firmly asked by her father to vacate the floor, so as to not endanger her other companions. Abigail did so, but not without many scowls and sullen grumblings muttered under her breath. Charles was nowhere to be found but, as this was not an irregular occurrence, nobody thought anything of it. Perhaps he had managed to smuggle a book into his waistcoat pocket. Ethan, who was too small to join in the dancing and too young to understand the intercourse of the elders, busied himself with a generous portion of the decadent fruit trifle which had been served to him by an elderly woman who could not resist an innocent and adorable face. And, alongside his dish of trifle, Ethan was also given, to his utmost delight, a bowl of *iced creams*. Luckily for Ethan his mother was unaware of the large quantity of sweet things he was rapidly consuming, otherwise it would have most certainly been confiscated from him.

Just as Eleanor was moving to stand to the side of the room after another lively polka, she once again, though this time even more intensified, felt eyes resting upon her - whose she knew not. She fleetingly scanned the room, searching questioningly for the culprit and, as she did so, her eyes locked with those of a young gentleman standing no more than a few metres away from her; a mere two couples separated them. He had the most piercing emerald green eyes she ever beheld and, although they now penetrated her own with an intense stare unlike any other Eleanor had witnessed before, they were not unpleasant, instead almost gentle. Before she could observe him any closer, she was pounced upon by her mother, who began to chaperone her back towards their table. Eleanor glanced fleetingly over her shoulder back to where he had stood no more than a moment ago, but he was gone.

At their table a man unknown to Eleanor was seated, conversing with her father. As she arrived at the table, the unfamiliar gentleman leapt to his feet and bowed respectfully. Eleanor nodded her head slightly in acknowledgment and curtsied prettily, wondering all the while who this man could be.

'Let me introduce Mr Henry Felton,' Mr Ashmore declared, also standing up. 'He is the son of a good friend of Kiran and has come to Mayhaven to take the waters a while. Mr Felton is also most interested in all things botanical and horticultural, so I am sure he will find plenty to occupy him here in Mayhaven. I have already offered my services and the usage of our library any time he should require it.'

Eleanor looked now with renewed interest at Mr Felton. He was tall and thin with a narrow oblong face and an unusually broad forehead. His beady, coffee brown eyes were framed by dark, bushy eyebrows, which unfortunately immediately drew the attention to the upper half of his face. His long, sleek hair was sandy blonde.

'Delighted madam,' he said courteously with a slight bow in Eleanor's direction.

'You're interested in botany?' Eleanor repeated. 'I studied the science myself a few years ago and found it most interesting, if not intermittently dull when studying the detailed fine structure of individual cells. I usually skip over those chapters. Trees and flowers are my favourite items of observation; I love watching them grow.'

Mr Felton reddened slightly, disconcerted by this intelligent and attractive young lady's knowledge. Eleanor, observing him closely, quickly concluded that Mr Felton, although ambitious and conscientious, was still somewhat immature, due to lack of experience. She was sure that this would all improve as his time in Mayhaven wore on and yet she somehow hoped that Mr Felton would not desire her father's assistance too often. Her train of thought was interrupted by Mr Felton turning to face her, having speedily overcome his embarrassment.

'Would you dance, Miss Ashmore?' he asked. Although groaning inwardly, Eleanor forced a polite smile and nod. As she once again walked onto the dance floor, she felt the eyes on her anew but had no time to dwell on the matter as the music had already begun and couples were starting to dance.

'You dance well, Miss Ashmore,' Mr Felton complimented after a few minutes of silence had passed between them. Surprised, it took Eleanor a few seconds to find her voice.

'Thank you,' she replied. 'Dancing is one of my passions.' And it was true. Eleanor had been born graceful, but also possessed good rhythmic senses and she enjoyed using this accomplishment as often as possible.

'I can tell,' he said. 'When you dance it is with energy and purpose. I am the same when making music.'

'Oh,' Eleanor exclaimed, now genuinely interested. 'Which instrument do you play?'

'Predominantly piano forte,' Mr Felton replied. 'Infrequently the clarinet. I find both instruments extremely satisfying to play, although the piano forte is my preferred choice.'

The gentleman then launched into a speech on musicality, frets, notation and the advantages to using tablature with stringed instruments. 'My parents are musicians, you see,' he concluded. 'Hence the slight fixation with music. I apologise if I ever seem overly-enthusiastic; when started on the topic of music I could enthuse for hours!'

'Do not unsettle yourself on my account,' Eleanor assured him. 'Your enthusiasm does not bother me, indeed quite the opposite; I admire it.'

Visibly relieved, Mr Felton untensed and silence relapsed between them until the dance ended.

'Thank you, Miss Ashmore, for this delightful dance,' Mr Felton said with a bow as the musicians ended the dance in a flourishing of hands and twiddling of strings. His hand lingered around Eleanor's waist as he turned to leave. Cordially, yet firmly Eleanor stepped back out of his arm's reach, curtsied and wished him a pleasant evening before determinedly walking off in the opposite direction, attempting to appear as nonchalant as possible. Reaching the opposite side of the room, Eleanor found a window which was slightly ajar and she leant closer to it and breathed deeply. She was half watching the dancers when she felt afresh someone's fixated gaze upon her.

Slightly disconcerted she made her way towards her parents. Only when she was all but standing next to them did she realise with a shock that the man stood but a short distance from her family was none other than the young gentleman whose eyes she had clandestinely admired just earlier. Now standing in such close proximity to him she was able to observe him properly.

The most striking thing that immediately attracted attention was his hair which, at first glance, seemed to be a tawny russet colour; but when the light shone against it, as now the chandelier behind him was doing, it became a fiery ginger. It was long, thick and tousled, just the tiniest bit wild, and his skin was also tawny. He had very little facial hair around his chin and mouth and the lines in his face which, though few were firm and chiselled, were predominantly centred around the jaw and cheekbones. Nearly bushy eyebrows that followed the slight curve of his eye merged into an unexceptional nose, beneath which full lips rested. His mouth seemed to be perpetually open due to an adorable upper lip which curled just slightly upwards, particularly when he smiled. The man carried himself with confidence and this gave the appearance of being tall, taller than he perhaps was. In reality he was not more than her father's height, roughly a head taller than herself. At that moment he seemed to be deep in conversation with an elderly gentleman, meaning he was thankfully unaware of Eleanor's scrutinising. The topic of their conversation she could, from her current position, not ascertain.

Eleanor's observations were cut short for Mrs Ashmore had spotted her and chose that instant to descend upon her yet again, Ethan's consumption of such a large quantity of desserts now known to her. Ethan was by now slightly hysterical and amusingly giddy as a result of the sugar and Abigail had, once again, caused an innocent and unsuspecting guest to trip, meaning that Mrs Ashmore was, to put it mildly, a little harassed and more than ready to remove her children from the scene.

'Eleanor!' Mrs Ashmore cried. 'Where is Charles? Ethan is quite lightheaded! What was he thinking of, eating so much sugar? An utterly nonsensical notion. He really should have known better. Has he really had such an inadequate upbringing? And where is Charles? Eleanor, we must leave now, I have no desire for the children to expire prematurely. The hour is late and the children are not accustomed to deprived sleep.'

She paused to draw breath.

'John!' she then called deafeningly to her husband, making Eleanor wince. Mrs Ashmore's spouse hastily snapped to attention, abandoning his drink and striding over.

'John, we must leave,' Mrs Ashmore flustered. 'Now. The children are out of control.'

'Right you are,' Mr Ashmore replied cheerily, not at all fazed by his wife's urgent and desperate tone. 'Come along Eleanor. We shall round the troops up while your mama pays our respects to the newlyweds.'

The two of them left Mrs Ashmore rushing off to say goodbye. From past experience Eleanor knew that they would not be seeing her mother for quite some time. As expected, Mr Ashmore and his children had taken their leave of friends and been sitting in the carriage waiting patiently, as patient as three exhausted children can be, for over half an hour before their mother finally made an appearance, accompanied by their aunt, with whom she was still talking animatedly.

However, Ethan's pitiful cries and Abigail's provoking tone soon caused Mrs Ashmore to end her conversation and hasten into the carriage. An air of tiredness and post wedding-excitement blues settled on the carriage as they journeyed home and it was with a joint sigh of relief that the family arrived at Felowspring Manor and could stumble up the steps and into their individual beds.

'Oh, I do love weddings!' Abigail murmured drowsily as she flung herself into bed a little later, allowing sleep to overtake her.

CHAPTER TWO

Second Sighting

The entire family was unpleasantly awoken in the early hours of the next morning - far too early by everyone's standards for the morning after a celebration - by an imposing sounding knock on the door. Francis was busy in the stables and so, at a loss as to who it could possibly be, Charles was appointed the undesired task of leaving the comfort and warmth of his bed to discover who their precocious visitor was. Highly displeased, Charles stomped down the stairs, fumbled with the lock and crossly swung the door open, stunned into silence at the sight of the person on their doorstep. Finding his tongue, he called breathlessly up the stairs.

'Mama! Papa! Come quickly! It's... It's... it's that man from yesterday!'

The urgency and distress in his voice at being abandoned with a man he barely knew while dressed in his nightclothes was easily identified and, throwing on their bodies any piece of clothing that lay close to hand, his mother and father hurried down, followed shortly by Eleanor, who was already dressed. Abigail rushed out of her room a few moments later; she had taken the time to dress herself slightly more thoroughly. She draped herself over the bannister and craned her neck to see who it was. Ethan, blissfully oblivious to everything around him, had not awoken and slept on.

Standing on the doorstep was none other than Mr Felton, his hat tucked under his arm, wearing a small, amused smile on his face in appreciation of being referred to as 'that man'. Eleanor groaned inwardly, she did not fully know why. That their new friend Mr Felton would not wait long before calling on them Eleanor had already guessed, but that he would be quite so forward as to appear at their house the very next day she had not suspected.

'Henry!' Mr Ashmore greeted in surprise. 'What on earth are you doing here? Shouldn't you be in bed or something?'

'Or something, yes,' Mr Felton agreed with a little laugh. 'Please forgive the disturbance.'

And here he bowed and smiled at Eleanor. She grimaced slightly.

'I hope I did not alarm you in any way,' he continued. 'I have always been an early riser and therefore I prefer to do my reading before the sun is high in the sky. I was wondering whether I would be able to take up the kind offer of the usage of your library?'

Mr Ashmore was too tired to argue so, with a nod of his head, he agreed.

'Eleanor, dear. Would you be so kind as to show Mr Felton the way?' Mr Ashmore turned to his eldest daughter, who, with the slightest nod of her head, complied with her father's wish.

'Now, you must excuse me,' announced Mr Ashmore, wrapping his emerald banyan tighter around him and stifling a yawn. 'I have never been an early riser, unlike some, and am most particular about my sleep. Unlike some, I also require at least one hour of moderate quiet in the morning, otherwise I am hardly fit for use.'

Without further ado the gentleman left them and returned to the master bedroom where he proceeded to dress before heading to his study to see to some of his more urgent matters of business before breakfast.

Abigail had now ventured down the stairs and peered around at the visitor from behind her mother's intimidating pink dressing gown.

'Ah, another one!' Mr Felton exclaimed.

'Yes, this is Abigail and this is Charles,' she explained, pushing Abigail forward and pulling Charles from behind the door.

'Eleanor you have met of course, and the youngest, Ethan, is still upstairs in bed,' Mrs Ashmore remarked cheerily. 'And of course, there is our dog Rumpus, Francis is out with the horses, Beatrice is folding clothes and Elizabelle is making breakfast. We don't count the livestock.'

'Ah!' Mr Felton nodded understandingly, though he wore a slightly bewildered look. Eleanor was just about to guide their guest to the library when her mother collared Mr Felton again.

'I suppose you have not broken your fast yet, Mr Felton?' she inquired, her maternal instinct, as ever, coming to the fore. She raised her auburn eyebrows expectantly, almost challengingly.

'No, Ma'am,' answered Mr Felton. 'I have not. My departure this morning was rather hurried, leaving no time for such pleasantries.'

'Surely food is more a necessity than a pleasantry,'

Eleanor remarked. Mr Felton turned to her with a patronising smile, which made Eleanor feel quite young and inexperienced.

'You are quite right, Miss,' he apologised. But the look in his eyes seemed to contradict the words of his mouth.

'You must eat with us,' Mrs Ashmore concluded. 'Food is healthy for the brain and will enable you to study more advantageously.'

'Thank you, Ma'am. You are most kind,' Mr Felton acknowledged graciously, with a slight bow. Eleanor knew it was unkind of her to think so, especially considering she was still in the process of becoming acquainted with him, but she sincerely hoped that Mr

Felton would not become a regular visitor to their home, however polite and chivalrous his manners seemed. Nevertheless, whatever Eleanor's sentiments were, she kept them to herself as best she could.

'I'll show you to the library now,' Eleanor offered, hurriedly marching off and refusing him the opportunity of offering profuse thanks once again.

'I don't like him, I wish he was not staying for breakfast,' muttered Abigail with a scowl on her face, as she watched him disappear along the corridor with Eleanor. Mrs Ashmore's smile vanished instantly as she rounded upon her daughter.

'You must not speak like that of one of our guests!' she rebuked hotly and Abigail was sent to her room in disgrace, to wait there until breakfast.

'You may sit on your bed in silence and contemplate the meaning of life!' Mrs Ashmore called after her daughter, as Abigail stomped back up the stairs in high dudgeon. A few moments later a door slammed. Charles quietly slunk away.

Meanwhile Eleanor led Mr Felton to the end of a spacious corridor, the walls on either side hung with paintings of the sun, sky and sea, and stopped at a pair of tall, wooden double doors. She swung them open, immediately flooding the hallway with light.

The library was without doubt one of the most pleasant rooms in the house. It was a slightly round room of a considerable size and yet they had still managed to fill every available space. From the tall ceiling to the floor the walls were lined with bookcases and shelves, each of them full to overflowing with books of every kind. All except for one wall, which boasted a magnificent bay window with a brightly cushioned window seat all along its edge. This immense amount of glass let in much natural light, making the library a beautifully well-lit and pleasant place to be. Also, on account of so many books of varying ages, the room had a slightly musty smell. To Eleanor it always smelt of adventures and mystery, romance and laughter; of so many stories and tales on those pages, just waiting to be discovered and experienced. They seemed to be calling out to her, almost begging to be picked up and freed from the covers that restricted them. When once she stopped Eleanor almost thought she could hear their faraway song.

Much to her delight and approval, Mr Felton seemed to feel similarly about this special room, for he also remained silent, observing and listening. This caused Eleanor's opinion of him to immediately improve tenfold. And when at last he did speak it was in a whisper, as if afraid to break the reverent moment.

'This is a breath-taking library,' Mr Felton praised in a low voice, moving to a shelf and stroking the cover of a book there, as though it were a genie's lamp.

'Thank you,' Eleanor replied with a smile. 'My mother's passion for books has helped us create such an extensive collection. She finds it as difficult to resist a book as she does a person standing on the front doorstep. In fact, she rarely returns from the local bookshop without a new addition to our ever-expanding library; she calls it giving them a home. The library is my favourite room to dream in.'

'Ah,' said Mr Felton sceptically and his countenance changed from one of wonder and appreciation to one of definite disapproval. It was clear from his expression that Mr Felton did not do a lot of dreaming which Eleanor, of course, could not at all understand. Her opinion of him sank once more, perhaps twentyfold, for it was her belief that a person who could not dream missed out on one of the greatest pleasures in life. To Eleanor, being able to transport herself in an instant to a different world, simply through the power of imagination, was not only a thrill and a joy, but also a vital ingredient for the accomplishing of anything and everything of real value and worth in this life. From an early age Eleanor's father had encouraged her to dream, and so she had grown accustomed to seeing and feeling in her dreams the fulfilment of her deepest desires and allowing those dreams to anchor her soul, to give her something to hold onto, an encouragement to come back to, as often as her heart needed it.

After spending a little time in her favourite room, Eleanor returned to the parlour, leaving Mr Felton, whose nose was already buried in a rather insipid botanical book, to his down-to-earth studies. The refreshing scent of black coffee in the morning air wafted through the house. Eleanor tilted her head back a little, as though this would help her to catch the scent more completely, and sniffed appreciatively. It was prognosticated that the weather would be surprisingly warm that day, so the French doors had already been flung wide so that the cool air could better permeate the house, thus framing the view of their back garden.

Eleanor had herself assisted in the landscaping of their stunning estate, which had taken years to plant, tend and beautify before it reached its current degree of high splendour. To the front of the manor house, green lawns with beds of controlled, semi-wild flowers and bedding plants could be seen. Neatly clipped yew and box hedges bordered gravel walkways, amidst compact stone statues and the occasional stone water feature. Tall ash trees bordered the gravel driveway leading up to Felowspring Manor, forming an emerald arch in the spring and a brilliant ruby one in the autumn. Off to the left of the house lay a beautiful rose garden and beyond that, close by the kitchen, a verdant vegetable plot with an abundant variety of herbs such as parsley, sage, rosemary, thyme, lavender, mint and dill, to name but a few.

Beyond this the estate boasted a sizeable orchard, each tree bursting with blossom or fruit. On the other side of the house were stables and pastures for the horses and for sheep. Adjacent to these lay a meadow of towering wild flowers of many kinds. In the summer the meadow became a favoured place for butterflies and when the flowers, in all their brightness and gaiety, were in full bloom and the meadow was covered with noiselessly fluttering butterflies , the effect was positively magical.

Around the back of the house there were even more tender green lawns, flowering bushes and majestic trees to be admired and off to one corner, hidden away, ran a bubbling, sparkling brook. What a delight this water was: in the summer, for paddling your feet in, and indeed all year round, for the sound the brook made as it pranced over pebble and stone was as soothing as a lullaby. This brook flowed through their land and out towards the centre of Felowspring, the village in which they lived, where it was joined by other brooks to become a stream.

It was upon this part of the garden that Eleanor was now looking, standing by the open windows of the parlour. Beyond these green lawns and peaceful waters came the wooded part of their estate. The most pleasant of walks could be made through those trees, whether with someone or just alone, with simply the old oaks and strong sycamores as companions.

Eleanor's moment of serenity with nature was all too soon obliterated by Charles who was testing his newest invention on Abigail. She, by the sounds of the agonised cries and frantic thumps, was not enjoying her brother's latest bright idea. Eleanor decided the best course of action was to leave and allow them time to work it out on their own, without her personal intervention. She was sure this would be the safest and most sensible course of action. A resounding slap, presumably originating from Abigail, followed by a howl from Charles confirmed Eleanor's suspicions and she hastily placed as much space between herself and the unpleasant noises as possible.

Eleanor emerged in the hallway just as her father reappeared.

'Ah, Eleanor, there you are,' her father greeted as he walked down the stairs, now properly dressed and fully awake. 'I trust our guest managed to find his way to the library.'

'Yes Papa,' she assured. 'And he also praised our tasteful furnishings; I think we have managed to impress him.' She grinned at her father. The library had been their special project together.

'Splendid, splendid,' he answered distractedly. His nose had now also detected that pleasant smell of breakfast.

'Come Lea, let us be first to the breakfast table.'

He winked and offered her his arm and the two of them strolled off towards the dining room and the ever-increasing smell of coffee and warm bread fresh out of the oven. Mr Felton arrived somewhat delayed, but, whatever minor feelings of annoyance the family might have felt due to his late arrival, they were forthwith replaced with exasperation and impatience after he had extensively apologised to each of them individually. Once they had all breakfasted Mr Felton bid them farewell, however not before requesting that the entire family come to dine with him the next day. Eleanor once again wondered whether they would now have the pleasure of seeing Mr Felton near to everyday.

'Well, Mr Felton,' Mrs Ashmore explained, somewhat

awkwardly. 'Of course, we would be more than glad to visit you in your own home but, you see, we are already elsewhere engaged tomorrow evening. We have been invited to a dance, a ball of sorts, you understand.'

It was clear that Mr Felton had not been invited, which was not surprising since he had only arrived a few days ago.

'But,' Mrs Ashmore continued 'the invitation did extend to any friend or acquaintance we wished to include in our party.' Fixedly ignoring Eleanor's silent plea, she finished: 'So I'm sure we would all be delighted to have you join us. Wouldn't we, children?' Mrs Ashmore asked pleasantly, but the children could sense the threatening undertone, daring them to answer wrongly.

'Yes, Mama,' they all chorused obediently, although rather lacking in enthusiasm. The younger three had nothing *against* Mr Felton but equally they had nothing for him. They found him fairly dull and uninteresting company. But their fear of what dreadful punishment their mother may issue, such as no pudding or no reading before bed, was greater than any personal preferences in regard to Mr Felton's company.

And so it was that the next evening found Eleanor mentally preparing herself for another night of Mr Felton's wearying and seemingly endless explanations of plant leaf structures. She sincerely hoped that some other young lady in attendance, there were sure to be plenty, would attract his attention. Eleanor had often been told that she should feel flattered when a young man so pointedly decided to converse with her, but somehow she was finding it incredibly difficult to feel flattered by a gentleman explaining how plants convert simple compounds into more intricate chemicals. Pushing such tedious thoughts aside she focused on the more important matter at hand - what to wear.

On this particular evening Eleanor decided to wear a modest cream dress with a bodice and sleeves of delicate lace and little pearl buttons sewn down the back. Due to the heat her hair had formed into tight curls and become laborious to tame, so she tied it back as best she could, a few stray wisps escaping and hanging loose around her face, framing it beautifully.

Their recent attendance at a wedding reception had done nothing to dampen the usual excitement and high spirits of the Ashmore household while preparations for any outing were underway. The house was a hub of noise; various frenzied shouts echoing from wall to wall, all of the voices intermingling, making it extremely difficult to decipher any intelligible sentence.

The ball was being held by their good friends the Laytons who lived no more than a mile away. Mr and Mrs Layton were both very agreeable and friendly. Mr Layton was a short, flat-footed, barrel-chested and balding man whose healthy appetite and appreciation of good food was outwardly visible. His wife Mrs Layton was not especially handsome, but she was stylish and notoriously picksome, on occasion somewhat mawkish and she possessed an incurable thirst for news. They had been blessed with only one child, a young girl by the name of Felicity, who was hopelessly scatter-brained, yet endearingly cheerful. And as her grandfather repeatedly, and quite aptly, described her: 'Generally speaking she is generally speaking.'

Felicity was short and plump and her cheeks were always rosy, the colour of ripe autumn apples, whether it was the height of summer or the middle of winter. Her strawberry blonde hair she always wore in two plaits on either side of her head and an ever-present twinkle in her eye betrayed an inner impishness.

Abigail and Felicity, who were both of a similar age and temperament, somehow invariably succeeded in conceiving a hare-brained game in a matter of minutes. Their 'games' usually required the support of various other family members who always pretended to dread having to help. Indeed, the adults acted quite immaturely when trying to avoid such escapades, using any excuse they could conjure up - any reason they could find to be elsewhere or unable to help - even using a torn fingernail or slight headache as a justification. All attempts at evading the girls 'games' were however consistently fruitless. And though the adults always protested at joining in the girl's games, deep down (despite all their objections) each one secretly enjoyed joining in, for it caused the playful child in all of them to rise up and, although they would never admit it, it was fun, once in a while, to become a child and believe once again in the magic of everyday things.

Mr Felton, who was to ride with the Ashmore's to the Layton's ball, arrived punctually, dressed in a crimson suit, which was rather too small for him, his hat tucked under his arm and his hair, still wet from being washed, smoothed back. And even Eleanor, rejoicing at the prospect of an evening full of friendship, music and dance, did not object to him immediately seeking her out and requesting the privilege of being able to sit next to her in the carriage (she refrained from telling him that the carriage journey was mere minutes long). In fact, Eleanor even felt brave enough to inquire about his studies. His expression when invited to share such information was one of great joy. Clearly he knew that this was the first time she had started such a conversation of her own accord (in fact it was probably the first time he had ever had such a conversation without himself being the initiator), and he promptly subjected her to what would have been a lengthy explanation of the advantages and disadvantages of studying the plants and trees in Mayhaven. She bore it stoically, even managing to appear interested and engaged. Luckily, Mr Felton was blissfully unaware that Eleanor's thoughts were very far away, daydreaming of the friends she would see again that evening and of the new acquaintances she could make.

Their departure was, as accustomed, delayed because Charles forgot they were going out that evening; he was not very enthused once reminded of the fact.

'Can I at least bring a book?' Charles insisted, while pulling on his shirt and flattening his hair with his hands. But the dangerous glint in his mother's eyes was all the answer he needed. Then Charles could not find his shoes. This complication was however easily resolved and the carriage laden with people soon embarked on its short journey. Although they arrived, surprisingly, precisely on time, numerous other carriages were already standing in front of the Layton's magnificent house, which was a prodigious size considering its usual number of occupants.

When the carriage halted Abigail and Ethan, after a frighteningly stern glare from their father, did not immediately leap out of the carriage but instead waited until a foreman had opened the door. Then, like two arrows released from a bow, they bounded out of their seats, pushing the unfortunate foreman against the carriage in their eagerness as they capered away, selectively choosing not to hear their mother's disapproving reprimand.

Charles did not follow his brother and sister. Indeed, he seemed reluctant to forsake his seat at all, not being overly fond of social gatherings. Instead, he sunk even deeper into his seat and pulled his hat over his face, as if hoping that his family may forget his existence and leave him behind. Alas for Charles, he had left far too marked an imprint on his parents' lives for them to have forgotten him, even if they had wanted to. Naturally, they did not want this and Eleanor, whom Charles immensely respected, succeeded in gently coaxing him out of his shell of refusal and persuading him to accompany them inside. Lively music was already playing, sending Mr Felton into ecstasies and people all around them were pressed against the wall in an attempt to evade the dancers.

Quietly slipping away from Mr Felton's side, Eleanor slowly made her way across the room to where the Laytons were standing. A dark-haired young man, whom everyone knew as Mr Joshua Ayles, was standing a few metres away from them, at the edge of the ballroom, observing the general goings-on. His eyes fell on Eleanor as she picked her way cautiously through the dancers and his blue eyes, which were the colour of the night sky – a deep, intense midnight blue - lit up like stars. The gentleman was tall, lithe and very handsome. His hair, which was thick and slightly tousled, was an ebony black. Despite the deep shade of his hair, his complexion was fair, like that of many northerners. His entire face, in particular his jawline, was chiselled and his dark eyebrows were furrowed, as if he were perpetually concentrating, or angry and distressed about something. Yet his face and his general countenance did not appear unwelcoming or harsh, in spite of his concentrated, tense look. Instead, it only added to the sense of mystery that seemed to surround him.

As he saw Eleanor his face broke into a smile and Eleanor, noticing him, returned the smile happily. Joshua Ayles was an old friend whom she had known for many years; she was always glad to see him. Eleanor changed her course slightly and headed for him, but then abruptly stopped in her tracks. She stared across the room motionless, as if transfixed. All around her everything continued; the couples whirled and the chatter persisted and yet she saw only the gentleman – the gentleman with tawny hair and emerald eyes - leaning composedly against the opposite wall. She was annoyed with herself for allowing the sight of him to unsettle her so, for he set her heart beating rapidly inside her chest like a butterfly frantic to escape. Indeed, she futilely reasoned with herself: I do not even know his name or from whence he came; but even as she thought this, she knew that neither name nor birthplace is really of any great importance. Despite herself, she found herself fighting to catch a glimpse of him again through the dancers. He must have sensed her searching gaze for suddenly he turned and caught her eye. Then, to Eleanor's acute alarm, he began to make his way towards her. Unsure of what to do and how to feel, Eleanor stood immobilised, watching him purposefully draw near. If Eleanor had not been so unobservant in her flustered state, she would most certainly have noticed that, however confident his general appearance may have seemed, the way he fiddled and adjusted his cravat with shaking hands as he walked towards her betrayed his ever-increasing nervousness.

He stood in front of Eleanor now, towering at least a head taller than her, and gazed down at her face. He had observed her on the day of the wedding reception at Faymor Hall but always only from afar, never daring to come too close. Now standing but a breath away from her he was struck by her natural and innocent beauty. With her face turned to the light, her pale complexion made her skin shine like moonlight, the humidity and excitement giving her cheeks a tint of blush. Her lips were lightly pressed together like the petals of a rose; Eleanor was beautiful, deep down to her soul.

She looked shyly up at him, her eyelids still partially closed, as if she did not dare to fully open them; and then their eyes met again.

For a reason entirely unknown to Eleanor she found herself panicking, and, as she looked deep into his eyes, she found that feeling reflected, that feeling of shock, as if, in that blink of an eye, their souls had exchanged something; something they could not at this moment fully understand. With impeccable timing, Mr Ashmore joined them.

'Ah, Edwards,' he greeted the handsome stranger. The man dragged his gaze away and turned to face Mr Ashmore, smiling a greeting. Eleanor's eyes grew wide and she glared at her father. How did he know this man? How dare he know him and not tell her!

'I see you've met the rose of Mayhaven, our Miss Ashmore. My eldest daughter,' he remarked proudly. 'Isn't she quite the belle of the ball?'

Mr Ashmore winked at his daughter. Eleanor's grunt of annoyance and embarrassment was barely audible. This rather muted response (when being teased by her father Eleanor would usually either exclaim loudly in irritation or resort to violence) was due to her excitement in discovering the stranger's name - Mr Edwards.

'Ah, but see, I'm embarrassing her again,' laughed Mr Ashmore. He fondly jostled his daughter, his eyes twinkling. He explained to the gentleman: 'As her father I have been given the honour of the paternal obligation of embarrassing her at every possible opportunity. Especially at social gatherings, in front of as many people as obtainable. But she *is* very patient with me,' he added, turning to Eleanor. 'Aren't you, my dear?'

Eleanor's eyes were filled with merriment and twinkling stars as she nodded.

'I know that it is meant well and that you enjoy it,' she

replied laughingly. 'And I also know that is a longing born into fathers to tease and embarrass their daughters.'

'Especially the eldest daughters I've heard,' Mr Ashmore added thoughtfully, winking at Mr Edwards. 'I think it's even been carefully studied. I mean,' he raised his eyebrows meaningfully at Eleanor, his face betraying nothing. 'In the light of these clearly *scientifically proven* facts, it's no wonder I tease you. I practically *have* to. It's in my very *bones*.'

He dramatically threw his arms about his body.

'You practically *don't* have to,' Eleanor said firmly, narrowing her eyes.

Rather too firmly until she noticed that Mr Ashmore had been, once again, teasing her. He flinched and took a step backwards as Eleanor moved her hand. Quite justifiably too, for half a second later Eleanor shot out her long fingertips and mercilessly tickled his neck. Mr Ashmore went purple with the effort of keeping quiet and not drawing attention to them as he fruitlessly tried to evade his daughter's vicious onslaught. It is not really done to tickle people at private balls, nor at public ones for that matter, but then the Ashmores did not greatly care whether something was 'done' or not - they did it anyway. The stranger seemed to be amused by the interaction and had visibly relaxed; his hands now rested by his sides and no longer shook.

'Well, I must leave you for the moment,' Mr Ashmore announced. 'The banquet table is beckoning, and I can no longer resist.' He kissed Eleanor on the cheek, bowed to Mr Edwards and left.

Silence once again reigned between them for some time.

'Will you... dance?' the handsome gentleman finally asked. He immediately coloured and hastily looked at the floor - he could only just keep from slapping himself for being so forward in marching across the room and asking this young lady to dance with him.

His heart, which had already sunk into his toes, had now as good as disappeared beneath the floorboards. 'I mean, I practically barked at her,' he raged internally. Truth be known, he dreaded hearing her refusal, however gentle and polite he was sure she would express it; he feared what she may say, how she would react to his bold approach. On the evening of the wedding at Faymor Hall he had, how ashamed he was to think of it now, been too nervous to speak to her. Too apprehensive even to observe her properly, choosing instead to hide among the shadows.

This evening the silent longing and mysterious attraction to this handsome young lady, an attraction that he could not fathom, had this time overcome any feelings of uncertainty. All these thoughts shot through his mind at an alarming speed in the interval of milliseconds before Eleanor replied. She smiled softly in response to his request and nodded - no words were needed - for her smile was the answer he was hoping for.

The musician's melody was slow and the steps of the dance were simple, allowing them both the luxury of consideration and speech as they began to dance. As they moved across the floor Eleanor was, for the first time that evening, able to appreciate once more the splendour and charm of the Layton's ballroom. By now the evening had darkened to night and the tall windows on either side of the room had been concealed behind heavy, red velvet curtains. A few hand-stitched tapestries (family heirlooms) were hung from brass rods on the walls and positioned between these were magnificent paintings of picturesque landscapes and portraits of men and women from days of old. A fair number of mirrors also ordained the walls, advantageously reflecting the candlelight. In the centre of the room hung a magnificent chandelier with arrays of hanging crystal prisms that scattered miniature rainbows whenever the light shone through them. This was complemented with smaller chandeliers that were distributed across the ballroom's expansive and ornate ceiling, providing an even distribution of warm light across the whole room. Quite adequate for a dance, and perfect for a ball.

As they danced together there were many curious murmurs and wild speculations as to who this amiable man dancing with their beloved Eleanor could be. Mr Edwards was the kind of gentleman who drew the gaze, even despite his humble attire. He seemed to radiate something which commanded attention - a kind of golden glow. He danced with grace and there was something regal about the way he held himself. It seemed that nobody really knew who he was. A few of the gentlemen who had already that evening conversed with Mr Edwards were immediately set upon by overly inquisitive and talebearing elderly ladies who were anxious to find out any snippet of interesting information before anyone else in Mayhaven. Alas, all the gentlemen could report was that he seemed quiet, honest and friendly enough. His good looks spoke for themselves. Temporarily satisfied with the knowledge they had gleaned, the ladies proceeded to scuttle around the ballroom, passing on the news and all the while sending furtive glances in the direction of Eleanor and Aiden (for this was the gentleman's Christian name).

The dance ended, everyone applauded the musicians and one another, and Aiden led Eleanor to one side of the room, to a more quiet and secluded area. A servant came with a tray of drinks and it was but a few moments before Mrs Ashmore and Mr Layton joined them.

'Mrs Ashmore, may I introduce Mr Aiden Edwards,'

Mr Layton announced. Mr Edwards bowed and Mrs Ashmore beamed at him.

'And where is it that you live?' Mrs Ashmore inquired, her curiosity fully awakened.

'Felowspring, Ma'am. Since Thursday of last week,' Aiden replied.

'Oh!' Mrs Ashmore enthused. 'How exciting! And have you been to Mayhaven before?'

Aiden looked across at Eleanor discreetly, not wishing to appear rude to Mrs Ashmore who was keeping up a steady flow of questioning. Eleanor's eyes were averted and she appeared deep in thought. The delicate silhouette of her face, from the apex of her head down to the elegant arch of her neck, was highlighted by a candle placed on a table behind her. As Eleanor looked up, he hastily turned away, not wishing her to see the unconcealable admiration in his eyes.

A very short time later Mr Layton excused both himself and Mr Edwards; there were still many people for him to be introduced to.

'Mrs Ashmore, Miss Ashmore,' Mr Edwards excused himself, bowing to each of the ladies before taking his leave of them. Eleanor's eyes followed him as he left.

Joshua had observed this entire interaction from afar, his eyes like chips of ice, as hard as stone. Wordlessly he turned and left, saddling his horse and riding off into the night; the dark coat of the stallion blurred into its master's and soon the night had swallowed them both entirely.

For Eleanor the remainder of the evening was uneventful, filled with much dancing and even more talk. And, although she looked for him, she did not see Mr Edwards again.

CHAPTER THREE

The Tea Party

Abigail flounced down to breakfast the next morning with a very exquisite lace shawl draped over her shoulders. She did a little twirl for her family's benefit. She looked very pretty in it, but also somewhat overdressed for breakfast.

'What do you think?' inquired Abigail expectantly.

'Very nice,' replied her father while holding his cup out and helping himself to seconds of coffee. Abigail pursed her lips.

'You weren't even looking,' she said in an accusing voice.

'I think it looks lovely,' said Mrs Ashmore warmly and rubbed Abigail affectionately on the arm in passing. 'Would you like some toast?' And she held up a laden plate.

'It's nice,' said Charles thickly through a mouthful of food, but Abigail clearly didn't think his opinion counted.

'What is it?' piped Ethan.

'What do you mean, what is it? It's a shawl!' replied

Abigail with an isn't-that-obvious look on her face.

'Yes, but what does it do?' pressed Ethan, a confused look on his face.

Charles cackled in the background.

'It's clothes Ethan, it's *fashion*,' snapped Abigail. 'It doesn't need to *do* anything.'

'Oh,' said Ethan, helping himself to a third piece of cinnamon toast, oblivious to Abigail's frosty tone.

Abigail collapsed into her seat looking disgruntled, but she cheered up after a couple of slices of honey cake.

Their conversation that morning, after covering vital

topics such as food, weather and other sundry matters, turned to what had been the talk of everyone the night before: The handsome gentleman Aiden who had, with his amiable manner and attractive appearance, captured everyone's attention. The mothers and daughters were especially pleased with this newcomer for he seemed a very favourable suitor and, though he knew it not, was already highly sought after by many of the ladies in Mayhaven.

'He seems very amiable, though not an overly enthusiastic dancer!' commented Mrs Ashmore.

'Did he dance with anyone else?' Abigail asked innocently.

'No, only with Eleanor,' replied her mother, pouring herself another cup of tea and stirring it reflectively. 'I wonder why he has come to Felowspring,' she mused.

'And I wonder why he did not dance with anyone else,' added Abigail, shooting her sister a mischievous look. Abigail may have been one of the most talkative of people, but one would be fooled to think she was not perceptive; Abigail had noticed the way the two young people had looked at each other.

Eleanor herself, although she would never give her sister the satisfaction of knowing, had wondered the same thing. Aiden had danced only once the entire evening, and that had been with her; Eleanor fairly shone when she thought of it.

Charles, as usual, had no opinion whatsoever. His response to being asked what he thought of Mr Edwards was rather lacking.

'Hm… Who? Mr Edwards? Who's that?' he had answered with complete ignorance.

'You know… the new man who danced with Eleanor…'

'Oh, you mean Mr Felton,' Charles replied.

'No, no, Mr *Edwards*... quite tall...,' Abigail tried to explain but, judging from Charles' blank expression, he had absolutely no recollection of ever seeing such a man.

'I liked him. I liked him very much,' Mrs Ashmore enthused. 'I think he will prove to be an extremely pleasant young man. Very agreeable. Don't you think?'

This last question was directed at Mr Ashmore who was unsuccessfully trying to drink his coffee. It had not yet reached what he called 'the drinkable temperature,' and so he was instead painfully sipping it.

'Hm? Oh yes, he is very nice,' Mr Ashmore agreed absentmindedly, still blowing on his coffee cup.

'Nice? Nice, Father?' Eleanor cried. 'Surely *nice* is not an appropriate word to describe him. It is an uninteresting, dull and *safe* word. Not at all adequate for describing Mr Edwards.'

All this Eleanor said in a voice surprisingly loaded with emotion and opinion which, for her, was most unusual. Eleanor herself knew this too and, after this unexpected outburst in Mr Edward's defence, she sank demurely back into her chair and hardly spoke at all for the rest of the meal, pointedly ignoring the victorious look from her sister and the bewildered ones from her brothers.

***

Later that day the Ashmores greeted another unexpected visitor on their doorstep, this one however much more welcomed than the last. Hailey Williams was one of Eleanor's closest friends, more like a sister to her, and always very gladly received in their home. Hailey was a good deal older than Eleanor physically, at least a decade. But then again, emotionally Eleanor was far advanced than conventional for her age.

Pretty enough and yet not possessing any striking features, Hailey was frequently overlooked in a crowd.

With a pale complexion, nut brown hair and deep-set eyes, she was considered mostly fair and moderately accomplished. A few years ago she had married her childhood love and, besides a few minor disagreements, which are only natural and anticipated in a healthy marriage, their relationship was thriving, much to Eleanor's joy.

Although Eleanor was of course delighted for her friend, marrying had meant Hailey moving away from Felowspring, to a little village called Talisbrook on the very outskirts of Mayhaven, making Hailey's visits infrequent. Marriage, as it does to all people, had changed Hailey, and Eleanor, however selfish the desire may be, longed to have her old friend back; the unchanged, carefree Hailey. But these melancholy reflections always dispersed, blown away on the wind of memories, as soon as Hailey was with her again.

Hailey's arrival was a breath of fresh air in what otherwise would have been an uneventful and rather mundane day for Eleanor. She rushed down the stairs and, overjoyed to see her friend again, greeted Hailey most affectionately, hugging her tightly before allowing her entrance to the house. Mrs Ashmore and Abigail hurried out of the second parlour to greet their guest with many exclamations of 'We haven't seen you in what feels like forever! It's been far too long' and 'Oh, it's so lovely to see you. Oh, and I do *love* your gown!'

Ethan ran full speed up the corridor to greet her, Rumpus barking beside him, and collided into Hailey's legs with a happy cry of welcome. Hailey had unfortunately not been able to make it to the ball the night before, so Ethan felt it his duty to relay a garbled account of the occurrences, as soon as he had disentangled himself from her dress.

'There was lots of food. I had roast beef and bread and

a soupy thing and lots of jelly with cake. And there was someone new, but I didn't really see him very much. But everyone likes him. Eleanor danced with him; I think he likes her. And it was *soooo* hot,' Ethan exclaimed and gasped for breath, as if remembering and reliving the heat of the ballroom. 'And I wasn't allowed to join in the dancing,' he finished indignantly.

'That all sounds marvellous,' Hailey laughed and patted him on the head, knowing she would get an understandable explanation from Eleanor in due course. Ethan grinned proudly, pleased to have been able to say something that adults found interesting. For him it was a rare occurrence.

The young boy skipped off, humming his theme tune to himself, in his mind already fighting off terrible enemies and fantastical beasts. Oh what a wonderful world he lived in, inside his head.

'Ethan dear, don't disappear!' his mother called after him. As you may remember, we were in the middle of French lessons in the parlour!'

Politely excusing herself Mrs Ashmore returned once again to the parlour and to Charles, with Abigail and a reluctant Ethan in tow. Once they were reinstalled Ethan leaned in to Charles.

'Why can't we have a governess like other people?' he whispered furtively. 'Mama's so strict!'

'Rubbish,' retorted Charles. 'Mama is no stricter than she needs to be, and I for one would much rather have her teaching us, than some poor governess who we do not know and who does not know us. As mama has always said "Train up a child in the way he should go: and when he is old he will not depart from it."'

'I know she always says that,' Ethan hissed. 'But what does it mean?'

'It means that because mama knows us best, she's the

best one to teach us!'

***

Eleanor interlaced her arms with Hailey's and they hurried to the library, hoping to find it a safe and quiet sanctuary, devoid of people. They were not disappointed and soon the two friends were both settled on the window seat with the sun warming their backs and the birds graciously supplying them with the sweetest kind of music. It did not take long for Eleanor to inform Hailey of all she had missed since her last visit. Hailey was particularly interested to hear about Mr Henry Felton and Mr Aiden Edwards and Eleanor painted as vivid a picture of the two gentlemen as she could.

'You must be careful, my dear friend!' Hailey exclaimed laughingly when Eleanor had finished her narrative. 'Or else you may find yourself falling for one of these amiable young men.' She grinned cheekily.

Eleanor bestowed Hailey with a withering look.

'My dear Hailey, I assure you I have no intention whatsoever of *falling* for anyone.'

'I'm delighted to hear it,' replied Hailey in a prim voice. 'I should hate to have to pick you up off the floor after you had fallen.'

She burst out laughing and Eleanor, shaking her head exasperatedly at Hailey, joined in, not being able to suppress her own laughter.

'I wish I could meet them both,' Hailey sighed a few moments later, somewhat regretfully. 'But Felowspring is so far away now and I so rarely have the use of the carriage. My darling husband works so hard but with no great profit to show for it. We can't even afford a maid yet, and there is so much work to be done in the house. I hardly know where to start! I was only able to come and visit you today because I was passing through Felowspring on my way to Denersdath, where, as you know, they sell the best linens and muslins in the region. I am in sore need of a new dress; and all our dining chairs require upholstering.' She sighed again.

For the first time Eleanor caught a glimpse of just how difficult matters were at the moment for Hailey and her husband and how challenging it must be for Hailey to set aside all her own wishes and desires because of her commitment to her husband.

'And,' Hailey continued, 'I do not wish to be the cause of any extra expense by paying for a ride with the stagecoach. You do understand don't you?' she asked anxiously. Eleanor, not wanting to trouble her friend with her own personal preferences, immediately cast such thoughts away and assured Hailey that she fully understood her situation, promising to visit her at her own home in Talisbrook more often instead.

Hailey's furrowed brow relaxed and it was clearly noticeable that she had been unduly worried that Eleanor would think her infrequent visits reflected a lack of desire to see her. The two of them had just begun to discuss which colour muslin would best suit Hailey's wallpaper when a sudden commotion elsewhere in the house, involving joyous shouts, frenzied stamping and excited yelps, attracted their attention. They did not have to wonder long what the reason could be, for Abigail took it upon herself to inform them in her typical exaggerated and theatrical manner. The unmistakable sound of feet thundering up the hallway was heard and moments later the doors were flung open.

'You'll never guess what!' the young girl cried, bursting into the room. She stood in front of them, hands akimbo, eyes sparkling and feet firmly placed on the floor, exulting in the superior feeling of knowing something they did not.

'No, you're right. We never will,' Eleanor agreed.

'Then I'll tell you,' Abigail pronounced dramatically, pausing for suspense. 'There is to be a tea party! A *garden* tea party.'

Abigail looked at Hailey and Eleanor, awaiting some shocked response or joyful outburst.

'Oh, is that all?' Eleanor responded mildly and turned back to Hailey in order to continue their discussion.

'Is that all?' repeated Abigail disbelievingly, her eyes wide.

'No, but you don't *understand*!' she exclaimed, deeply exasperated and disappointed by their controlled reaction to her oh-so-exciting news. 'There is to be a tea party *here*. In our house. *Tomorrow*!'

'Here?' Eleanor repeated sceptically, her eyebrows raised. She and Hailey exchanged looks. They had never held a tea party at their house before. Mrs Ashmore, despite immensely enjoying social gatherings, especially when tea and cakes and sunshine were involved, found it much more of a challenge to host such events herself, not an impossibility, merely a challenge.

'Are you quite sure?' Eleanor asked again. Abigail gave her a withering look as if not understanding why on earth Eleanor would not immediately believe what she said.

'*Yes*,' Abigail replied with slow deliberation, like explaining something to a simple-minded child. 'I am *very* sure.'

Eleanor swiped at her sister playfully and Abigail dodged and darted out of the room laughing, her auburn hair streaming behind her.

'Come on, *come on*!' she called back to them as she capered up the hallway.

Hailey and Eleanor turned to each other and exchanged questioning glances again, both wondering what had brought on this sudden spasm. Without further delay they trooped down the corridors and into the lovely, stone-floored kitchen where the rest of the family had already gathered. A thick smell of spicy stew filled the room, making their mouths water in anticipation of their evening meal. Mrs Ashmore was already deep in conversation with Elizabelle, their incredible house help and cook rolled into one.

Elizabelle was slightly short and the tiniest bit plump ('Only because of my height!' she would often say. 'If I had been that bit taller, everything would have stretched and been in nice, even proportions!') Her fuzzy hair was as soft as swansdown and as white as snow on Christmas morning. Wrinkles around her eyes and mouth were testimony to her ready smile and she was as lovable as a baby chick, and about as stern as one too. The kitchen was undoubtedly her domain, but Eleanor was often to be found alongside Elizabelle, the two of them working culinary wonders with their gifted hands.

'Mama,' Abigail butted in, causing Elizabelle and Mrs Ashmore to look up with a start. 'Eleanor did not believe me. You know, about the tea party being here. Tell her that it is true.'

'It is perfectly true, Eleanor dear,' Mrs Ashmore confirmed, returning to the ever-growing shopping list she was compiling with Elizabelle's assistance. Scribbling one last item on the last tiny corner of space on the otherwise filled scrap of paper, Mrs Ashmore straightened up with a satisfied nod.

'Good,' she murmured, more to herself than anyone else. 'Now, what shall we do about drinks?'

'But why, Mama? Why are we suddenly hosting a tea party? *Tomorrow?* There must be a reason,' pressed Eleanor, certain that there was an ulterior motive behind this sudden plan.

'Am I not allowed to host a tea party for all our good

friends? I merely thought it would be a nice idea.' Mrs Ashmore smiled disarmingly at her daughter but Eleanor was not fooled for a minute. As if struck by an insignificant afterthought her mother added nonchalantly: 'And of course, it will also be a lovely opportunity to become better acquainted with Mr Edwards.'

Eleanor groaned and sank down heavily into one of the wooden chairs around the table, her forehead falling into her hands in an attempt to hide her cheeks which were reddened with embarrassment.

'Mama, how many friends have been invited?' she asked.

'Oh, not that many,' her mother answered airily.

'Mama…,' Eleanor repeated.

'Only about twenty,' she replied sheepishly. Eleanor groaned again.

'But do not trouble yourself,' Mrs Ashmore continued, 'for no one will suspect the real reason for arranging such a tea party, not with such a number of people in attendance. And,' she added on a brighter note, 'after we have become better acquainted with Mr Edwards we shall be able to invite him personally.'

'Why this expeditious eagerness to gain Mr Edward's friendship?' Eleanor questioned suspiciously.

'No reason,' she shrugged. 'I simply think him a very interesting and admirable young man.'

'You've met him once Mama!'

'Which is why I can hardly invite him over on his own,' Mrs Ashmore retorted. 'And besides, I do also genuinely want to invite our friends here for a change. I have been meaning to do so for some time, but for me there was never sufficient motivation or reason. And Mr Edwards, and let us not forget Mr Felton, have both arrived so recently. They have not been officially welcomed to Mayhaven or Felowspring. Now is the perfect time; the weather is heavenly, the early fruit is ripe, the flowers are blossoming, spirits are high! And I *want* to hold a tea party which is a wonder in itself.'

Eleanor couldn't reasonably argue with that and so, having no other option but to accept her mother's explanation, Eleanor let the matter rest.

Hailey assured Eleanor that she and her husband would make every effort to attend the momentous Ashmore tea party the next day. Farewell had never been so painless before, the expectancy of tomorrow clouding the very thought of sorrow ordinarily caused by having to say goodbye. Hailey was cheerily waved away and, as if they had in the past few days not already had their complete share of excitement, the house became once again utter pandemonium, every family member eager to assist with either baking, decorating or even, for the first and possibly last time, cleaning.

Charles and Ethan were given large handfuls of invitations to deliver.

'Race you,' Charles whispered to Ethan and the two boys darted out of the door and off down the driveway.

It was an extremely exhausted, yet triumphant family that yawned their way into bed that evening, a sense of a job well done prevailing over all of them. They did not believe in doing things by halves; it was either everything or nothing - there was no in between.

***

The next morning Eleanor, only half-awake, agitatedly thrashed around with the bedcovers, hoping the beautiful dream she had just lost would come tumbling out from between the linen folds. Much to her disappointment it did not, but through her violent movement she had fully awakened herself. She lay for a moment, her eyes flitting to the window where the curtains were open just a crack, letting a shaft of light stream into the room and dance over her.

She smiled and stretched herself lazily until the sudden recollection of what was to take place that day hit her with such a force that she bounded out of bed with an energy most unusual for Eleanor in the morning. The view out the window revealed a delightfully sunny July morning, much to Eleanor's joy; a garden party that has to move indoors because of rain is somehow not the same as a garden party that takes place - as intended - outdoors, especially on such a glorious day as this. Her joy however soon turned to alarm as she comprehended just how high the sun had already risen; a glance at the clock confirmed her fears and without so much as a look in the mirror she threw on her clothes and dashed down the stairs in a most undignified manner, coming to a halt outside the dining room, only to find her entire family still seated at the table, leisurely breakfasting.

'Ah there you are,' Mr Ashmore greeted, momentarily looking up from his plate. 'We managed to save some food for you,' he glanced at the boys 'but only just.'

He indicated with his head. Eleanor took up her place at the table and began to hurriedly butter a slice of toast whilst decapitating her soft-boiled egg. She glanced around the table at her family, some of whom had finished eating and were gazing out of the window whilst others were helping themselves to fourth slices of honey cake, before casually asking, 'Shouldn't we be preparing or something?' still slightly puzzled at her family's relaxed attitude in regard to time.

'Yes, we'll start soon I expect,' replied Mrs Ashmore taking a sip from her cup. 'The guests are not expected for another… '

She glanced at the longcase clock in the corner of the room and her eyes went painfully wide. She leapt up from the table, upsetting much of the crockery, smashing two dishes, spilling Mr Ashmore's coffee all over his clean shirt and disturbing the dog, before rushing out of the room, shouting hysterically for Elizabelle as she did so.

'*And* that's my cue to leave,' Mr Ashmore announced, futilely attempting to sponge off the deep brown coffee marks spread all over his white shirt as he walked to the door. He still had some matters of business to attend to before helping with the tea party preparations.

'Now don't kick up any larks,' he instructed his youngest offspring, fixing each of them with a warning look. 'In fact, even better, go and make yourself useful to your mother. I shall see you all shortly!'

And with a last wink at Eleanor he exited the room, heading with all haste to his study before anyone could ensnare him in a job that they 'could not possibly complete without him'.

Eleanor hurriedly finished the remainder of her meal and sought out her mother in an attempt to soothe her nerves and assist Elizabelle with any tasks that needed completing. Eleanor was a talented baker and had, over the years, built up an extensive repertoire of cakes, biscuits and pastries. Soon Eleanor and Elizabelle had once more worked wonders in the kitchen and an abundance of delicious foods were now being arranged outside on a long table in the shade of an obliging oak tree: dainty finger sandwiches, sugar biscuits, fresh meringue with clotted cream and strawberry preserve, lavender shortbread, lavender madeleines, rum cake, saffron cake, plumb cake, hartshorn jelly, cranberry jelly, syllabub and an eye-catching centrepiece of peaches, pomegranates, cherries, oranges, mint leaves, nut tartlets and marzipan sweets, arranged artistically on crystal glass salvers. The sight and smell of such delicacies made the mouth water and, in the end, Mr Ashmore had to be posted at the long table (with a book for company) so as to fend off anybody, including the dog, trying to pinch the cakes.

A few white circular tables accompanied with matching seats had been spread around at a comfortable distance from the food. Mrs Ashmore's very best china tea sets in pomona and pale primrose yellow with intricate hand painted gold leaf patterns (which were an ancient family heirloom and always considered too nice to be used) had been dusted and polished especially for the occasion. Petite lace doilies had been placed under the cake stands and tea sets and several magnificent bouquets of vibrant wildflowers - Abigail's contribution - had been distributed along the length of the table. A couple of gay blankets had been spread on the grass and then littered with cushions. Eventually everything, down to the last silver spoon, was in place and the overall appearance was surprisingly grand.

And so it was that, as the first guests began to arrive that afternoon, the whole family was standing neatly in a line, all dressed in their best clothes with their faces shining, ready to receive everyone. Mr and Mrs Layton were the first to arrive, with their daughter in tow. Felicity was wearing an outrageously pink dress and matching hat, precariously balanced on the side of her head. With joint shrieks, Abigail and Felicity leapt to greet each other. Then Hailey and her husband Richard Williams came, closely followed by the Halfords and the Whithams.

Mr Felton was precisely punctual, greeting everyone with a genteel smile and courteous bow. Shortly after him came Mr Edwards - the last guest to arrive. Against her intentions - and she fought viciously to repress it - Eleanor found her heart begin to beat faster as she saw him.

'I think we are all here now!' announced Mr Ashmore, surveying the group gathered at the front of Felowspring Manor. After offering Mrs Layton his arm, he proceeded to lead the party around the outside of the house towards the rear, where a large lawn, dappled shade from beech trees and flowering philadelphus and hydrangea bushes awaited them - the perfect location for a tea party. Eleanor found herself face to face with Mr Edwards as the group began to move off around the house. The gentleman bowed and Eleanor nodded shortly before walking on. Mr Felton appeared at her side a moment later, arm outstretched gallantly, and promptly engaged her in conversation.

Soon everyone was peacefully settled - some seated, some preferring to wander freely among the trees - and a gentle hum of pleasant conversation filled the air. Tea was brought out and everyone exclaimed with delight at the sophisticated tea sets, much to Mrs Ashmore's satisfaction. She took great pride in announcing that they had been in the family for centuries. Plates were loaded up with sandwiches, cakes and biscuits of every kind; each one was pronounced delicious and quite the best they had ever eaten. Eleanor glowed with concealed pleasure and contentment at the reception of her culinary skills.

Once everyone had drunk and eaten to their hearts content and mouths were no longer occupied with consuming good food, conversation was recommenced. A quiet game of croquet began over in one corner of the lawn. Meanwhile Abigail and Felicity Layton disappeared off to the brook to dabble their feet in the delightfully cool water and the boys ran into the house to fetch their rackets so that they might have a match of battledore and shuttlecock.

Aiden doubted whether he dare seat himself at Miss

Ashmore's table. Her reception of him that day had been cool and lacking any kind of emotion and he had not trusted himself to greet her suitably, for the sight of her had discomposed him – his power of self-control rapidly diminishing. However, Aiden's abhorrence of the very idea of acting in a cowardly manner was much greater and so he hastily, yet as composedly as possible, occupied the last available seat at her table.

'Ah! Mr Edwards!' Mr Layton greeted. 'We are just talking about how fortunate we have been with the weather today, and… '

The rest of his sentence was a blur of strung together words which Aiden did not manage to take in, for, with the initial intention of obtaining from Eleanor's countenance whether the conversation also bored her, he was struck afresh with Miss Ashmore's innocent beauty. Her hair, which tumbled down in waves around her narrow shoulders, seemed to him more beautiful than the ocean breaking upon the shore, and her dress, a delicate lavender shade, seemed to echo the beauty of the flowers all around her. A gentle blush tinged her cheeks and the curving lines of her soft pink lips rested in a small smile. Little did Aiden perceive the reason for the darkening of her normally so pale complexion. Eleanor had sensed his tender scrutiny and, although also listening to the general conversation at the table, the very thought of his soft, intense eyes resting on her had caused her face to flush.

'Are you quite well, Miss Ashmore?' Mr Felton inquired, turning in his chair in order to look at her properly. 'You have remained positively silent. In fact, I don't think I have heard you speak one full sentence so far this afternoon.'

This was not quite true.

'I do not feel the urge and necessity of constant conversation when I am in the company of others,'

Eleanor answered politely.

'But surely polite conversation at such an event can be considered a beneficial and positive element?' Mr Felton countered, raising an eyebrow.

'Polite conversation, yes. But while I have nothing of any interest or importance to say I find it unnecessary to fill the ears of my fellow companions with needless information and noise,' she responded.

The ghost of a smile hovered over Aiden's lips - his upper lip slightly curling - and it made Eleanor smile too. Mr Felton seemed to perceive Eleanor and Aiden's silent conversation and he turned again to Eleanor in an attempt to capture her full attention.

'Miss Ashmore, I understand that many of these, may I add extremely delicious cakes, were made by your own fair hands?'

'Yes,' Eleanor replied softly, uneasy at being pushed into the centre of attention. She muttered something scarcely intelligible about only helping, but Mr Felton ignored it.

'They are truly superb, as I'm sure we all agree,' Mr Felton praised.

He glanced round the table, searching for affirmation of his statement. Everyone nodded and unanimously agreed. Hailey, seeing how uncomfortable Eleanor was to be talked about so, took pity on her and abruptly changed the subject.

'Mr Edwards, do you sing?' she inquired, this being the first question that came to mind.

'Yes, ma'am I do, though infrequently I confess,' Mr Edwards answered.

Mrs Ashmore, only arriving on the scene in time to hear the end of Mr Edwards' sentence, immediately cried out.

'Oh, singing, how delightful!' she enthused, fully

aware of the rarity of a man who can not only sing but also admit to the fact. 'You know, Eleanor plays the piano beautifully. You must sing for us! And I am sure Eleanor will be more than willing to supply you with instrumental accompaniment.'

Mr Edwards appeared slightly uneasy at this suggestion but he courteously replied, 'It would be my pleasure', noting how Eleanor's face came alive at the very mention of music.

'Will you?' Mr Edwards asked, turning now to Eleanor, his gaze guarded yet hopeful. She nodded, and politely, yet somewhat curtly replied - 'If you wish.' - and then stood and left the table.

Silently he watched her leave, in his head viciously reprimanding himself for expecting more than such a cordial and indifferent reply from such an accomplished and attractive young lady. His outer semblance may have appeared undisturbed but inside he shook and trembled, even such a brief intercourse with her - merely a few words - causing his heartbeat to quicken and the blood to surge through his body. Aiden observed her from a distance now; the way the wind whirled with her hair in the gentle breeze, the way her graceful steps and movements were like a dance. She was talking to Mr Felton now who had followed her as she left the table – something he had said causing her to laugh, lighting her whole face up - and a pang of red-hot jealousy shot through him. The feeling was so intense that it physically hurt him, making him gasp and clench his teeth - he turned away.

At that moment Francis strode towards Mr Ashmore, a look of urgency on his face; everyone turned to look at him curiously.

'It's the sheep, master,' Francis said in a low voice. 'They've got out and I cannot round 'em up again. I'm mighty sorry to disturb you, only I've been trying this last half hour with no success.'

Mr Ashmore patted him on the arm.

'Don't worry, we'll get the rascals back soon enough. I shall be with you in just a moment.'

'Can I be of assistance?' Mr Edwards volunteered, stepping forward. 'I have some experience with sheep.'

'Splendid Edwards! We could certainly use another pair of competent hands,' replied Mr Ashmore gratefully and the three men set off.

Eleanor saw Aiden leave with them. However detached she had deluded to be, she had known every movement he made, her eyes being strangely familiar with his ever-changing position, always inconspicuously knowing where to rest to find him.

After the menfolk had been absent for some time Eleanor slipped off to see how they were faring. Quietly she approached the meadow where the sheep were pastured. Mr Edwards was just helping Francis to lift a heavy fence post, which had fallen askew, back into place. The sheep were contentedly milling around nearby, methodically munching grass.

'He's so far beneath my touch,' Eleanor thought with a jolt, watching him lift another heavy fence post before straightening up and brushing his hair aside with the back of his hand. He glanced in the direction of the stables where she was standing and Eleanor flattened herself against the wall, heart pounding. After a couple of minutes had passed, she ventured to peer out again and saw him shake hands with Mr Ashmore and Francis before leaving.

Eleanor slowly wandered back, swiping absent-mindedly at a bush as she passed around the house. She joined the others just in time to hear the end of their speculative chatter. Hailey was conversing with Mrs

Layton and Mrs Whitham: 'Perhaps he is not a gentleman after all?' Mrs Whitham was saying thoughtfully. 'If he has knowledge and experience with *sheep*?'

'And he is not staying in a very *costly* house, is he? That at least does not indicate great wealth, does it?' added Mrs Layton.

Eleanor felt a strange sensation rise up in her as she listened.

'And yet,' interjected Hailey. 'Is his manner not that of a gentleman's? Is his conduct and character not unquestionably noble, whether he is of birth a gentleman or not?'

The other two ladies nodded vigorously in agreement and thus was their conversation ended. If Hailey had not defended Mr Edwards, Eleanor felt sure she would have rashly burst into the conversation and passionately defended him herself. Why should she care whether he was a gentleman by blood or not?!

***

By early evening all the guests had taken their leave, each one individually thanking the Ashmores for such good food and even better conversation. The frugal remains of cakes and biscuits were then cleared away to the safety of the kitchen larder. The younger children were, to their great dismay, promptly sent to bed, giving their parents and eldest sister the much-required space from people that is essential after such a day in society. Mrs Ashmore's unending supply of words had officially ended. She preferred now to meticulously study the very dull wallpaper in the parlour, eyes staring unseeingly ahead of her, all of her facial muscles slack, shoulders slumped; this is what Mrs Ashmore looked like when she was tired. With her now in a somewhat mentally vacant state, Mr Edwards and the ulterior motive behind the tea party were not discussed, for Mr Ashmore and Eleanor were definitely not going to initiate such a discussion of their own accord.

After wordlessly staring at each other's weary and morbid faces for over half an hour, Eleanor, tiring of such a cheerful occupation in the evening, kissed her parents goodnight, readied herself for slumber and indulged in the comfort of a good book before slipping off into dreams.

CHAPTER FOUR

Wanted And Unwanted Intrusions

The next few days were, for the Ashmores, relatively uneventful. Abigail and Ethan, after completing their lessons, disappeared for the majority of sunlight hours, occupying themselves with drawing, playing cards and reading, thus freeing their mother from the responsibility of continually attending to them. Equally, Charles was utterly content to withdraw himself to the habitual refuge of his bedroom for hours on end, provided he was punctually notified in time for meals. Mr Ashmore was busy most of the day in his study, discussing the development of some new properties with Matthew, his estate manager. With no social gatherings or tasks impending Eleanor was presented with an adequate and most welcome amount of free time, which she took great joy in filling with pleasant occupations such as expanding her culinary repertoire with Elizabelle, improving her musical prowess, and painting. The climbing rose which grew over the wooden arbour in the garden was in full bloom and under its wings, cocooned by its rich fragrance, she delighted to sit with her small easel and paper, with the sun beaming down on her from a cloudless sky, feeling the grass beneath her bare feet and the gentle rustle of a breeze wafting through her hair as she painted.

Most days Eleanor would also go walking, while the agreeable weather allowed it. For her there was no greater pleasure than being able to drift along as slowly as she pleased for as long as she chose, deep in thought, in the woods or across the fields. She met not one soul on her solitary wanderings, and she would not have it any other way. These were Eleanor's personal times for dreaming herself away into sequences of events that may never take place outside of her wishful imagination. However unlikely her daydreams might be, they never ceased to lift her spirits and the hope always stayed with her that maybe, one day, those dreams would become reality.

After some time spent wandering the fields alone she would more often than not loop round and walk back through the village of Felowspring, past its friendly cottages and houses, sometimes stopping at the post office or calling in on the Laytons with a message from her parents.

A few days later Eleanor returned from one of these wanderings on a particularly warm summer's day and, as she walked up the long driveway under the canopy of emerald green leaves, the dappled sunlight, which was only just pressing through the dense foliage, played patterns all over her face. Skipping up the steps to the manor and slipping in through the unlocked front door Eleanor unfastened her shawl. It was only as she reached up to hang it by the door that she noticed a hat and jacket hung beside her father's which she did not recognise.

'Who has come to call I wonder?' Eleanor mused. Spurred on by the welcome prospect of friendly company and intelligent discourse she hurried to her room to wash her face and check her reflection in the mirror before noiselessly padding down the stairs and up the corridors to the parlour, where she was sure the family would be entertaining their guest.

The parlour was a light and airy room, very well-suited to entertaining guests and hosting social gatherings. It was also perfect for convening in as a family in the evenings to read, talk and play games, or for retreating to during the day when one was in need of some time alone spent in pleasant, plush surroundings.

All the walls of the room were wood-panelled, painted white with intricate embellishments of gold leaf and carvings, with the exception of one wall which was elegantly covered with chinoiserie wallpaper. The floral, hand-painted motif of the paper was pale sage green and lent the room an exotic, sumptuous feel. As for the furnishings in the room, these were equally luxurious. Damask armchairs and a damask chaise sofa were arranged around a large low table. Each of these was upholstered in the same colour as the curtains which hung on either side of the French windows - a pale Wedgewood blue. Matching cushions were scattered liberally along the chaise sofa and on the armchairs, and at each end of the sofa was a bolster for utmost comfort. A cream Axminister carpet covered the entirety of the floor and the low, gleamingly polished table in the centre of the room was never to be seen without a bunch of flowers gracing it.

It was not Eleanor's intention to arrive in the parlour unnoticed, but her lightness of foot allowed her silent movement throughout the house and she often remained undetected by all members of the family, excepting Rumpus, until the very last minute.

Consequently, Eleanor was standing in the doorway, already half in the room, before its inhabitants, who all had their backs turned to her, became aware of her presence. The occupant of the high-backed damask armchair in the corner of the room instantaneously leapt up and swung around as soon as Eleanor was detected and she realised with a shock that it was none other than Mr Edwards. He bowed gallantly.

'Mr Edwards!' She sank into a deep, slightly unsteady curtsy, flustered by this unanticipated visit.

'Eleanor, you have arrived quite fittingly!' her mother exclaimed, beckoning her over and patting the seat beside her. 'We were just in the middle of telling Mr Edwards the story of Felowspring Manor.'

Still a little flustered, Eleanor allowed herself to be seated, her unwavering gaze fixed on the window directly in front of her as she listened to her father's rendering of the tale. Mr Edwards appeared most interested and asked many questions concerning the architectural structure of the house and discovery of the grounds, all of which Mr Ashmore willingly answered, with more enthusiasm than he addressed any other subject.

This house had been Mr Ashmore's aspiration since young adulthood, so the fruition of that long-awaited dream was a matter he never tired of discussing. When the Ashmores had first found and purchased the expansive portion of land, the shell of a building already situated near its centre had been in a pitiful state of ruin. However, with a very clear vision, the young John Ashmore had set about bringing his desire to reality. And, being convinced that all is possible for those who believe, he successfully directed the construction of the impressive building which they now called home, surrounded as it now was with lovingly cared for gardens and well-tended grounds.

Just as the discourse gradually drew to a close between the two gentlemen a light rap sounded on the parlour door and Elizabelle ushered in Mr Ayles, who had clearly ridden there, for his dark hair was windswept and in his hands he clutched his riding crop and gloves. He bowed to the occupants of the room who had all risen to their feet to greet him.

'I have come to apologise for not being able to accept your invitation to attend the tea party,' Mr Ayles explained. 'I was away on business in Wenerfield and have only just returned.'

'Then we shall have to plan another one for when you are able to attend,' responded Eleanor enthusiastically, her mind already leaping to a new recipe she had found in a magazine; she was sure Joshua would enjoy it.

'We would not ordinarily have planned something at such short notice,' added Mrs Ashmore. 'But I was eager to welcome Mr Felton and Mr Edwards to Felowspring while they were still freshly arrived. I don't believe you have been introduced yet?'

Mrs Ashmore turned to Mr Edwards who had remained silent until now. He stepped forward and bowed shortly. Mr Ayles had not noticed Aiden's presence in the room. He returned the bow, just as shortly, and all of a sudden it seemed as if the atmosphere in the room had tensed.

'Would you like to eat with us? We were just about to have a light repast, you would be most welcome to join us!' invited Mrs Ashmore, opening the parlour door and beckoning him forward with her hand.

'No thank you ma'am,' Mr Ayles replied. 'I cannot stay for long. I did not wish to disturb you.' His eyes flicked briefly to Aiden who held his gaze, and then to Eleanor.

'If you'll excuse me,' he muttered, face downcast, brow furrowed, and he left the room.

There was a joyous cry of 'Joshua!' heard from the hallway and some moments later Ethan hurried in, a radiant smile on his face, to inform them that the food was on the table. They hastily adjourned to the dining room where a light luncheon of fresh homegrown salad, crusty bread, cold beef and creamy cheese had been set out. Eleanor and Mrs Ashmore found their appetites somewhat abated because of the heat but everyone else was not in the least influenced by something as trivial as the weather and fell to with zeal.

After their youthful appetites had been sated, Abigail, Charles and Ethan drifted off, leaving the grown-ups to their own amusement.

A welcome breeze, one of those sublime ones where there is just the right amount of warmth and coolness hidden in it, had begun to waft through the grass outside, creating waves of verdure, and the leaves of the trees above rustled ever so gently.

***

Aiden and Eleanor left the house in each other's company a little later, and, after strolling a while through the orderly walkways bordered by neatly clipped yew and buxus to the front of the house, they headed past the stables and in the direction of the woods. Conversing together they discovered, to their mutual surprise, that the words flowed easily and the conversation was unexpectedly refreshing even though they did not talk of many consequential matters, just light conversation as between friends. As they entered the woods a companionable quiet descended and for quite some time neither spoke, though much passed between them without their feeling the need to verbalise it.

Finally, Aiden broke the silence by asking Eleanor questions about herself and her family, about Mayhaven and Felowspring and many other things. Eleanor answered all these questions readily and as they walked she found it hard to stop her gaze from wandering to his face, his strong profile silhouetted against the backdrop of the forest.

They reached a small clearing in the woods with a stunning panoramic opening, revealing miles upon miles of fields, hedgerows and rolling hills. A narrow wooden bench, which was bathed in warm sunlight due to a convenient thinning out of foliage directly above, looked out over this scenic view. Crude steps, blanketed in moss, were roughly hewn out of the rock and led up to this vantage point. Aiden's first consideration was Miss Ashmore's wellbeing and so he leapt up the steps ahead of her before turning around to offer his hand in assistance. She gratefully accepted and, with Mr Edwards' attentive assistance, allowed herself to be guided safely to the summit of the stairs.

As she attained the top Eleanor became acutely aware of her own hand still held in his. She looked up and met his gaze and then for many long moments they stood, their eyes speaking louder than their voices ever could.

Suddenly Eleanor, almost ashamed, hastily looked away and withdrew her hand. So intense was his gaze that she felt bare before him, exposed and defenceless. For it is true that sustained eye contact, that lasts just seconds too long, can be more intimate than words could ever be.

***

The sun had already begun to sink, giving the clouds an innocently pink lining, when Eleanor and Aiden turned towards home, neither speaking until they had reached the steps leading to the front door . Eleanor was already standing on the highest step, her hand resting on the door handle when she felt Mr Edwards gently take her hand from behind. Eleanor suppressed a gasp and swung around.

'Will you excuse me from the rest of your family?' he asked. 'The hour is late and I must take my leave of you all now.'

Eleanor merely nodded, once again robbed of the power of speech. Aiden bent ever so slightly forward, as if to kiss the surface of her hand, but, catching himself, he let her hand slip through his and walked away, not looking back once. Eleanor released the slow shuddering breath she had not realised she had been holding and gradually turned the handle to open the door.

Dinner was just about to be served, candles were being lit and the tantalising smells of breadcrumbed asparagus and venison pie were spreading from room to room, more speedily summoning people to the table than any dinner bell could have.

After delivering Aiden's message to her parents Eleanor rushed up the stairs to change. Once in her room however she slowed her pace, drifting over to the open window and perching on the edge she allowed the cool evening breeze to refresh her flushed face and dance through her hair. Eleanor, leaning out, was just in time to see the sun sink behind the horizon, surrounded by pink and purple tinted clouds, bathing the distant hills in a soft red light. She exhaled slowly, taking in the vibrant colours of the sky.

Eleanor loved her home. She loved the hills and valleys, the fields full of flowers, the tall trees and pretty houses. But sometimes, on occasions such as this, Eleanor longed to be somewhere else. It was when the wind danced in her hair, when the sweet smell of wild flowers surrounded her, when the sun set on the horizon or when she could almost smell the salty scent of the sea, that was when she felt the compelling urge to explore faraway lands and return with tales of mystery and adventure. But the feeling passed soon enough, as the excitement and fresh air of the day had by now awakened her appetite. She firmly shut the window, changed and returned to her family.

Later, after a pleasant evening of games over a glass of burgundy (and brandy for Mr Ashmore), Eleanor threw herself between the comfort of her soft, linen bed sheets and feather-filled pillows, promptly drifting off into a fitful night's sleep.

***

The next morning they once again received a visit from Mr Felton who, after paying his respects to them all, withdrew himself to the library to continue his studies. He did not reappear for many hours. In fact, Eleanor was in the process of rehearsing a new composition on the pianoforte when Mr Felton chose to silently enter the room and position himself behind her, shocking Eleanor to the extent that she completely lost her place and brought her hands clashing down on the keys in a discordant cacophony of jumbled notes.

'Beautiful playing,' he murmured admiringly, leaning forward.

And then, in a furtive whisper, his mouth so close to her ear that she could feel his breath on her skin: 'But not nearly as beautiful as you.'

His voice was silky smooth like honey but with a bitter aftertaste. Eleanor shuddered with repulsion and, after a moment's pause, rose to her feet, excused herself and hurriedly left, leaving Mr Felton standing speechless in the centre of the room. He narrowed his eyes; he had not expected such resistance.

Eleanor immediately sought out the rest of her family. There was safety in numbers and Eleanor knew that Mr Felton would not be so foolish as to continue his amorous advances with others in the room. Indeed, she was not at all surprised to hear the main door bang shut seconds later - Mr Henry Felton had exited the building. Sometime later Eleanor retired to the sanctuary of her beloved library, and, as she entered it, closed the tall doors behind her, and leant her head back against the wood, she felt as if the entire room bent in to embrace her.

CHAPTER FIVE

Open Hearts

A respectful rap on the study door disturbed Mr Ashmore's intricate thought processes and, upon opening the door, he was a little taken aback to see that his visitor was Mr Edwards. He showed him in and indicated to an armchair by the stone fireplace, opposite his own desk. Mr Edwards seated himself.

Mr Ashmore's study was tucked away in the quietest part of the house, with a window overlooking the wooded area of their estate. All of the walls were oak panelled, a splendid rich brown, as were the bookcases and shelves. Two deep damask armchairs, the kind you sink into when you sit down and have to heave yourself out of to stand up, were placed on either side of the oak desk. Varnished floorboards were partially covered by a thick Persian rug, of a similar deep red to the armchairs. Papers littered the desk surface and every shelf overflowed with books and files and broken ornaments, given to him by his family, which he had yet to fix. A deep stone fireplace with a basket grate was set into one wall; the entire room had a pleasantly *manly* feel to it.

'Well, Mr Edwards. This *is* an unexpected pleasure,' pronounced Mr Ashmore warmly, also seating himself and leaning forward, his hands resting on the desk surface. 'How can I be of assistance?'

'I have come to ask if I might be able to look at some of the deeds for properties in the area,' the gentleman replied. Mr Ashmore owned a great deal of the properties in Felowspring.

'Certainly!' exclaimed Mr Ashmore obligingly. After a brief discussion on the type and size of property Aiden was looking for, Mr Ashmore pulled out the bottom drawer of his desk and fished through the papers he had stashed there. A few moments later he laid a heap of selected papers in front of Aiden.

'Those should give you something to look at for now,' Mr Ashmore said.

He stood up, his fingers quickly scanning across the many files he had accumulated, and he heaved an exceptionally thick leather-bound file off one of the top shelves of his bookcase. He opened it on his desk with a resounding thump.

'In the meantime,' he added, already flicking through the pages. 'I'll have a look for some more in here.'

The two gentlemen set to and soon the only sound to be heard was the gentle rustle of pages being turned and papers being rearranged. Mr Ashmore was able to retrieve a couple more deeds and Aiden poured over them with a look of intent concentration and deliberation. Eventually he straightened up, still holding a number of selected papers in his hands.

'May I borrow these?' he asked.

'Certainly,' replied Mr Ashmore generously, tidying up the remaining papers and putting his desk back in order. Aiden tucked the deeds carefully into his coat pocket and assisted with the tidying up.

'You must have luncheon with us today,' Mr Ashmore invited.

There was a sudden flutter in Aiden's stomach, quite unaccounted for. But he answered, 'Thank you, Sir. I would be very happy to,' with a slight bow of his head.

Mr Ashmore waved aside the thanks with a flick of his hand, knocking over a pile of books as he did so; Aiden swiftly bent down to retrieve them.

A bell went at that very moment, ending their already substantially concluded conversation. The two men did not need telling twice; they abandoned the room with all haste.

Eleanor, guided by her stomach, which had been telling her for the past half hour that sustenance would greatly be appreciated any time soon, also punctually reacted to the announcement of food, exiting the library in a matter of seconds. She made her way along the hallway as speedily as a gentlewoman can, only to be drastically impeded in her progress by nearly colliding with some unfortunate individual who had been standing innocently just on the other side of the corner she had hastened around. To her surprise she realised the person was Aiden and, as she sank into a deep curtsy of apology, her face colouring, she wondered if she was condemned to forever come upon him unawares.

'I am—,' she began to apologise, but was interrupted by Mr Edwards.

'No, please forgive me. I seem to have lost my way to the dining room. Your father was so kind as to invite me to dine with you again today, but I was so distracted by the paintings hung in this corridor that I completely forgot to follow him.'

He smiled bashfully at her and Eleanor realised for the first time how beautiful he looked when he smiled. She suddenly had the irresistible longing to make him smile once again, for her to be the reason for that instantaneous bright smile which lit up his whole countenance.

A second ring of the bell which seemed to say 'you're keeping us waiting' distracted Eleanor and she forced herself to ignore this urge and, before she could change her mind and linger longer in the corridor alone with him, she briskly led the way, Mr Edwards striding along beside her.

Mrs Ashmore was only too pleased that Mr Edwards was once again a visitor in their home and made this very clear through her warm greeting.

Luncheon was a leisurely affair with much light banter and afterwards everyone gathered in the parlour for some informal and intelligent discourse. The French windows had been opened wide to circulate fresh air throughout the house. This meant that, although they were in actuality seated indoors, they were also able to appreciate the delightful smells and breezes of outdoors.

Eleanor, after refusing an offer of a chair from Mr Edwards, seated herself in her favourite childhood seat: the lap of her father. While Mrs Ashmore initiated a rather one-sided conversation with Mr Edwards about animals (one-sided only because Aiden could not multi-task), Eleanor attempted to suppress her laughter so as not to interfere with the talk whilst simultaneously evading her father's vagarious fingers which threatened to tickle her at any moment.

Aiden, despite giving the appearance of listening to Mrs Ashmore (who was currently speaking rather heatedly about the cruelty shown to nesting birds in the area), was actually observing the light-hearted play betwixt father and daughter. He looked at Eleanor and unconsciously smiled, but quickly glanced away when she noticed.

Ethan, who had by now concluded that Aiden was not an enemy and could therefore be trusted, decided to clamber onto his mother's lap. With a gasp of awe Ethan spotted the sword Aiden had propped against the wall upon entering the parlour. The young boy's eyes went from the sword to Aiden's face and then back to the sword, his little mouth open in dumbstruck wonderment. All shyness now utterly discarded, Ethan engaged him in a complex conversation about weapons of warfare.

After the man and the boy had conspiratorially discussed some secret matter of military operations for a few minutes Ethan dashed out of the room, returning after a few minutes, staggering under the weight of a substantial collection of wooden swords, daggers, arrows, spears and various other forms of munition. Then followed the serious procedure of choosing the appropriate weaponry, and then, out in the garden, a battle commenced.

On many occasions the spectators (Eleanor, Mrs Ashmore, Mr Ashmore and Abigail) had to close their eyes or stifle screams as each opponent fought on heroically. That is to say, Ethan fought ruthlessly and unsparingly, battering his adversary brutally, while Aiden tried his best to not inflict any genuine injuries upon his young friend while deflecting Ethan's frenzied onslaught. Finally the battle ended when Ethan dramatically flung his sword at Aiden's legs while Aiden issued a genuine cry of anguish. Thankfully no real damage was done and, as Ethan forced his defeated foe to beg on his knees for mercy, Aiden's gasped response was full of merriment and laughter. His face however was covered with sweat and his shirt and waistcoat had picked up a good deal of dust and grass during the fight. He rubbed a grubby hand across his equally grubby face and Eleanor, immediately noticing his predicament, arose and offered to assist him.

Not so far away, in a convenient proximity to the kitchen, a stone well had been dug, supplying the household with an unceasing supply of fresh, ice cold water.

As Aiden, on Eleanor's instruction, took off his waistcoat, his shirt sticking to his chest with sweat, she could not help but notice his well-built body. Rapidly looking away she devotedly focused all her attention on drawing up a pail of water and wetting her handkerchief in the refreshing liquid before handing it to Aiden. As she used some of the water to scrub his waistcoat, in an attempt to clean it of its marks, she could feel his eyes on her, scrutinising her every movement.

'Thank you for joining Ethan in his games,' Eleanor said. She looked up and smiled gratefully at him. 'I am sure it will be all he talks about for the coming few days.'

Aiden laughed.

'I assure you, I did not see it as an obligation. I thoroughly enjoyed the experience, however painful it proved to be.'

As he laughed, Eleanor felt an inexplicable thrill rush through her body, causing her to shiver and, as their gaze met, there was laughter in his eyes and she could see his searching gaze penetrating her; what he sought for she did not know. He spoke again, his voice trembling with emotion, the nature of which Eleanor could not tell.

'Your eyes are like a walled terrace, a secret garden,' he murmured softly. 'Would you let me climb over that wall and into your heart?' he added in a whisper.

A gentle breeze rustled the leaves of the trees and swept through their hair and Eleanor, Aiden's words caught on the wind, couldn't be sure of what he had just uttered.

Ethan chose that moment to sneak up on Aiden and slash at his legs with a wooden cutlass, causing him to cry out and diverting his attention.

Seizing the distraction, Eleanor slipped away, the noise of her light footsteps and the gentle swishing of her skirts masked by her brother's war cries. She safely reached her bedroom without any undesired hindrances and, quite overcome by the combined effect of a sudden burst of exercise and a bewildered heart, she crumpled into a heap by the foot of her bed, like a puppet whose strings have gone slack. The sounds of play battle and laughter - Aiden's laughter - carried up through her open window on the soft summer breeze, kissing her ears like a butterfly, the melody as beautiful to her as any sublime musical composition.

Throwing herself onto her bed she gazed up at the ceiling. As she lay there, examining her heart, she sought to ascertain from the confused jumble of thoughts, feelings and fears stored up inside her what the true desires of her heart were. She had for some time not allowed them to see the light of day, choosing instead to repress and contain everything within her until the storm inside became too much for her to weather. And now all those feelings and thoughts burst forth in violent, yet somehow strangely refreshing waves.

With a shock she realised the simple answer to all the confusion inside of her - she loved him.

To be in love, Eleanor realised, was not exactly the fairy tale feeling she had been led to expect. It was more like a beautiful and yet bittersweet combination of breathless captivation, pain and dreamlike surrender; like the first summer's eve, when you can almost taste the sweetness, yet madness of new hope, warmth and adventure.

The simple realisation and acceptance of the fact that she loved him disentangled Eleanor's intricately woven heart as harmlessly as only love can. She was suddenly filled with an excitement at the infinite possibilities of love. But what if he did not love her? Her heart sank a little. Then Eleanor remembered that her feelings were not wholly dependent upon his returned affections. She loved him and would continue to love him, whether he returned the sentiment or not.

Such a lightness filled her, a happiness from head to toe, and she laughed out loud. Eleanor threw her arms around her shoulders and hugged herself tight, just letting that happiness course through her.

The noises outside reminded her that she ought to be downstairs with her family and so she straightened her hair and generally made herself presentable before joining them once more. They had by now retired again indoors, Abigail amusing herself with a book while Ethan and Charles chose to scheme together.

'I have the ears of a hawk,' warned Abigail as her brothers whispered together, occasionally sending her furtive glances.

'It's the *eyes* of a hawk actually,' corrected Charles and Ethan chuckled appreciatively. Abigail did not deign to respond, but returned to her book with an indifferent sniff.

As Eleanor entered the room, Aiden's eyes were immediately drawn to her. Trying to restrain his gaze, he returned his focus to his conversation with Mr Ashmore. For a while the two gentlemen were the only ones who spoke, the ladies being content to listen. Eleanor found that her clarified heart and mind now allowed her to perceive and understand her feelings more readily. As Aiden relaxed again into his conversation with her father, Eleanor was able to observe the softness with which he spoke, the gentleness of his manners and the wisdom in his words. All these little details Eleanor absorbed and delighted in.

Mr Edwards regretfully took his leave of them soon after, explaining his departure with the expected arrival of a good friend.

'Give our regards to your friend, whoever he may be!' Mrs Ashmore called cheerily after him, as the entire family stood on the steps to wave him off.

'Oh, isn't he lovely!' she exclaimed a few moments later after they had all entered the house again and shut the door. Charles rolled his eyes.

As Aiden briskly walked away from their estate, throwing fleeting glances behind him, he fancied he saw Eleanor's figure highlighted in one of the downstairs windows, watching him, but when he looked again she was gone, like an elusive dream.

The gentleman's journey was thankfully not a long one and he arrived moments before a knock on the door heralded the arrival of his visitor. A friend of many years, Raymond was a roguish looking young man with welcoming eyes, a ready smile and a word of wisdom for every occasion; he knew Aiden better than most. They were true blood brothers - a rare yet beautiful species.

They greeted each other with that commonly known and universally used greeting unique to men: a hearty hug, manly handshake and comradely slaps on the back. The two men proceeded to shed their outdoor coats, unfasten their ties and loosen the top buttons of their shirts and waistcoats. Only then did they feel comfortable enough to relax and converse.

'Well, how is Mayhaven? Will it do?' Raymond inquired while allowing himself the liberty of opening Aiden's best bottle of wine (what Raymond didn't know is that it was his best and only bottle of wine) and pouring himself a generous mug full, for Aiden did not have any wine glasses.

'I think so,' Aiden replied carefully.

'And where have you just returned from?' his friend continued.

Raymond's eyes twinkled with mischief and good humour as he poured his friend a comparatively small mug of the red liquid.

'Nowhere particular,' Aiden responded nonchalantly, accepting the offered drink of his own wine and staring very hard at its content, deliberately avoiding his friend's searching gaze. But his normal behaviour was too familiar for Raymond to overlook such atypical conduct; and Aiden was most definitely behaving abnormally. Raymond decided however to say nothing, choosing instead to steadfastly bore his eyes into Aiden until his conscience would give him no peace, which Raymond knew from experience never took long with an honest heart like Aiden's.

'I have just returned from the Ashmore estate,' he said.

'And the Ashmores are…?' prompted Raymond expectantly, taking a generous draught of his wine.

'The Ashmores are one of the most wealthy and influential families in Mayhaven, alongside the Laytons. Mr Layton is the man to whom I first wrote before coming here. He invited me to the wedding I told you of, and it was during the ball at his house that I first became acquainted with the Ashmores.'

'And why were you with them this fine evening?'

Aiden looked down.

'I confess I went there today not only to inquire about properties, but also to see Mr Ashmore's daughter.'

'Ah,' said Raymond in the tone of one who has suddenly understood everything very clearly. 'Ah. So what you are telling me… or trying to tell me… is that you have fallen for Miss Ashmore?'

'Yes, I suppose that is what I am trying to say,' Aiden agreed, his upper lip curling into a small smile.

'But, Aiden,' Raymond responded reasonably. 'You met her how long ago…? A week… a little more perhaps, at the very most? And you fancy you love her?'

'Yes I do,' Aiden replied steadily. 'I do love her.'

Raymond ran a hand through his hair and gave his friend a slightly despairing look.

'I wouldn't expect you to understand Ray,' Aiden said quietly. 'I know you doubt, I know you repudiate the very suggestion that it would be possible for two people, two strangers, to fall in love after a fleeting look, a brief discourse and a polite introduction. That two souls could possibly connect by merely noticing each other. Remember that we are not merely a body but a spirit, with a soul of depth and feelings. And surely, when such a connection of souls, even between seeming strangers, is made, then a bond has been created and in that essential moment in time, *love has begun.*'

Unnoticed to Aiden his voice had been increasing in volume and passion.

'I'm in love with her Ray, truly I am!' The earnest plea in his voice for his friend to understand was clearly identifiable. 'And it is a true and honest and devoted love.'

'I do not doubt you,' Raymond replied after a long pause and Aiden leant back in his chair relieved. 'But does she know of your feelings? Have you told her of your affections and made them clear to her?'

'No,' Aiden confessed slowly, his eyes downcast. 'Not entirely.'

'Then you must - as soon as possible!' declared Raymond, equally caught up in the energy and emotion flowing from his friend. 'Tell her, tell her tomorrow! Don't delay, who knows but that there may be other admirers; if you wait too long you may lose her forever.'

He leaned across the table and gripped Aiden's shoulder in an attempt to more effectively portray the urgency of the situation.

'Yes I should,' agreed Aiden nodding, his eyes staring unseeingly at the table in front of him. 'And I will.' There was a firmness, a resoluteness, in his voice.

Raymond loosened his grip on Aiden's shoulder before encouragingly slapping him on the back.

'Sleep is what you need now, my friend,' Raymond wisely suggested. He did not wait for a reply, for he knew it would be a long time in coming since Aiden was still leaning back in his chair in a stupor, a distant look in his eyes.

Raymond decided to show himself the way to the guest bedroom. But before he left, he cast a worried look at his friend. Should he remind him? But Raymond could not bring himself to spoil his friend's happiness, however temporary it may need to be.

A few minutes later Aiden looked around the room as if awaking from a dream, only to realise that he was now alone and that the sun had already finished its descent for the day. Once in his bedroom he opened the window and gulped big breaths of air in an effort to clear his head and keep himself calm. He stood at the window, clutching the frame, his breath coming thick and uncertain, his eyes shining with a mixture of hope and joy, of slight despair and above all, love. The mere thought of her soft, questioning eyes, the image of her face in his mind caused his heart to quicken and the blood to coarse through his veins, such was the intense passion within him. No matter how hard he tried to focus on anything else, every other thing seemed unimportant and meaningless in comparison; he could think only of her.

But then, unwanted and unwelcome, another thought slipped into his mind. Another place, another person, another purpose. His shoulders slumped heavily and he ran a hand agitatedly through his hair. Turning slowly away from the window he laid himself gingerly down on the fragile wooden frame and thin mattress that served adequately as a bed. Alas, the turmoil in his mind allowed him no rest until the early hours of the following morning.

CHAPTER SIX

Sudden Farewell

It was Eleanor's unpleasant task to forsake her bed far too early for her liking to answer a knock at the door.

'It must only be shortly after dawn,' she grouchily and incorrectly estimated as she traipsed down the stairs, pulling a shawl tightly around her shoulders.

This time it was not their near-constant companion of late, Mr Henry Felton, but a vastly more interesting messenger, a young errand boy with an abundance of freckles. He had a note addressed to Mr and Mrs Ashmore.

Eleanor's disgruntled expression instantly vanished to be replaced with a ready smile for the boy, followed by an eager curiosity as she accepted the note.

'Thank you James,' she said, and the boy, with a quick grin, darted off. Eleanor slowly shut the door, studying the handwriting of the addressee in an attempt to identify its sender.

'Eleanor? What is it dear?'

A faint, drowsy call wafted down to her from Mrs Ashmore whose extremely proficient ears had detected the engaging sounds of news, even in slumber.

'A note Mama! May I open it?' Eleanor called back. Not waiting for a reply she tore open the seal.

'It is from Mr Edwards, Mama!' the delight in her voice unconcealable. 'He requests the honour of dining with us this evening.'

'This evening!' Mrs Ashmore repeated in a rather higher tone of voice than usual. She appeared at the bannister above Eleanor, wrapping her pink dressing gown tighter around her body.

'But we have not made preparations! The manor is in a disastrous state and I'm sure we have nothing edible in the house!'

The good lady paused briefly.

'What day is it today?' she questioned urgently.

'Tuesday, Mama.'

This response disconcerted Mrs Ashmore considerably, causing her to groan deeply.

'Tuesday is Elizabelle *and* Beatrice's day off! And Mr Edwards is coming to dine! And now we have no servants to help us! Why can they not be present when they are so direly needed!'

Noting her daughters' mildly reproving look Mrs Ashmore softened her voice slightly. 'I know that it is not their fault, dear. But why, oh why must Tuesday be their free day? Now who will tidy and cook?'

'Mama, apart from plumping a few cushions and drawing the curtains the house is ready to receive visitors. Elizabelle has already prepared most of the food for the day and I am fully capable of making a fresh salad! We will not starve, Mama.'

Suitably pacified, Mrs Ashmore nodded her agreement and withdrew herself. Seizing the opportunity of solitude, Eleanor rushed up the stairs to dress, the letter still clutched in her hand. Taking more than her accustomed amount of time to prepare herself, paying particular attention to the minor details of her appearance, she chose a sweet rose gown and hung a string of pearls around her pale neck. The precious stones glistened as the sunlight caught them. She then went to the garden where Francis was already standing knee-deep in some bushes, shears in one hand and some pruned branches in the other. He was wearing his ever-present pear green greatcoat, his long mane of greying hair tied back into a ponytail at the nape of his neck.

'Good mornin' Miss Eleanor!' he called, waving the branches clutched in his hand in greeting. Eleanor waved back cheerily and skipped over to him.

'I was just looking for...' she began, but she did not need to finish, Francis already knew. From one of the enormous pockets of his greatcoat he drew out a single salmon rosebud, exquisitely delicate and perfect; not one petal was damaged. Motioning for Eleanor to turn he softly tucked the rosebud into the folds of her braid.

'There Miss, 'ow's that,' he asked, smiling at her.

Eleanor's cheeks were flushed and her eyes shone with pleasure; pleasure at this glorious day and the thought of seeing Mr Edwards again.

'Perfect, thank you Francis,' Eleanor replied beamingly and kissed him on the cheek, before returning to the house.

The remainder of Eleanor's day was spent in the pleasant and undisturbed atmosphere of the kitchen. As far as kitchens go, theirs was surely one of the finest and nicest specimens, with its cool, smooth flagstone floor and broad window positioned above the butlers sink, so that one might contemplate the swaying trees and bright flowers and herbs while one worked. Big bunches of lavender, sage and rosemary hung above the old oak table in the centre of the kitchen. The work surfaces were marble and all the handles of the panelled, full-height cabinets and the bridge tap were of burnished brass.

The rest of the family chose wisely to give Eleanor a wide berth whilst her culinary creations were in progress, knowing that they might otherwise be appointed distasteful tasks such as the washing of dishes. Appetising smells soon began to spread throughout the house, urging the family on to finish their various household tasks.

As Eleanor baked, weighing out various ingredients and stirring numerous pans full of delicious concoctions, she lazily mused about the possible reasons for Aiden's prompt revisit. She did not want to speculate, and yet she could not completely repress the inkling that she might be the reason for his ever-increasing desire to call upon them.

A knock at the door, followed by a brief ring of the bell, sent the entire household dashing frantically about, doing seemingly everything and yet somehow achieving nothing Ethan and Abigail crashed into each other, Charles nearly fell down the stairs, Mrs Ashmore began issuing instructions hysterically, Mr Ashmore attempted to calm and quiet the dog and Eleanor dropped an ancestral bowl of soft fruit on the flagstone floor, smashing it to smithereens.

Mr Edwards was left patiently standing outside for some time before they were all in a halfway suitable state to receive him. If he had been puzzled by the noises he had heard issuing from behind the closed door he was too polite to comment. When the door was finally opened to him, he amiably greeted Mr and Mrs Ashmore and their two youngest offspring who were still mournfully rubbing their bruised heads; behind them he could just make out Charles on the floor, inspecting his bruised leg.

'My eldest daughter is still occupied in the kitchen, preparing dinner,' Mrs Ashmore informed him. 'But she should be able to join us presently. Why don't we withdraw to the parlour in the meantime?'

'I think I should like to first see if I can be of any assistance to Miss Ashmore if possible,' Aiden responded politely. 'I would not like to sit at leisure while Miss Ashmore labours alone.'

'Of course you may. I'm sure Eleanor would be

delighted to receive you in the kitchen.'

With a slight bow Aiden headed for the kitchen.

Eleanor was in the process of assembling the components of a supplementary fruit salad when she perceived the presence of another person in the room. Eleanor could barely save herself from once again dropping the bowl in her hands. Upon seeing Aiden in the doorway she immediately placed the fruit bowl on the worktop and removed her apron before curtsying. She self-consciously brushed back her hair and smoothed out the fabric of her dress. It was some minutes before Aiden, wholly lost in gazing at her, realised that her inactivity was due to his lack of response. He swept off his hat and bowed, his gaze never leaving her face.

'I...,' he gestured vaguely with his hat in an attempt to explain. 'I wanted to inquire if you were in need of any assistance.'

He gulped, all his uneasiness rising anew at the sight of her. He pressed his hands firmly against his hat so that she might not notice how they shook.

'No, thank you,' Eleanor replied, unable to conceal a small smile of pleasure at Mr Edwards' particular thoughtfulness and consideration to her wellbeing. 'I am very nearly finished in here. But thank you,' she repeated and quickly turned back to her washing and chopping.

'I hope we did not delay your ability to receive your friend yesterday,' Eleanor remarked. Aiden moved a few steps closer to Eleanor and her heartbeat quickened noticeably.

'No, not at all. I arrived in impeccable time,' he answered.

Eleanor made as if to leave, the finished salad in her arms, but was smoothly interrupted by Aiden who wordlessly relieved her of her burden and, after waiting for her to exit the room first, proceeded to accompany her to the dining room where the rest of the food had already accumulated. He gently set the bowl in amongst various other dishes.

'I wonder,' Aiden said, without turning around, not trusting himself to speak coherently when looking at her. 'I wonder whether I may once again request your sole company in a turn through the woods this evening.'

Eleanor's hands trembled.

'You may,' she forced herself to say, as calmly as possible.

'Thank you,' he replied simply, inclining his head ever so slightly towards her, his upper lip curling in a bashful smile.

'Ah! There you are!' Mrs Ashmore exclaimed, bursting into the room and causing them both to jump, as if caught in a guilty act.

'Hello Mama,' Eleanor greeted, self-consciously fiddling with the braid in her hair. 'Everyone can come in now, the food is ready.'

'Everyone' had been waiting in earshot so before the words had fully left Eleanor's mouth there was a mad stampede to the table. That is, Charles, Abigail, Ethan and Rumpus stampeded; Mr Ashmore's entrance was rather more dignified.

A fresh salmagundi salad of apples, cucumbers, celery, chives and duck with a dressing of oil, vinegar and lemon, cold slices of ham and beef, crusty bread and savoury veal pastries disappeared speedily from serving platters to plates and from plates to mouths with very little time in between. Then the desserts appeared, sweet puddings of soufflé, raspberry cream and fruit. It did not take long for these to also vanish into seemingly hollow stomachs and soon there was nothing to show for all of Eleanor's work in the kitchen.

'Thank you, Lea, that was most enjoyable,' Mr

Ashmore praised, folding his arms across his stomach and leaning back with a contented little sigh. His statement was confirmed by various grunts from around the table. More words were not obtainable, for everyone had been lulled into an extreme feeling of drowsiness due to the comforting warmth of the weather and satisfying nourishment.

For the remainder of the evening no one seemed in the least inclined to do anything more than flop around like a herd of seals, occasionally exerting themselves to the extent of talking to each other, however finding everything else far too strenuous. A pack of cards was produced some time later with a tray of sugar biscuits and sweet meats and a bottle of claret (with lemonade for the children) and a few merry rounds of Vingt-Un were played.

As the sun began its descent in the heavens and the birdsong diminished to a sporadic chirp, Aiden, who had spent the whole evening dwelling on what he planned to say to Miss Ashmore, arose and extended a hand towards Eleanor. She slipped her own tremulous hand into his and the gentle touch of her soft skin on his sent thrills through his entire body. In that moment he suddenly yearned for her more than ever before. He longed to reach out his arms and enclose her in a passionate embrace, to sense her heart beat against his chest. And he longed for *her*; not merely a body but a spirit and a soul full of light, love and moonlit dreams, of kindness, grace and a lionheart.

The two of them slipped out through the open French windows of the parlour and walked through the garden. The night had now thrown its starry cloak across the heavens, veiling everything in a silver darkness and the moon cast dreams of hope and magical fantasy into the unbarred hearts of already slumbering souls. Neither of them spoke, both preferring the words of the night and whisperings of the moon to mere human interaction.

Then without warning, Aiden whispered to her. 'You haven't perceived it, have you?'

He turned to look at Eleanor and then gazed back up at the sickle moon which was surrounded by a halo of soft light; Eleanor also looked up.

'You haven't noticed how alike you and the moon are. You shine so bright, full of love, like the moon, unveiling the beauty of the darkness and guiding those who have gone astray to the light. And yet…' Aiden paused, seeming unsure of how to go on. '...And yet, you hide your feelings away, like the dark side of the moon - as if you fear a thief in the night. However, I'm sure that one day, you *will* discard the veil and radiate so brightly, like the full moon rising at last, that I think it shall become hard to look away.'

Aiden's eyes were on Eleanor now and he brushed a strand of hair behind her ear and leaned in towards her, his face merely inches away from her own. He looked into her eyes and could see the night sky reflected in them. His hand still rested tenderly on her cheek as their faces slowly drew closer, until their moonlit shadows had melted into one. She could feel his breath on her lips, his mouth almost touching her own - when he suddenly paused and stepped back, his hand falling to his side. And there was a deep pain in his gaze. Then he cast his eyes down, turned and walked a few paces away from her before stopping in his tracks and looking back at her again, one more time.

'Please forgive me,' he whispered, half turning his head towards her, unshed tears glistening in the corners of his eyes and then, without another word, Aiden turned and left.

Eleanor's eyes went wide with stunned bewilderment as she watched him walk along the gravel path before swiftly fading into the darkening night. She caught hold of an obliging tree to steady herself, her breath coming shakingly in short bursts, and for some time she was incapable of doing or thinking anything coherently.

But then came the onslaught of painfully unknown questions from which she could have no relief. What had she done? Where had he gone? Had she in any way offended or discouraged him? Maybe his particularised attention had meant nothing more than a companionable friendship, but why should he then depart so strangely and suddenly? Perhaps his attentive study of her had been for some other reason. All these tormenting speculations filled her mind and her emotionally wearied legs collapsed under the burden of so many doubts and unanswered questions. She sank down into the grass and buried her fingers in its long blades.

The occurrences of the day had, to say the least, left her mentally dazed and physically drained and, summoning the remains of her depleted strength, she pushed herself up and headed for the ajar French windows.

Slipping through the house and up the stairs Eleanor reached safely and unheeded the security of her room. She lowered herself onto the edge of her bed and forced herself to try and repress her feelings and questions for the present, in a wild hope that it would enable her to sleep.

Eleanor was however to be disappointed. For tedious hours on end, she sat immobile on the edge of her bed, the shores of sleep distant oceans away until a lone wave finally took pity on her and swept her away.

***

Her few hours of precious sleep did little to freshen Eleanor. Indeed, the next morning she felt even more fatigued than the night before. Utterly lacking even the tiniest shimmer of energy or motivation, she wearily dressed, taking care however to apply a little rouge to her cheeks in the hope that her restless night would pass unobserved by her family. And so, with a pasted-on smile which looked reasonably convincing she greeted her parents at the breakfast table and compelled herself to eat a small portion of food.

'Oh, Eleanor, I almost forgot,' her father remarked offhandedly. He peered over his glasses at her. 'Mr Felton left a note with Francis yesterday evening, surprisingly late. He is coming to dine with us today.'

Eleanor failed to hide a grimace and looked somewhat dejectedly at her father.

'Very well father. But why do you tell me this so specifically and not the others? I'm sure Mr Felton will excuse my absence for a while during his stay here, for I am rather weary and would prefer to withdraw myself to my room or the library for the greater portion of the day.'

Eleanor also did not wish to give Mr Felton any opportunity to find her alone again. The memory of his last visit was still uncomfortably vivid in her mind and she was determined not to make the same mistake twice.

'Well...' Mr Ashmore began, somewhat apologetically. He avoided eye contact and began to vigorously polish his glasses with the sleeve of his shirt. 'Well, I'm afraid that will be most inconvenient'.

He became even more engrossed with polishing his glasses. 'For Mr Felton specifically requested your attendance.' Mr Ashmore cleared his throat uneasily. 'And a private interview.'

All eyes around the table moved to rest on Eleanor.

'*Ooooh!* I bet he—' Abigail began, before a sharp tap on the arm from her mother and a kick under the table from Charles silenced her. The meaningful look Abigail gave her elder sister was however worse than anything she could have said.

'Well, I shall inform Elizabelle of the addition to our party,' Mrs Ashmore said with a cheerful smile, hoping to break the awkward silence. Her smile faded at the sadly lacking response. Rumpus was the only one unaffected by this exchange. He continued his duty of cleaning up all the stray crumbs as if nothing had been spoken; his enthusiastic snorts and were the only noises in the otherwise silent room.

Finally Eleanor pushed her uneaten food away from her, stood up and moved towards the door.

'Where are you going?' Mrs Ashmore questioned hurriedly, spinning round in her chair.

'Outside.'

'To do what?'

'For a walk.'

'And where?'

Eleanor gestured vaguely with her hand. 'Somewhere. Not far.'

Her mother frowned disbelievingly but consented.

'But make sure you are here when Mr Felton arrives!' she called after her daughter's rapidly receding figure. Eleanor pretended not to hear.

***

The fine weather had continued to persist and all of nature rejoiced at the sunshine. Every flower seemed to bloom brighter than ever before and the sky that morning seemed freshly washed, painted a brilliant ocean blue; not a cloud was in sight. The birds felt it too and joined the rejoicing by melodiously chirping for all they were worth. The beauty of that day though was unfortunately entirely wasted on Eleanor. She had chosen to walk the same way she and Aiden had walked only the night before, along the gravel path which led through the flower beds and bushes, alongside the lawn to the front of the house. But now Eleanor saw neither the flowers nor the trees nor the sky - she saw only the path they had walked together.

After some time she remembered, with an unpleasant jolt, that Mr Felton would undoubtedly be waiting for her when she returned. She dreaded what he could have to say to her. The limited and unwanted introduction to his feelings for her, which she had already received on their last meeting, gave her reason to feel disturbed at the prospect of once again being forced into a room alone with him. It never occurred to her to confide these feelings and fears in her parents.

Eleanor however had no time to dwell on such unpleasant thoughts for she accurately deciphered from Ethan’s demented leaping and waving that a certain Mr Henry Felton had already arrived. Ethan rushed out to meet her as she neared the house.

'He's here! And he's waiting for you in the library!' Ethan gasped urgently, momentarily stopping his leaping. His sandy hair had flopped over his eyes and he impatiently shoved it back with his forearm. Seizing her hand he attempted to drag his sister along in an effort to hasten their progress. Eleanor would however not be disturbed and stubbornly refused to hurry, choosing first to stop and smell the roses, drink a glass of cool water drawn from the stone well and straighten her hair. After that the dreaded interview could not be realistically delayed any longer.

***

Eleanor entered the library quietly. Mr Felton stood by the bay window, his narrow frame hunched together. He turned at the quiet click of the door shutting and hastily moved towards her, as if eager to finish his task as speedily as possible.

'Madam,' he bowed courteously. Eleanor eyed him

warily, as a chick may eye a fox. She did not return the greeting but waited silently for him to continue.

'Madam, you cannot be in any doubt as to why I requested a private interview.'

He raised his eyebrows expectantly. Eleanor perceived that he wished to place words in her mouth and so she acted as though ignorant, assuming a vacant expression.

'Sir, you are mistaken,' she replied. 'I do not know to what I owe this honour.'

Her response was not entirely free of sarcasm, however it was utterly lost on Mr Felton who merely accepted her statement self-righteously.

'I have never been a man of indecisiveness,' Mr Felton continued, beginning to pace around the room, his hands clasped behind his bony back like an army sergeant on parade. 'And, this being so, I always, bar a few insignificant exceptions, which is naturally only to be expected, get that which I desire. In this case, that is you.'

Eleanor flushed hot with indignation at her sex been talked about as nothing more than merchandise that can be 'got' as a man wishes.

Her body language and general demeanour were screaming for him to stop, to save them both the pain and embarrassment, but alas, Mr Felton was too engrossed in his dramatically pre-written, and what he supposed to be romantic confession of love, that he completely missed these signals.

'I know you may think me hasty,' Mr Felton resumed. 'We have been acquainted for a mere few weeks, but with matters of the heart time is irrelevant.'

He sniffed conceitedly as if he were an expert in such matters. Eleanor very much doubted that Mr Felton knew anything about the heart besides knowing that it is a life essential, blood pumping organ. She however quickly reprimanded herself for thinking so harshly.

Finally Mr Felton turned to look at Eleanor, proving that he was talking to her and not, as Eleanor had sometimes thought, the bookcase.

'Eleanor, you,' he reached forward and grasped her hand. 'You, with your beauty and calm serenity, and the evident efficiency and ease with which you accomplish all your tasks, have wholly convinced me that I could never need more in a bride than what I find contained in you.'

He leant down as if to kiss her hand, but Eleanor hastily placed it out of his reach and averted her head, disgusted with his petty proposal.

'I am flattered by your considerate words,' Eleanor began.

Mr Felton bowed gallantly.

'And I know,' Eleanor continued, and here she spoke with entire sincerity, looking him full in the eye, 'truly I know to appreciate these intentions which I do not doubt were made for some of the very best reasons.'

She struggled to find the words.

'But - I am unable to accept.'

'Unable?' Mr Felton repeated disbelievingly. 'Unable?'

His demeanour changed unpleasantly and he took a step towards her. 'I was not aware of your engagement to another man.'

'You have been rightly informed,' Eleanor agreed. 'I am not engaged.'

'And yet,' Mr Felton repeated. 'You are - *unable* - to accept my proposal.'

'Yes, indeed,' she repeated firmly.

'Is there another man?' he inquired viciously, as if daring her to name the culprit. 'Has another man secured your affections?'

He almost grabbed Eleanor in his temper.

'No other man has confessed his love to me,' she

answered, taking a cautionary step back.

'Then why?' Mr Felton asked through gritted teeth. 'How dare you refuse me?'

'Sir, you surely cannot expect me to marry when my heart does not contain any feelings of love towards you.'

Mr Felton looked at Eleanor pityingly.

'Worse things have happened than a woman marrying for reasons other than love, I am sure,' he replied scathingly.

'I could not and I will not,' Eleanor contradicted firmly.

'That is not the only reason, is it?' Mr Felton prompted, his voice now so bitter that Eleanor could almost taste it. 'There is someone else who has led you to foolishly turn down my offer, is there not? There is someone else in your mind right now, as we speak.'

His eyes bore into her and Eleanor coloured at the truth of these words.

'It is true. I cannot marry you while I love another man,' Eleanor confessed. It was the first time she had verbally proclaimed herself to be in love and the feeling, although it contained so much pain and confusion, was also liberating. A slight smile came to her as she now thought of Mr Edwards, for the very thought of him gave her much needed strength.

Mr Felton let out a sudden agonised shriek. He slammed his hand against a chair, sending it toppling to the floor with a crash.

'You have no idea what you do to me,' he cried with the voice of one in the utmost despair. He dashed a hand dramatically across his brow and through his hair. 'How you tear my heart apart, ruthlessly destroying my dreams. And now you stand there smiling?!'

'I truly had no idea that my refusal would cause you so much grief,' Eleanor said, moving towards him anxiously, now genuinely distressed for afflicting so much pain as he claimed to feel on anyone. 'I assure you, now that I am aware of the extremity of your discomfort I will without delay endeavour to ease your anguish by softening my refusal through explanation.'

Mr Felton's face distorted into an ugly grimace. Now he had seen that dramatic distress would not persuade her to change her mind, he dropped all pretence.

'No you wouldn't,' he growled. 'You wouldn't try and help me. You care nothing for others, only for yourself!'

He took a step towards her, his body trembling with an uncontrolled anger and Eleanor trembled as well, fearful of what this man may do in his current state. Nevertheless, she refused to submit to his menace and attempt to instil fear in her.

Eleanor was disgusted with him. His behaviour was most immature; a true gentleman would accept a lady's refusal, however disappointed he may be and would not behave like an untamed wild animal or unruly child when they did not get what they wanted. Eleanor realised that Mr Felton was nothing more than a fraud; a counterfeit, who could flaunt his perfect manners to the highest extent and yet who possessed such a repulsive character.

'I have made my decision,' Eleanor cried. 'Do you think I would be willing to throw away my life for a man who cares nothing for my feelings?'

'You would do well to remember your place,' Mr Felton spat. 'Men are superior to women in every way. If I wished, I could force you to do whatever I please.' He took another step towards her, his fists clenched. 'Greatness is determined neither by sex, nor the ability to dominate others. It is determined by a person's character, the nobility of their conduct, the wisdom in their conversation. A true gentleman would never treat a woman like she was merchandise, nor rant and rave in the manner which you have done,' Eleanor finished.

Mr Felton was entirely unable to respond to these last remarks, for he felt a sudden and terrible conviction; he opened his mouth but no words would come; he remained rooted to the spot, staring at her. Eleanor, strengthened by the truth of her own words, met his gaze with steady eyes. And so they stood until finally Mr Felton, feeling defeated, charged past her and dashed out of the room, slamming the door in a final burst of heated anger at the humiliation he felt. Eleanor was shaken but this was a victorious moment; she had not bowed to intimidation and, mixed in with all the other emotions, she now also felt relieved and elated.

Some moments later Mr Ashmore poked his head around the library door while softly tapping on the door frame.

'May I come in?' he asked tentatively.

Eleanor nodded and her father walked over and wrapped her up in a comforting, supporting embrace. Although Eleanor was a fully grown and mature woman, there were still some things that could only be fixed and put back into perspective by simply holding her father's hand or feeling his strong arms around her. She allowed her head to fall wearily against his chest.

After a few moments Mr Ashmore held his daughter at arm's length and chucked her gently under the chin.

'Come on beauty, smile,' he whispered.

Eleanor made an effort, for her father's benefit, but her attempt was rather wan, not reaching her eyes.

'We have received an invitation to dinner at the Laytons on the morrow,' Mr Ashmore continued, in a less than successful endeavour to cheer her up. 'But I understand if you would rather stay at home. I can excuse you and I am sure they will understand… '

'I will come, Papa,' Eleanor interrupted. 'What I am in need of is diversion, not solitude. Solitude would only bestow upon me time to dwell on and possibly worsen matters.'

'Very well,' her father agreed. Then he added: 'Let's go for a walk.' He took her hand and the two of them headed for the garden.

***

Eleanor returned from the walk somewhat revived and things improved as the day wore on. She helped Elizabelle with the preparation of dinner; time spent in the kitchen with Elizabelle was always a healing tonic for Eleanor, and today was no exception. They prepared a chicken fricassee with golden crusty pastry and vegetables drowned in a buttery sauce and Eleanor decided to try out a new recipe for their last course. The recipe had been given to her by the Layton's cook and was for a sweet dessert called blancmange. It required cream, sugar and a thickening agent, and was often flavoured subtly with almond. This mixture was prepared, strained and then poured into moulds to set before being turned out and appropriately garnished.

Eleanor set to with a will and Elizabelle, more out of curiosity than necessity, aided her. What with Elizabelle's expert experience in cooking and Eleanor's unending inspiration and creativity the Ashmores were certainly never short of new delectable dishes and toothsome puddings. Nobody complained.

***

The Ashmore family were to be exposed once more the next evening to exceptional cuisine, this time at the Laytons, whose cook had lived in France for some years, where he had spent most of his time accumulating convenient knowledge, techniques and recipes.

As the Ashmore carriage halted in front of the

Layton's house the two families came together in an outbreak of shouts, shoulder slaps, hugs, kisses and joyous exclamations. They were all ushered in, their coats and hats were whisked away by waiting servants and very soon they were all seated at the long polished dining table with its many golden candle holders burning bright with tall beeswax candles.

As dinner was served Mrs Layton was full of news and the latest gossip, which was all well-meant and shared eagerly with Mrs Ashmore. Their husbands meanwhile chose to remain silent, neither of them even attempting to fathom what their wives were talking about. Most of this chatter washed in through Eleanor's one ear and out through the other without her retaining so much as a phrase or topic of what was said. However, one name caused her to stiffen and suddenly pay acute attention to every word that was uttered.

'See, I knew you would be shocked!' Mrs Layton was saying, pausing to take a sip of her burgundy. 'Indeed, I am sure everyone was when they heard. Nobody would have suspected that Mr Edwards would leave so unexpectedly! And we all thought he was so well settled and welcomed. They say he left on horseback at night the day before yesterday, without even waiting to pack. There must have been some vastly important reason for his departure. He left his friend to collect his belongings and send them on after him and now his house is shut up and abandoned!' Mrs Layton laughed slightly hysterically and shook her head. 'Now what do you think of that?'

One would never have guessed from Eleanor's outward appearance how deeply startled and dismayed she was at this unanticipated information. Her pulse raced as she remembered him being swallowed into the dense darkness of that night, after leaving her. She had been the last person he conversed with. Surely she was the cause for his leaving. But it was not knowing this for certain that most unsettled her. It was the uncertainty, the thick mist of ambiguous misgivings settling heavily upon her, that began to torment her to the point of being unbearable.

Mrs Ashmore was very disappointed and equally confused at hearing this news and she turned to Eleanor, studying her demeanour for any tell-tale signs of distress. Eleanor however studiously glued her eyes to the table, refusing to look up. She picked up her wine glass and tried to nonchalantly take a sip, as if she had not at all heard their discussion. As if, even if she had heard, she could not care less.

And, as Eleanor had never voiced or explicitly shown her feelings for Aiden, her mother concluded that perhaps there was no great attachment between her daughter and the said gentleman. And so she turned her attention back to their friends and dismissed that momentary maternal concern from her mind with a light sigh of relief.

The rest of the evening was nigh on torture to Eleanor, for she was obliged to listen to and on occasion participate in conversations, speculations and general ventilations about Mr Aiden Edwards. Every aspect of him, his character, manners and appearance were all discussed meticulously for what felt like hours on end. At one point Eleanor felt she could not bear it a minute longer and asked if she might be excused.

'Of course dear! Maurice is in the kitchen, I'm sure he would like to see you!' Mrs Layton exclaimed and Eleanor nodded gratefully and escaped.

Maurice, their cook, had an exciting new recipe for his young friend to try: bouillabaisse, a French fish stew.

'It is a trifle troublesome to make here in Mayhaven, with such abounding varieties of fish not being readily available,' Maurice explained. 'But it is nevertheless a fine recipe.'

Eleanor thanked him for the recipe, and, after refusing the tray of canelés he offered, knelt down by the fireplace to stroke Caesar, the Layton's little ginger kitten. After a little while she again joined the rest of the party, where her mother and Mrs Layton had moved on from discussing Mr Edwards' house and whether he had taken *everything* with him, to the length of his hair and his preferred choice of food.

Just then a heated quarrel broke out amongst the children (Charles had allegedly cheated in a game of chess with Felicity), reminding the adults of their obligation as parents and cutting their conversation short.

After promises to meet again the next day had been made by the womenfolk, the Ashmore family took their leave. Francis had the carriage ready and waiting for them. He helped the rest of the family clamber in, then he leapt up onto the driver's seat and extended his hand down towards Eleanor. He assisted her up and Eleanor rode home beside him; his merry smile and mere presence were more comforting to her than she could say.

CHAPTER SEVEN

To The Sea

For many days after they received the news of Aiden's departure Eleanor was in unusually low spirits, her normal quietness now increased to the extent of hardly any speech at all. Her family knew not what was wrong with her and she would not tell them. They suspected it to be a combination of various matters but were never given so much as a hint from Eleanor, however much they artfully questioned or blatantly asked. And so they left her alone, knowing she would return to her normal self in her own good time.

When troubles threatened to overwhelm Eleanor, she sought refuge in her dreams. Those were days when she would drift along in a haze, seemingly oblivious to the everyday, worldly things around her, her mind focused on her own fairy tale world. During this time Eleanor would fully allow her imagination to run wild, dreaming of beauty, adventure, love and peace in her land where anything was possible for those who believed and had the courage to dream. On these days her eyes carried a faraway look, as if she had caught a glimpse of a different world, just out of reach, on the borders of fantasy and reality. She also reflected upon deep matters during those days. It somehow seemed the appropriate thing to do, to match her deep mood.

But these phases of intense deepness always ended. The dark clouds would break and the sun would once more shine through and all would be well again. For surely there is nothing that a little love and kindness and fresh air, rounded off with lashings of good food, company and laughter, will not cure. That is certainly what the Ashmore family believed and their method had not failed to date, so it must therefore be a good one. One often does find that the simplest, nicest methods are best.

In the general spirit of fresh air and good food, Mrs Ashmore decided that it would be a very good thing for them all to go on a holiday to the seaside. She made the grave mistake of first proposing her brain-child at the breakfast table. Not only did it raise the customary shouts, clamour and prevailing noise of a meal in the Ashmore household from an only just bearable buzz to an intense throb; it also meant that now Mr Ashmore was subject to repeated reminders, suggestions, questions and, on occasion, downright blackmail and threats as to whether and when they were going on their holiday, and this not only from his wife but also Charles, Ethan and Abigail. Even Eleanor had innocently questioned her father over a walk the next day whether he had yet made his mind up. Mr Ashmore was certain that Rumpus would have joined in and voiced his opinion too, if he possibly could have. The Ashmore household was, after all, a household brimming with opinions about all and sundry and to therefore have a dog who tried to participate seemed only proper and fitting. And indeed Rumpus tried. He would often bark and howl and whine when his younger masters and mistresses raised their voices, but he soon stopped if a well-aimed slipper indicated in no uncertain terms the displeasure of his owners. Rumpus was however a rather peculiar specimen and either suffered from short term memory loss or extreme stubbornness. Time after time he would bark and howl, have a slipper thrown at him, whine indignantly, lie down in a high dudgeon for a few minutes and then the process would repeat itself.

It was some days before Mr Ashmore gave his answer and consent to the suggestion. This announcement also occurred at the breakfast table. As may be imagined, the result was one of much exultant shouts, shrieks and thanks from all sides.

Charles, abandoning his slice of thickly buttered toast, was immediately struck by the idea of investigating and, if possible, inventing a mechanical contrivance which would use the power and energy flowing in the waves of the sea to make his newest creation, an engine made of discarded carriage parts, work.

'Papa, may I borrow a book of yours? And your tools? And your candelabrum?' Charles asked eagerly.

'My dear boy,' his father replied. 'If you take my candles how am I supposed to have any light to work in my study?'

'You don't need to work,' suggested Charles hopefully, already halfway out of the door on his way to his father's study.

'If you take my candelabrum, I shall not be able to arrange this holiday, for that requires light,' Mr Ashmore answered firmly. 'I must research suitable means of transport and accommodation, which area is most pleasant at this time of year, and then write many letters. But you can still take it if you desire and we shall simply not go.'

Mr Ashmore looked decidedly too pleased at the prospect of not being able to go. He leant back, folded his arms across his chest and raised his eyebrows meaningfully at his eldest son. Charles released his hold on the door handle and ruefully returned to his place at the table.

'Abigail,' he whispered to his younger sister a few moments later, after checking that his parents weren't looking. 'May I have the candles in your room?'

Later that day Francis heaved several immense pine wood trunks down from above the stables where they had been, judging from the measurable coat of dust which ensconced them, not touched for some time. With some difficulty he carried the cumbersome objects into the hallway, but made a sharp exit again when Abigail appeared with several dresses in her hands, asking him which ones he thought she ought to pack.

'I favour the canary one I think, although the coquelicot is also very pretty… What do you think Francis?'

A look of alarm had entered the man's face and he had hurriedly sidled out of the front door, muttering something about the sheep.

***

The household was a hive of preparation and excitement over the following weeks. Mrs Ashmore assured Eleanor that every household was always in such an uproar before going on holiday, but somehow Eleanor very much doubted the truth of that statement.

Looking around the day before they were scheduled to leave, Eleanor found it hard to believe that any other house in the world could possibly be in more disarray, and looking less like they were leaving the very next morning, than the Ashmore house. The floors of every room were, as Abigail called it, a dump-pit. Stockings and petticoats and every imaginable piece of clothing were scattered around, half-packed and half-empty valises and trunks were lying about in all the wrong places and to round it all off, Rumpus had decided he was bored and had dashed into each of the rooms, pinched some piece of clothing, and made good his escape. At that very moment he was haring through the hallway with a mouthful of stolen items, half-running and half-sliding. His long, greying fur, although giving him an undoubtable air of deluded importance and grandeur was also an impediment to him, especially on the polished wooden floor of the hallway and the flagstones in the kitchen of their home. His paws could find next to no grip due to the long strands of hair which grew between his claws and the pads of his feet and he would slip and slide around until he reached the carpeted areas of the house where he could once again prance along in his usual fashion.

Now the unfortunate dog skidded recklessly around the slippery corner leading into the kitchen, his feet scrabbling furiously as he attempted to maintain his balance and at the same time keep up his breakneck speed. He failed miserably and, his legs sliding away from underneath him as he rounded the corner, he crashed into the pantry door, sending reverberations up and down the corridors. He lay there unmoving for a few moments, amidst a pile of stockings and other sundry articles of clothing, and then, as if sensing danger, he sprang up, staggered around dizzily, fell over again, leapt up once more, frantically pattered around gathering up his precious stolen treasure and disappeared through the kitchen and out of the open back door which led to the herb, vegetable and fruit plots. His hunter's sixth sense appeared to have served him well for a few seconds later Charles, Ethan, Elizabelle, Abigail *and* Mrs Ashmore all stormed around the very same corner, shouting encouragement and insults at each other as they went.

'Careful of that slippery bit there near the door!'

'Be careful yourself, gollumpus. I can look after myself.'

'Oh no you can't.'

'Oh yes I can.'

'Shut up you two and focus on catching that thieving rascal.'

'Well done, well done, dears. You are all doing splendidly!' Mrs Ashmore cried from the rear of the wrathful little troupe, wanting also to participate in the racket by adding her maternal shout of encouragement.

By the time they reached the kitchen garden 'that thieving rascal' was already well away, leaving in his wake a trail of undergarments. Everyone, for Charles immediately set about forming a committee by enlisting, whether willing or not, every member of the family, spent the next half hour retrieving the stolen articles from the four corners of their garden.

Eleanor wearily picked up a striped petticoat, sodden with dog saliva, from behind a peony bush. Above her Ethan had climbed up a pear tree to pick a solitary pear, altogether distracted from the original purpose of their mission, whilst Charles was overviewing the entire proceedings from the comfort of a cushioned armchair which he had dragged out from the parlour, much to the disapproval of Elizabelle. Charles was always extremely good at coming up with amazingly unrealistic ideas and schemes. He would then animate some poor unsuspecting victim, invariably his younger brother, until they agreed to assist him. Then followed the forming of a committee to do all the strenuous work, meaning he, Charles, could survey the proceedings from a more *leisurely* position.

Mr Ashmore, more for his own amusement than any other reason, and perhaps also out of pity, had joined the merry gathering of searchers. He was standing by Charles now with an entertained yet also slightly despairing smile on his face.

Mrs Ashmore had by now cornered the offending creature with her weapon of choice, an obliging broom, and was fiercely reprimanding him.

'You disgraceful animal. You ought to know better. This has been going on for far too long, do you hear me?

And it has to stop!'

Eleanor wondered whether she ought to remind her mother that he could not understand a word she was saying, being only an animal; an especially thick-headed one at that. But Mrs Ashmore seemed to be enjoying herself so much - stabbing in the direction of the miscreant with her broom and releasing all her pent-up vexation at him in no uncertain terms - that Eleanor had not the heart to spoil her fun. The hound in question was wagging his tail happily, apparently rather amused by all the fuss he had caused. And, fortunately for him, Mrs Ashmore's aim was so poor that she could most probably not have touched him even if she had desired to. As it was, she preferred to simply punctuate each sentence with a ferocious stab from her broom in his direction.

Abigail had long since abandoned Charles' committee and was now back in her room, putting the final touches to her valise and laying out a few last-minute dresses which had yet to be packed into one of the big, old trunks.

In short, the family was anything but ready for their departure the next day.

***

It had been decided that they would stay at the coastal fishing town of Southcliffe. The journey would undoubtedly be a long one, really too long for Mrs Ashmore's liking, but Mr Ashmore and his eldest daughter had done all the appropriate research and had quite fallen in love with Southcliffe from the information they had gleaned about it. They had even found a sketch of the cove and cliffs in Southcliffe in one of the books in their library. This illustration had been passed around and poured over by everyone until that page in the book was creased and covered in marks where inquisitive fingers had traced the outlines of the image.

With both Eleanor and her father's persuasive skills, combined with extravagantly lavish descriptions, Mrs Ashmore had found she had no chance of resisting. And so letters had been written and dispatched and enquiries had been made and accepted and it was all settled that they were to stay in a charming little cottage with a promised view of the sea.

'Little cottage?' Mrs Ashmore had repeated dubiously when Eleanor read the description of their holiday cottage to her. Twenty years earlier Mrs Ashmore would have cried with ecstasy and youthful joy at the prospect of staying in a little cottage by the sea. But now, more than a score of years later, with a veritable rabble of children to manage and a peculiar dog to contend with, she did not relish the prospect with quite so many romantic and happy musings.

'They say little because they must Mama,' Eleanor assured. 'A cottage must somehow always be described as little. Can you imagine a big cottage being advertised? No, a cottage should always be small and homely and cosy. But the man whom we wrote to assured us that this particular cottage is by no means small. Quite large enough to accommodate us for our stay. We shall be very happy and content there Mama, I am sure. Rumpus will stay here with Francis and Elizabelle; everything is arranged now.' And indeed it was.

By some miracle everyone found themselves in the carriage the next morning, all fed, watered and packed, and with eyes shining as bright as stars, filled with merry expectations and excitement. They were going on holiday, the sun was shining, a grand adventure was just beginning and all was well with the world.

The journey *was* long and no small number of stops were required. They stayed at an inn overnight; and to be sure, after nearly an entire two days spent in the confining and somewhat claustrophobic carriage, it is not surprising that everyone's nerves were starting to fray as the sun set. But then, delightful hope and happiness arose in them again for they all, one by one, stuck their noses in the air and sniffed and smelled it. Smelled that smell. That beautiful, unique, invigorating smell which can only be found where the waves break against the sand and the moon controls the tide and, as Abigail fancied, the fairies chase the wind and there is magic to be found in every moonlit walk along the shore; that smell, which somehow manages to remind each and every one of us of some exquisite happy memory from long ago, containing the power to refresh wearied spirits. To Eleanor, the smell of the sea was a fragrance full of passionate romance and adventure and star-streaked mystery; a smell which causes worries and burdens to diminish in size until they are blown away by the ocean breeze like a mere grain of sand. And in their place come dreams. Beautiful, daring dreams, full of colour and excitement and adventure and all things good. Dreams which are a glorious mixture of everything you love, every good memory of beautiful things that have happened and every hope and wish for things to come.

Each member of the family stuck their noses in the air and sniffed and then inhaled deeply and then sniffed again, just to make certain they had not been mistaken. Parents and children alike shuffled along the seats towards the windows of the carriage and somehow succeeded in crushing their heads together to the extent that every one of them was able to look out, just as they rounded a sharp bend in the road and beheld the sea. There is something about seeing the sea for the first time again when you have not seen it for such a long time.

However, for once, the Ashmore family did not express their emotions through noise and shouting, but each one chose a deeper way of responding to the first glimpse of the sea. Charles clenched his fists tightly and grinned. Abigail squealed just a little and then let out a contented little sigh. She was quite a romantic at heart, but was going through a phase of perceiving everything to do with *love* and *feelings* as horribly embarrassing. Ethan smiled a grim, satisfied smile. Here was a place finally worthy of an adventure-seeking, courageous knight-cum-pirate such as himself. Here he could at last find a quest to embark upon. The young boy's bright eyes gleamed with excitement. Mr Ashmore quietly reached out and grasped his wife's hand, tenderly squeezing it. Mrs Ashmore turned around and smiled equally tenderly at her husband. The sea air was already working its magic on her and she felt young again. Young and free. Just for that moment at least, she allowed herself to forget her motherly responsibilities and become a spirited, young woman once more. She was once again skilled and handsome and hopelessly in love, and she was ecstatically happy - no dream was too big, no cage could restrict her. She was entirely free to once more embrace that feeling of being able to do anything.

Truth be known, she was still just as skilled and in love now as she had been then. She had simply grown in maturity. Her eyes now radiated wisdom and inner strength and she was still handsome, especially when she laughed and felt relaxed enough to let her hair hang loosely around her shoulders. Mrs Ashmore, or Olivia Jane Ashmore, had thick, wavy auburn hair which perfectly suited her temperament; Eleanor thought her mother was altogether beautiful. Sometimes, on occasions such as now, when Olivia was calm and did not have little people constantly demanding things of her, when her hair was hanging down her back with the sun shining through it, making it look like fiery liquid gold, when she was laughing and filled with the joys of life and love, she would look to Eleanor like a radiant queen. And that was just the way Mr Ashmore saw his wife. No matter how much patience and quiet humility had been and still would be required of him in their marriage, Olivia remained the love of John's life. They were one flesh - soulmates and best friends. Olivia was his radiant bride, no matter how many years passed, and she would always remain so.

And Eleanor? As Eleanor beheld the sea, she felt a sudden surge of emotion wash over her, like a mighty ocean wave crashing against the rocky cliffs of her heart. She felt joy and passion and excitement rise up in her, but also a painful longing for a person who had, without explanation, so suddenly left, taking with him a part of her she had not even known was hers to give.

Who would think that simply a glance of the raging, mysterious, endless sea could create so many varied responses in a matter of moments?

***

Only a few bends of the road later they reached their destination. The carriage halted quite a way from the door of the cottage, for the singular way of reaching the low, stone wall which marked the edge of the little garden attached to the cottage was a narrow, steep path only accessible on foot. The path wound up to a weather-beaten, yet freshly varnished gate in a small gap in the stone wall. The garden beyond consisted of a few gnarled and knotted apple trees which formed a kind of miniature orchard to the left of the cottage, and a wild meadow of various grasses, reeds and some hardy, determined-to-live flowers to the right.

The cottage itself was everything a seaside cottage ought to be. From the thatched roof to the climbing roses which stretched over the little wooden front door and from the quaint chimneys, which were only just visible from the front of the house to the east side of the building, which was entirely mantled by centuries old ivy. Here in Southcliffe summer ended earlier and already the ivy was changing from a summery emerald green to a brilliant ruby red. A few stubborn leaves still lingered in the memory of summer, longing for warmth and the lush green colour they were so accustomed to, but these were few and far between and from a distance that side of the cottage wall looked like it was ensconced in a velvet curtain of fervent ruby.

The cottage altogether charmed the Ashmores, each person seeing in it exactly what their heart longed for - be that adventure, inspiration, comfort or rest. Francis and Elizabelle had stayed on in Felowspring to take care of Felowspring Manor in their absence and Mr Ashmore had hired a larger, more comfortable coach - well-suited for longer journeys - to convey them and all their luggage to Southcliffe. Their driver, who had been hired with the coach, leapt down now and helped them drag their trunks and valises up the narrow path until a substantial heap of belongings had accumulated on the doorstep of the cottage.

'Thank you, Tom!' called Mr Ashmore after the disappearing figure of the driver. Tom, without turning, waved his hand enthusiastically in acknowledgment.

'Well, here we are!' Mr Ashmore declared as he retrieved the key from under the customary and somehow ever-present flowerpot by the doorstep. He unlocked the door and pushed it open.

'Now, let us organise the luggage first before we madly thrash about...' But his words fell on deaf ears as the entire family did exactly that - madly thrashed about. There is no enjoyment quite like being able to dash through a completely unknown, unexplored house and being able to open every door and peer in every cupboard and jump on every bed. It is an enjoyment which will, or at least should never cease to be thrilling while it lasts. And it lasted rather a long time for, as the man who had helped them rent it had so aptly described, the cottage was not a cottage as far as the size was concerned. Besides the normal necessities such as kitchen, dining room, parlour and pantry, there were numerous bedrooms of varying shapes and sizes, a rather dangerous looking but none the less thrilling attic which stretched along the entire length of the thatched roof, the customary deep and dark cellars which are always simply begging to be explored *at once* and, of course, the garden.

After all these exhilarating discoveries had been made and everyone's curiosity was, at least for the present, sated, then came the ceremonial distribution of bags and bedrooms, a most important and to-be-taken-seriously procedure for the Ashmores. Charles, Abigail and Ethan seemed to be of the opinion that, if they were not allocated the rooms which they desired, then the whole holiday would be utterly ruined.

'I want the big one with the big bed at the end of the corridor!' Abigail pronounced, flicking her long hair back with a toss of her head. 'The bed is *beautiful*, just like a princess bed! *And* there is a large wardrobe for clothes. Come, you must all see it.'

It was clearly the prospect of having her own wardrobe which had clinched it for Abigail. But her father had to disappoint her.

'I think you'll find that the bedroom in question is the master bedroom and therefore intended for the master of the family.'

'But Papa, we don't have a master,' protested Abigail, pouting slightly.

Abigail had the kind of face which, when she was in a

good mood, was beautiful and joyous to behold, and when she was in a bad mood, looked worse than a toad with a sore throat, or so Charles described it. Right now her countenance was in no man's land.

'Oh yes we do,' counteracted Mr Ashmore. 'I am the husband of my wife and the father of my children and am therefore head of the house and master, and must therefore occupy the master's bedroom.'

Abigail's bottom lip stuck out further. Her countenance had now stepped over into enemy territory. 'But… but it has a nice big bed. *And* the nice wardrobe - with a *mirror* inside it,' she reasoned, a pleading tone creeping into her voice.

'The bed is big because two people are supposed to sleep in it,' said Mr Ashmore. Now Abigail's bottom lip was stuck out as far as it would possibly go. However, she soon forgot her woes when she saw the room she was to sleep in. It overlooked the apple orchard to the west of the cottage. From her window she could actually reach out and touch the branches of the fruit trees and, if she could persuade Charles to build her a harvesting contraption, she was sure she would even be able to pick apples from the comfort of her bed.

'I could have a midnight feast of apples if I so desired,' pondered Abigail dreamily, now fully reconciled to not having the master's bedroom. 'With only the fairies for company,' she added. And so she was happy.

Charles and Ethan were to share a room, as was their custom. Their allocated bedroom was large and peculiarly shaped. The entire room was painted and furnished in every possible shade of blue. Indeed, the room seemed to perfectly reflect the view from their bedroom window. That side of the cottage looked out entirely to sea and one could see the waves crashing against the shore and the seagulls soaring just above the surface of the mighty water. Ethan fancied he could even see the foam being created by the force of the waves. It altogether suited the boys splendidly, for it meant Charles could execute his scientific observations of the waves from a place of comfort and warmth and Ethan could listen to the sound of the sea at night and imagine himself voyaging across the oceans in a pirate ship. He could also wake up in the morning and immediately look out upon the sea to see if any ships had been wrecked that night. Yes, the boys were also perfectly content.

As is to be assumed, Mr and Mrs Ashmore occupied the master's bedroom and found it much to their liking. It was cosy and furnished prettily, with just a hint of the roughness and wildness of the waves.

Eleanor's bedroom was equally perfect. One corner of the expansive attic had been enclosed and converted into a bedroom and it was into this room which Eleanor now entered. The serenity and pleasant peace of this space immediately struck her like a breath of fresh air. In the few weeks before their seaside holiday Eleanor had had little to no time or inclination to dream about what her possible bedroom by the sea might look like, but standing now in the middle of that tranquil little room at the very summit of the quaint cottage, slowly turning around so she could inspect it from every angle, she found it to be perfect. If she had dreamed of a perfect seaside bedroom, it would surely have been just like this one.

The supporting rafters of the ceiling substantially shrunk the collective size of the room, for in some corners one could barely stand, so great was the slant of the ceiling. But Eleanor did not mind. Far from it. She had never slept in an attic room before but had somehow always longed to. There was a certain romance attached to sleeping in a cosy little attic room at the top of the house, away from everyone else. One was closest to the moon and the host of singing stars up there.

Whitewashed walls, a few pieces of wooden, also whitewashed, furniture and a handful of ornaments that paid homage to the location, such as a cluster of shells, a painting of the waves and a beautiful piece of sun-bleached driftwood, were all the decorations the room required. The only source of natural light in that little room was a sizeable window right above the bed, which had been made to follow the general slant of the roof.

Eleanor leapt upon her bed with all the zeal and excitement of a six-year-old and pounced feverishly upon the latch of the window. The latch was stiff and the hinges were rusty but, with an energetic heave, she was able to push the window open, prop it up with the provided metal rod and stick her head out. With her feet now firmly planted on her bed, Eleanor was able to stand upright and have her body from the waist down, inside the room and the rest outside. The sun had just drowned, way out there among the waves of the reckless sea, awaiting the dawn for its resurrection, while now the moon and stars all appeared to burst forth, at last released from the shadows of the bright daylight which had kept them hidden and encaged all that day. It was as if the entire starry host of the night sky let out a deep breath, finally able to exhale freely. Eleanor felt that breath and rejoiced in it. She knew how the stars and the moon felt. She could relate to them deeply and she shared their joy at being released now, as the moon danced on the waves below.

***

The next morning dawned radiant and shining, with a slight shimmer of moonbeams still caught in the waves and the swaying leaves of the trees.

Eleanor awoke to the sun shining directly onto her

face through her dear slanted window which had the night before enabled her to become one with the night sky. To be kissed tenderly awake by the sun is surely the most pleasant way to wake up, at least so Eleanor thought, and she swung out of her bed with the glow of the sun's loving embrace still lingering on her cheeks and the starlight of midnight shining bright in her eyes.

Skipping expectantly down the stairs to the cottage kitchen, Eleanor found she was the first to arise and, happily embracing this unexpected opportunity of exploring this beautiful place on her own, she grabbed her shawl, which she had so hastily discarded by the front door the evening before, and dashed down the steep lane to the gate in the stone wall.

Gleefully unlatching the gate Eleanor found herself on the rough road the carriage had brought them along only yesterday. Except now, in the light of the early morning, everything looked different and, if at all possible, even more exciting and breath-taking than it had done in the fading light of yesterday's evening. Eleanor already knew that the road to the right led along the shore a short way and then back onto the main road headed in the direction of home. And so her course for that morning's adventure was clear - to the left it was.

The day had now fully sprung and everything was awakening, wide-eyed and eager for what may come. The earth seemed to be singing. Drops of dew glistened on new-born leaves, shining like pearls in the early sunlight of the morning, full of humble beauty. Wind, fresh and pure, rustled the branches of the trees overhead, causing the grass below to dance to earth's eternal love song to its Creator. Flowers, bright and beautiful, as many different kinds as there are expressions of love, bloomed in the most unexpected places, alongside a dirt track or in the harsh, forsaken cracks of a cliff, proving again and again that life - precious life - can be found in all places, however unlikely or dark the surroundings may seem.

Eleanor heard creation's love song that morning, loud and clear. She could see the waters of the ocean stretching out below her, seemingly endless. She could hear the waves crashing against the cliffs and the harmony of two love birds in a fir tree above her. Even the grass seemed to be singing that morning and Eleanor, grateful for such a pure unique tune, decided to accompany creation. So she danced, clasping her dress in her hands and swirling around and around. She allowed the beauty of the moment to fill her being and she danced with all the passion of the seas and wildness of the wind and grace of the moon and love of the sun. She danced as she had never danced before, and she cared not whether anyone saw her. She was alive and she was free. She was young and would be forever. Right in that moment, Eleanor decided she would never grow old. Mature, yes. Gain knowledge and experience, yes. But grow old? Never. Childhood was too sweet.

Eleanor continued her dancing and twirling until the fir trees to her left and right thinned out and she was able to see for miles around. She was now nearing the cliffs which bordered on the sea and, with one final burst of joy, one final leap and twirl to the finishing notes of creation's melody for her that morning, her harmony with the wind and waves ended.

Breathless and beaming Eleanor stood by the edge of the cliff, allowing the cool ocean breeze to waft over her face and through her loose hair.

Down below, in a sheltered and secluded cove which had been created by the surrounding cliffs, was the little village of Southcliffe. Its inhabitants lived in cottages and small houses, much like the one the Ashmores were staying in. The houses which were closest to the open sea were built on stilts to avoid damage on any particularly stormy, starless nights. From what Eleanor had discovered in her research about Southcliffe, the village had a small population and supported, subsequently, very few shops. A bakery, a butcher, a grocer and an unending supply of fresh fish were all the people of Southcliffe required to live and anything else that was needed was supplied by the generous occupants of the other little seaside villages nearby. And this was precisely what the Ashmores had desired - a holiday consisting of fresh air and simplicity, and of that there was ample to be found in Southcliffe.

Eleanor's heart thrilled and her imagination soared when she saw Southcliffe nestled in the cove below, but then her head caught up and, on a more practical level, she wondered how the villagers got in and out of their secluded home. Straining her eyes, Eleanor looked all around her for a way to descend and, lo and behold, a little way off was an excellently engineered staircase. Steps were partially hewn into the bare rock and, in some places, where the rock had crumbled too much, these steps were supported by planks of wood which had been painted in such a shade of grey that they entirely camouflaged with the cliff.

Eager to try out this peculiar staircase Eleanor skipped forward and began to descend. To her surprise, and relief, the cunning villagers of Southcliffe had added to the staircase a bannister of sorts, making the descent a less precarious experience. Thus Eleanor safely reached the bottom of the cove that was Southcliffe and, with much self-control, she resisted the temptation of further exploration and instead, with a little laugh, did an about-turn and scuttled back up the steps, before running all the way home, back through the fir trees, up the steep path and into the house.

Breathless, but with a full heart, shining eyes and her tangled hair flying, Eleanor burst into the cottage kitchen, impeccably arriving just in time for breakfast.

CHAPTER EIGHT

Southcliffe

The next week provided for the Ashmores a much-needed recreation and rest from their normal and sometimes hectic daily routine. Within a few short days they had visited Southcliffe, tucked away in its private, enchanting cove, numerous times and had dined every night so far at the local and beloved inn 'The Homely Inn'. It was just as simple and homely as its name strongly suggested. The inn, which was situated right on the edge of the village, was raised up on stilts and had a broad driftwood staircase leading up to its ever-open front doors. The roof extended on one side of the building, providing a sheltered overhang under which tables and chairs were neatly arranged. Every evening lanterns were hung from the external beams, placed on each table and all along the edge of the driftwood staircase. Flanked on either side by the sandy beach with the ocean stretching ahead and quaint seaside cottages behind, 'The Homely Inn' was idyllically located.

The villagers, who were regulars at the inn, were passionately hospitable, with open hearts full of generosity and good stories. Their brown, weather-beaten faces, warm ruddy cheeks and bright eyes contrasted strongly with the cool, pastel tones of the ocean and cliffs which encompassed them. The inn food, although nothing fancy, was delicious and comforting, and seafood, naturally, featured heavily on the menu. This was a most luxurious and pleasant change for the Ashmores, since fresh fish was one of the few things one could not readily obtain in Mayhaven.

The weather had so far held well for the Ashmores, enabling them to take walks together as a family and also indulge in individual exploration to their heart's content.

Eleanor's favourite spot to walk, reflect and dream were the cliffs where she had danced that first glorious morning when it had seemed that the whole world danced with her. Now she would often slip away at a convenient time of day and walk alone along the edge of those rugged, majestic cliffs, which were every bit as dangerous and beautiful as the mighty ocean waves pounding below.

Aiden, she had come to realise, was very much like the ocean. He was calm and quiet, like the gentle, foamy wakes that kiss the sandy shores, and yet there was much more to him. His soul was as deep as the ocean whose beautiful depths remain hidden from those who only look upon the surface, not daring to dive below. In the depths there was another side of him to be discovered - one of fervour and feeling, a place which was intensely *alive*.

The profound insights into Eleanor's soul which Aiden had voiced on more than one occasion had sparked in her a flame of curiosity. And, as the troubled waters of her soul began to settle, no longer crashing within her, she saw the moon reflected in her being. Oh, how she hoped that the sinking moon would once again meet upon and kiss the incoming waves of the ocean.

Eleanor, reflecting on it, realised that Aiden's observations were true. That she did hide away her feelings in the shadows, rarely telling anyone what it was that oppressed or troubled her. It was a weakness of hers, she knew. It pained her to think of him and to think that she could have perhaps prevented his tide washing out of her life, leaving in its wake only the waves of sweet reminiscence. Yes, Eleanor had much time to think.

Perhaps she ought to strive for a greater openness with people, especially her parents? Had she but known how her parents longed for complete transparency with their eldest daughter, for her to trust them enough to confide in them that which she told no one else, Eleanor's everyday life could have been much less burdensome. But Eleanor did not know it and so, however much she tried to be open about her feelings, there was always that one thing which occupied her thoughts like a shadow that refused to be swept away.

On her solitary strolls Eleanor did not only reflect on deep, emotional matters of the heart, but also revelled in the freedom she had to simply dream. Her surroundings were ideal for such a pleasant occupation, for Southcliffe, and indeed the coast in general, was a place practically leaking with dreams and inspiration. It was on one such walk that Eleanor met a familiar face, whom she had certainly not expected to see this far away from home.

She had just descended the cliff staircase into the very heart of Southcliffe, with the initial purpose of acquiring some fresh fish for their dinner that evening, when a tall handsome young man with dark hair, flashing eyes and a stern brow strode past her, as deeply sunk in his own thoughts as Eleanor had been in hers only moments earlier.

'Joshua!' Eleanor cried in surprise.

Joshua, for indeed it was he, spun around. He had certainly been oblivious to who or what went on around him, but that voice he would recognise anywhere. That voice which was as sweet to him as the most harmonious birdsong that had ever blessed the ears of any mortal being.

'Miss Ashmore!' he exclaimed, bowing.

Eleanor curtsied automatically and eagerly began her enquiries as to why he was in Southcliffe and where he was staying and how long he had been here and whether he would not come and call on them at their seaside cottage on the very outskirts of that ring of cliffs. All the while she was speaking her eyes were sparkling with eagerness and surprise at meeting her friend here so unexpectedly; and the cool sea breeze as well as her enthusiastic questioning had brought a rosy blush to her cheeks.

The past few weeks had been entirely beautiful for Eleanor, giving her sufficient time to not only reflect and dream, but also eat good food and enjoy the company of her family. The last item had been executed in manageable spurts, although Eleanor had to confess that her family, in particular her two youngest siblings, had been doing exceptionally well on this holiday. Ethan and Abigail had, so far, been very perceptive and understanding of their parents' need for space and quiet and had most days occupied themselves productively with their own adventures.

Even Charles had been surprisingly active, first building a contraption for Abigail with which she could pick apples from her bedroom window, then assisting Ethan in building a pirate ship out of sticks and lashings of string - it actually floated.

Eleanor's heart and soul had now been greatly refreshed and this was visible from the outside too. Her hair, which had a slightly wild and untamed edge due to the ferocity of the wind around the coast, was practically shining. It whipped around her face as she stood there speaking now with Joshua and the overwhelming effect was one of wild beauty and a free spirit.

Joshua smiled at Eleanor as she talked on and only partially heard the information she so gladly bestowed upon him. There was nothing lukewarm or passive about Joshua. He was full of an intense passion and also pain, a deep pain which still clung to his heart and refused to let go. But somehow, despite, or maybe because of that almost ever-present pain and a deep brooding look, it was delightfully glorious when he did smile, for he did so with all of his heart.

'I am here visiting an old friend,' Joshua informed her. 'He suggested that the sea air may do me good. I have been here for a week already and travel back most probably in a few days, it is not definitely settled yet. I may choose to linger here a little longer.'

He smiled again and Eleanor smiled back. Joshua's gaze was very intent and Eleanor averted her eyes after a few moments.

'I hope you will come and call on us,' Eleanor said sincerely, while studying the weather-beaten cobbles between her shoes. 'We are staying in the rather large cottage on the border of Southcliffe, just up there, beyond that cluster of fir trees.'

She looked up and pointed in the direction she meant.

'We do not leave for another week. I know Mama and Papa would be overjoyed to see you,' Eleanor urged. 'As would the others, especially Ethan.'

Ethan harboured a deep admiration and respect for Joshua; he truly had a loyal and ardent admirer in the youngest Master Ashmore. Maybe it was Joshua's dark hair and penetrating eyes, which made him appear to Ethan's fanciful young eyes, like a roguish pirate or gallant fighter. Or maybe it was simply something deeper which Ethan's unpolluted, innocent and therefore highly perceptive heart had sensed - a kindred spirit and fellow adventurer. Whatever it was, Ethan was always in a state of almost nonsensical excitement when he knew Joshua was due to come and dine with them. Ethan would then spend most of the evening gazing at Joshua in open-eyed, unconcealed wonder.

'It would be my pleasure,' Joshua responded earnestly. Eleanor nodded her thanks, smiled her pleasure and turned to leave.

'Where are you going?' Joshua asked before she had time to take a step away from him.

'To the market and then back to the cottage.'

'My friend's house is up that way. Won't you let me accompany you a little way?'

Eleanor smiled again and nodded and took the gentleman's offered arm and together the two friends walked up the quaint cobbled lane leading from the beach to the marketplace of Southcliffe.

***

'I'm back!' Eleanor cried as she opened the front door of the cottage, cast aside her shawl and carried her parcel of fresh mackerel and herring, most likely only fished that very morning, into the kitchen, where her parents were standing over the range. Her mother was attempting a baked apple pudding and her father was standing at his wife's shoulder, taking his delegated role as official taster very seriously, as he always did. The sound of laughter wafted in through the open kitchen window, alluding to the fact that Eleanor's siblings were amusing themselves peaceably in the garden at the back of the house.

Almost without thinking Eleanor went to the oven and took out the pastry base which was on the point of burning and placed it on the wide window sill to cool a little.

'I was trying to make it to your recipe Eleanor,' Mrs Ashmore added, somewhat anxiously. 'Is it acceptable?'

Deftly nabbing a piece of the stewing apple from over her mother's shoulder and chewing reflectively, Eleanor added a dash of cinnamon, a sprinkling of nutmeg, a slice of lemon-peel shredded fine and a little of her special concoction of moondust and love, which she carried with her always. Trying the apple mixture again after she had made these minor adjustments, Eleanor smacked her lips appreciatively and signalled with her eyes to her father who, following his daughter's example, stuck a sizeable spoon into the pan and critically chewed on his mouthful for an excessive amount of time.

'Delicious!' he pronounced at last and Eleanor let out a satisfied little sigh. Mrs Ashmore in her turn also tried the apple mixture and agreed wholeheartedly with her husband.

The mixture was then poured into the nicely browned pastry case and Eleanor, quickly stirring a handful of oats and a pinch of salt into the prepared topping, sprinkled the crumble over the top of the fruit and slid the tray into the waiting oven with practised ease.

Mrs Ashmore did not in the least mind Eleanor taking over any and *all* culinary responsibilities. She found little to no joy in cooking, cleaning or in fact any activity performed in the kitchen besides that of eating and possibly preparing cold meats and bread for luncheon or supper. She had only been attempting to make a pie because of Eleanor's prolonged absence and her own maternal interest in avoiding, if possible, an emotional breakdown from her children, owing to a lack of nourishment.

Extremely aromatic and mouth-watering fragrances were soon ensuing from the oven and these succeeded in rounding up Ethan, Abigail and Charles in record time.

The pudding, which was then served with the obligatory lashings of thick golden custard, was pronounced unanimously delicious and after their repast the happy family sat around chatting and laughing together, simply because they could. Eleanor related her morning's expedition and the unexpected meeting of Mr Joshua Ayles.

'Really? Here in Southcliffe? Fancy the odds of that!' exclaimed Mrs Ashmore wonderingly.

'Ah yes, he's a grand chap is Joshua,' said Mr Ashmore.

'Yes, he's lovely,' agreed Mrs Ashmore enthusiastically. 'It's a pity we have not seen more of him lately really. But having said that, we were in the company of both Mr Felton and Mr Edwards a good deal. Ah well,' she sighed, remembering that Mr Edwards had left Mayhaven to go goodness knows where for heaven knew how long.

Eleanor winced slightly at the mention of Mr Edward's, as if the wave of bittersweet and still rather too fresh memories which washed over her with all the suddenness and strength of the ocean had slashed against her face - unforgiving and unforgetting.

'I'll be back in a moment,' Eleanor muttered, no longer desiring to sit in the merry gathering around the table and participate in their carefree banter and chatter.

She stood up, left the room and slowly ascended the staircase to her attic bedroom. Pacing around she found herself to be restless and, thinking that the fresh, invigorating sea breeze may enliven her, she stood upon her bed, opened the window and inhaled deeply. She could see much from her lofty vantage point: to her left the little apple orchard belonging to the cottage and beyond that a small pine forest, directly ahead she could see smaller hills and rocky mounds which stretched into the great cliffs surrounding Southcliffe, which sheltered Southcliffe as an eagle may protect its young under sheltering wings of safety and comfort, and to the right stretched the sea.

Her eyes wandered from the distant hills to the gate and up the winding stone path. It was then that Eleanor realised with a start that someone was walking up the path that very moment. Straining her eyes, Eleanor identified their unexpected visitor and was glad at heart; the sight of him enlivened her even more than the fresh air had done. She hurriedly closed the window while calling to her family to ready themselves. Eleanor rushed down the stairs as composedly and hastily as she was able to without losing her dignity. She obtained the hallway just as Mr Ashmore opened the door for their visitor.

'Joshua, come in, come in!' Mr Ashmore greeted, opening the door wider and beckoning him in.

'We were just talking about you!' added Mrs Ashmore, peering over her husband's shoulder. She made it sound as if it were a reassuring statement to be told that one is being talked about without one actually being present.

Joshua entered and shook Mr Ashmore's hand warmly before kissing Mrs Ashmore's hand with all the gallantry and respect as though she were the queen herself. And in a way she was the queen of her own little kingdom, so, considering this, his manner towards her was not at all unfitting.

Charles, Abigail and Ethan all appeared at the same time, charging in from the kitchen where they had been vying over who was to scrape the apple pan. Charles had won purely through size and strength, but had graciously condescended to allow his younger siblings a lick of the spoon, such was the great feeling of love and generosity flowing from his heart. Abigail curtsied at Joshua and Charles bowed, but Ethan, his happiness entirely overcoming any nervosity, leapt forward eagerly. Joshua swept Ethan up in a bear hug and twirled him around. Joshua was very fond of the little chap - fonder than he cared to admit.

'If I were ever to have a son,' the young man had once mused after spending a day with the Ashmore family, 'then I would care for him and love him with every fibre of my being.'

It was in the middle of this fond reunion and display of affection between the gentleman and the boy that Joshua became aware of Eleanor standing on the bottom step of the staircase.

'Miss Ashmore,' he bowed, taking her outstretched hand and lightly brushing his lips across the surface. His eyes met hers - the midnight, starless ones and the moon-filled radiant ones - and Eleanor found herself blushing. It was the first time, she realised, that Joshua had greeted her in this fashion.

'Mr Ayles,' Eleanor curtsied in reply.

No one else was aware of the well-concealed depth and intensity of emotion radiating from Mr Ayles' eyes. No one that is, except for Eleanor. In that instant, the brief touch of the back of her hand on his lips, the locking of eyes and souls, Eleanor felt certain she had caught a glimpse of his heart. The heart which Joshua strived so hard to keep hidden away so that none may discover its secrets.

Mrs Ashmore ushered the gentleman into the living room and Ethan clung to the young man's arm while Mr Ashmore took his hat and coat. Everyone continued as if nothing, at least nothing of any great significance, had occurred, and in a way it hadn't. Everyone continued in the natural, heady world but Eleanor found she was unable to transfer so easily between the two realms. She lingered still in that world of the heart and soul, just a little longer.

Mr Ayles' visit was brief but he left with a solemn promise to call upon them again soon. If his friend had no previous arrangements lined up for him, then he would call the very next day. And it would appear that Joshua's friend was lenient for the next morning, and a day shrouded in mystery and mist it certainly was, saw Mr

Ayles once again walking up the stone path to the 'little big' seaside cottage.

He stayed all that morning, spending some time with Ethan, playing pirates, and some time conversing with Mr Ashmore. It had been a long time since the two gentlemen had had the liberty of sitting at leisure with no impending event to pressure them, and for them to be able to talk of whatever lay on their hearts as men to discuss.

Eleanor delighted in the opportunity of cooking for their guest and hopefully blessing him through her cooking. She was not yet entirely sure whether she agreed with the statement that the way to a man's heart is through his stomach, but she had no doubt that good nourishment certainly helped, if for no other reason than the fact that food is necessary to staying compos mentis!

And Eleanor certainly did them proud. She had that morning, on her now obligatory daily stroll to Southcliffe, obtained some more fresh mackerel which she had then endeavoured to cook as skilfully as possible. She had added flavour through herbs and butter, and yet the freshness of the fish was still retained. Neither her family nor their honoured guest were scant in their praise of the meal. Served with roast potatoes and heavily buttered vegetables and garnished with a light dressing of fennel, mint and lemon slices, the fish was pronounced perfect and altogether delectable.

Eleanor then had the pleasure of seeing the look of surprised delight on her family's faces as she placed the dessert on the table - a respectable dish of trifle, simply oozing with fresh cream, whipped syllabub and fruit. This was served with even more raspberry flavoured cream, additional fruit and custard or a small portion of iced creams. Although most chose a delicious combination of all three.

'If you are in doubt and you can't choose between several good things, have everything, that's what I always say. You can never have too much of a good thing.' These were Mr Ashmore's words of wisdom for them at the dinner table that day, as he helped himself generously to the iced creams, poured a good glug of cream on top and proceeded to spoon copious amounts of custard over everything.

'I travel back tomorrow,' Joshua informed them later that afternoon, when they were all resting lazily after their midday meal.

'Oh,' said Mr Ashmore, sitting up. 'Why do you not wait a day or two longer and travel back with us? You would be more than welcome and an invaluable asset to our conversation and general company.'

'Thank you, sir. I would be glad to,' replied Joshua gratefully with a slight bow of his head. Pleased, Mr Ashmore sank back into his chair with a contented little sigh.

Joshua looked around the room and his eyes, as they so often did, came to rest on Eleanor, who was at that moment braiding her younger sister's hair. She was concentrating on the task at hand and had a focused, determined look on her face. There was one strand of her hair which was continually falling in front of her face and obscuring her vision and time and time again she would brush it back behind her ear, only for it to slip out again moments later. Eleanor deftly braided her sister's long thick hair, and as Joshua watched her - watched her slender fingers flicking to and fro and the strand of hair slipping in front of her face and her eyes focusing intently on the task at hand - he smiled to himself. At last Eleanor finished the braid in Abigail's hair and turned around. She met Joshua's eyes, but alas, he found he could not avert his gaze speedily enough to conceal the fact that he had been observing her from a distance. Eleanor, however, smiled merrily at him and he found himself smiling back.

***

Two days later the morning dawned bright and beautiful with not a cloud in the sky, a most unusual phenomenon for that region. Eleanor had taken her last walk to the cliffs and the sea that morning. The entire family, Mr Ayles included, had dined out at 'The Homely Inn' for the last time the evening before and now everyone was saying goodbye to their dear 'little big' seaside cottage.

Eleanor, although she had greatly enjoyed and benefited from her stay by the sea, was now ready to go home and, as her father always remarked, this is most certainly a good sign. It indicates that one has stayed exactly the right amount of time in a place and that one's home is exactly as it ought to be, for one should always be glad at heart to be able to return. And so it was with every member of the Ashmore family that sunny morning. They all left Southcliffe in the company of Mr Ayles, who insisted on riding alongside the carriage on horseback, with hearts full of happy memories, but each one of them ready now to return home.

CHAPTER NINE

New Seasons And New Faces

The weeks passed and the weather had begun to fluctuate, heralding the changing of the seasons, and the mornings had grown crisp and the evenings dark. The leaves changed from emerald to orange, clinging on to their branches resolutely until a sudden harsh breeze swept them away. The apples in the orchard ripened, were promptly harvested and the brimming baskets were whisked away into the kitchen where they were transformed into delectable puddings, preserves and pies. And sometime later, in the misty morning month of November, Felowspring welcomed some more new faces to Mayhaven.

Eleanor and Abigail were strolling through the village arm in arm, having delivered a basket of the large, rosy apples to Elizabelle's sister, when they witnessed first-hand the arrival of a spectacular, maroon-coloured barouche, drawn by four fine horses. It drove past them and around a bend in the road just ahead of them. The two young ladies curiously hurried forwards and saw that the carriage had halted a little way up the road, outside one of the empty properties in Felowspring. A few moments later a young gentleman leapt out and held out his hand to whoever remained in the carriage. Cautiously a tall, bony lady dressed in very dark colours stepped out, followed immediately by a pretty young lady with golden hair, clutching a parasol. The young lady smiled gratefully at the man who had helped her out and the man smiled back readily before extending an arm each to the two ladies. They then proceeded to walk up the path towards the house with great dignity. The door was opened for them by a maid who had clearly been preparing the house for their arrival. They then disappeared from view.

Abigail and Eleanor exchanged excited glances before scurrying back home. Abigail outran Eleanor, but they both burst into the house together and rushed to find their mother, who was discussing meal plans with Elizabelle in the kitchen. They eagerly related to her everything they had seen. Eleanor began the narrative but was soon interrupted by Abigail who could barely contain herself.

'And that house has been unoccupied for years, hasn't it Mama!' exclaimed Abigail, doing a little jig. 'And they had such a lovely carriage with such handsome horses!'

'It was a barouche Mama,' Eleanor added for clarification. 'And a splendid one at that.'

'Oh I am so excited!' squealed Abigail, unbuttoning her jacket and flinging it across the back of a chair. She then collapsed into the chair for a moment before leaping up again.

'I must go and tell Papa!' she exclaimed and rushed out of the room.

'I'm not sure he'll be that interested…' began Eleanor but trailed off. Abigail had already left.

***

The Ashmores were not kept in suspense for too long. Mr Ashmore took it upon himself to walk into the village a few days later and call upon the new occupants of the house. As one of the most respected and looked-to men in the village he felt it was his duty. It was a fine house, not oversized but with generous rooms, tall ceilings and grand furnishings, and it had a pretty little garden with some well-established fruit trees, as well as a little portion of the brook which flowed through the Ashmore's estate cutting across one corner of the property. He was graciously received, his call was brief and he left shortly afterwards, but only after securing a time at which the newcomers were to dine with them at their estate.

Upon his return Mr Ashmore refused to answer any of his family's eager and inquisitive questions about their appearance, character or conversation, simply replying: 'You shall see for yourself soon enough.'

And soon enough they did. Mr and Mrs Layton, and Felicity of course, had also been invited to dine with them. They had already arrived and were sitting comfortably with the rest of the family in the parlour. Mr Layton was mildly curious as to who their new neighbours were but Mrs Layton, much like Abigail, could barely contain herself.

A knock sounded at the door and all the occupants of the parlour leapt to their feet and waited expectantly as Elizabelle took their guests jackets and showed them in.

First came the tall, bony lady; she was most definitely the older one. Her raven hair was scraped back into a tight bun on the top of her head and two identical ringlets hung by the side of her face. She walked with unmistakable grace and held herself very erect, her extremely long neck meaning she had to look down her nose at most people. Her thin lips, which were not much more than a mere pencil line, were pursed and her cheeks looked as if she were perpetually sucking a lemon. An exquisite cashmere shawl of dark Prussian blue was arranged around her bony shoulders and the hem of her evening gown was embroidered with finest lace. Despite her slightly haughty and severe appearance she curtsied graciously at them all and Eleanor noticed with a wave of compassion that the lady's hands shook slightly with nerves as she seated herself gingerly on a pouffe.

Close by her side came the younger lady who could

not have been more than nineteen years of age; she introduced herself as Miss Charlotte Langlois. She was pale and delicate, as fragile as a snowflake resting on a rosebud, with extremely petite features and innocently blue eyes. Her stature was equally petite and her hair was a very fine golden colour. She seemed to Eleanor like a doll. Not a heavily painted Russian doll, but more of a delicate, pristine china doll, each limb so fragile that one feared to touch it lest one, by merely handling it, broke some part of it. She was dressed in a very fine gown of pale primrose silk, elegantly trimmed with lace and brocaded with silken flowers. In her hair she wore a petite feather headdress, and her hands were adorned with gloves, of the same primrose silk as her dress.

The young lady was very softly spoken and, as she now introduced her companion as 'Miss Remonde Bucheron,' and thanked them all for their kindness in inviting them both to dine, she spoke with an unmistakable French accent.

Miss Charlotte Langlois and Miss Remonde Bucheron had barely seated themselves when Elizabelle reappeared in the doorway to announce that dinner was served. Everyone arose eagerly and followed Mr and Mrs Ashmore who, arm in arm, led the way to the dining room.

***

Dinner was a delicious affair: chestnut soup with fresh rolls, roasted pheasant, jugs of rich gravy and redcurrant jelly, bacon pasties, buttered root vegetables, sautéed potatoes, barberry ices and hartshorn jelly were washed down with glasses of burgundy and claret.

Their special guests, though not hugely talkative themselves, ate heartily in a very sophisticated way, and seemed to enjoy listening to the merry chatter of their hosts. Abigail was bursting to ask the two ladies many questions, but she had been strictly lectured not to.

Although Eleanor had to confess that she too was vastly curious.

'Did you travel alone?' Mr Layton inquired, looking first at Miss Charlotte Langlois, then at Miss Remonde Bucheron.

Charlotte glanced fleetingly at Remonde, who gave the slightest nod of her head.

'No,' replied Charlotte in her gentle French lisp. 'We were accompanied by a friend of ours - a gentleman - but he was merely our escort. He left the very next day, after he was suitably convinced of our ability to settle here.'

'What a pity we could not meet him!' exclaimed Mrs Ashmore. 'But I daresay he may visit again?'

Charlotte smiled her agreement, but it was a forced, tense smile.

***

The two ladies did not stay long. Mr Ashmore tried to tempt them with a game of Vingt-Un, but they explained they were still much fatigued from their journey (Abigail and Mrs Layton had to bite their tongues to not ask where they had journeyed from). And so the two women graciously and elegantly thanked their hosts for the pleasant evening and soon their fine carriage had disappeared down the drive.

When the remainder of the little party had once again congregated in the parlour after bidding them farewell Mrs Layton exhaled loudly.

'Well,' she said meaningfully.

'They were both French, were they not Papa?' asked Eleanor.

'Yes, I think they were,' agreed Mr Ashmore slowly.

'She had a beautiful dress on,' mused Abigail lazily.

'Don't you think of anything but dresses and hair?' retorted Charles from behind a book. Abigail was about to retaliate with an equally loaded statement about reading and books, but a gentle nudge and small shake of the head from Eleanor stopped her. Abigail instead contented herself with sniffing haughtily and pointedly ignoring her brother for a couple of minutes.

'Well, I should like to have a round of Vingt-Un,' declared Mr Ashmore, producing the cards and beginning to deal hands. 'Olivia my dear, will you join us?'

Soon everyone was gathered around the low table in the parlour, either participating or observing the game; and the sound of their happy laughter and conversation carried on long into the night.

***

Miss Charlotte Langlois and Miss Remonde Bucheron were the first new inhabitants the little village had had since the arrival of Mr Felton and Mr Edwards, which was by now some time ago by their standards, and their appearance kindled an excited fire of speculative gossip which spread by word of mouth, in the form of scuttling old ladies, so speedily that the entire population of Felowspring knew of their arrival before more than a week had passed. The fact that they were French undoubtedly added another layer of intrigue and interest; what were they doing here?

Coincidentally, that very next week there was to be a celebration held in the village hall, marking the beginning of winter; it was fondly referred to by all in the area as the 'Winter Party'.

The apprehensive wait before the cold months and also the duration of winter can be dreary and dispiriting but this celebration endeavoured to remind the people of the pleasures of winter which often tended to be forgotten, overshadowed by gloomy thoughts of heavy snow and freezing cold.

Eleanor had previously, like so many other people,

grudgingly tolerated winter and clung to the hopeful promise of daylight and warm sun in the spring, but now she was endeavouring to embrace the chilly weather by focusing on the comforts instead of the gloom. The clean, vivid smell of the cold or the crisp, fragile light in the mornings or the soft, knitted clothes she wore in layers, innocently dressed for warmth, or the honeyed sweetness of steaming puddings and the spicy, festive smell of cinnamon and Christmas. These were all things beautifully unique to winter.

Eleanor looked forward to the Winter Party with great eagerness, as did all her family. They had all been busy these past few weeks with soaking fruit for rich Christmas cakes and puddings and baking all manner of delicious wintery delicacies and preserved spreads for the Winter Party. Elizabelle had guarded the precious and hopefully delicious baked goods as fiercely as a mother duck protects its chicks and none of the family, not even Mr Ashmore, had been allowed to taste them. This of course only added to their anticipation and excitement for that special evening's festivities.

***

The day came, as crisp and cold and perfectly appropriate for their Winter Party as they could have hoped. All day people of every age, shape and size hurried about, making last-minute preparations. The village hall, which was much like an oversized barn in shape and appearance, with the wooden rafters and supporting beams of the tall ceiling clearly visible, had been transformed with supplementary tapestries and draperies on the walls and across the windows. Small bunches of evergreen branches interspersed with mistletoe had been secured to the backs of chairs and a magnificent arrangement of evergreen branches, mistletoe and holly had been skilfully woven and suspended from the rafters above their heads.

Furthermore, the village supply of beeswax candles had been ruthlessly raided so that, when the evening came, the hall was aglow with warm candlelight and dancing flames which waved merrily out of the windows as a welcome to anyone outside. The villagers wound through the streets into the brightly lit and festively decorated hall where the smells of comforting food and merry strains of music were already escaping through the continually opening and equally speedily shutting doors.

Young Master Whitham had been assigned the much sought-after job of door keeper and bodyguard and he was taking his job very seriously.

'But what are you guarding?' Felicity Layton had questioned him innocently as she tripped up the stairs with her parents. She was wearing a flouncy and very girlish pink frock, trimmed with tulle and she had an adorable and equally pink fluffy wrap covering her shoulders. It did not look particularly appropriate for the occasion - she looked more like she was going to a garden party in the height of summer - but somehow, she still looked exactly right. Wearing anything else she would simply not look like Felicity.

'I mean, whose body are you guarding?' Felicity pressed, eyes wide.

But young Master Whitham was taking his job far too seriously to indulge in idle chatter with a little girl. Even if the little girl was his second cousin twice removed and more than two years his senior. He bestowed upon her a remarkably withering look, at least remarkable for someone of his age.

'I have been given the most important task of assuring that these doors are opened only to allow the guests access to the building,' the young boy explained. 'In that way I am endeavouring to contain every ounce of warmth so as to provide all the guests a more enjoyable experience.'

He puffed out his chest to about twice its original size and managed to pull himself a whole two feet taller, at least that is what he thought he managed to do. But Felicity was not impressed. She just laughed and ruffled his hair and hurried through the door he had opened for her.

Her parents however did not belittle him so. Mrs Layton showered praise and love upon the diligent doorkeeper and told him how well he was doing and how fine he did look and after they too had entered the building young Master Whitham decided that he rather preferred Felicity's conduct to that of her mother's.

***

Many of the villagers quietly (or not so quietly) hoped that the highly intriguing Miss Langlois and Miss Bucheron would accept their invitation to attend the annual celebration. And they were not to be disappointed, for the French ladies soon joined the merry gathering in the town hall. Many heads turned as the two ladies entered the room, but, remembering their manners, most of them hastily looked away again.

Everyone was dressed in their finest and best; even Francis had discarded his greatcoat and donned an olive-green waistcoat, white shirt and maroon breeches, his grey mane neatly combed and, as always, tied back at the nape of his neck.

The musicians had arranged themselves comfortably in one corner of the room and the occasional pluck and twang could be heard as they prepared. Suddenly they were ready and the opening chords of the quadrille were sounding through the hall.

A swift flurry of movement surged through the room as the floor was cleared and partners were found for the first dance.

'Hurry!' squealed Eleanor, skipping past Mr Layton and taking her place opposite her partner, a cheerful, ruddy and powerfully built farmer boy.

Eleanor looked over her shoulder and saw a young man ask Charlotte to dance; she seemed remarkably flustered and unsure. Glancing about her frantically as if searching for an escape, Charlotte's eyes met Eleanor's and Eleanor gave her an encouraging smile and vigorous nod of the head. A few moments later Charlotte was standing next to Eleanor, curtsying to her partner and beginning to dance.

***

A fair few gallops, waltzes and polkas were played before a halt was called and everyone streamed eagerly to the food. Eleanor cast about her, searching for Charlotte in the surging body of people. She spotted her, stood at the very edge of the mass with her companion Remonde, both of them slightly tense, standing very erect, hands clasped in front of them, eyes flicking restlessly about them.

'Welcome!' Eleanor exclaimed warmly, pressing her way towards them. 'I hope you've been enjoying yourselves this evening and haven't felt too lost! We in Felowspring are exceedingly fond of our Winter Party. And we must introduce you both to some more people; everyone is so eager to make your acquaintances.'

'Really?' questioned Remonde, her pointy eyebrows raised. Her French accent was undisguisable - particularly noticeable in the way she emphasised *every* individual letter and syllable of a word - but she spoke with extreme deliberation and sophistication.

Eleanor nodded emphatically.

'Definitely,' she replied.

'Anyway, I expect you're both hungry,' Eleanor hinted

hopefully, not wanting to appear greedy but finding the nagging hunger signals in her stomach and enticing smells increasingly hard to ignore. Charlotte responded with an almost inaudible murmur of something and Eleanor noticed that the young lady's hands were shaking slightly. Eleanor's face softened sympathetically, and she decided that food would be the best way forward.

'I know *I* am exceedingly hungry,' Eleanor stated, choosing the more blatantly obvious route instead. 'Let me find you both something to eat and drink.'

The food had been set out buffet-style on a long trestle table in an adjoining room. Jars of gypsophila and evergreen pine branches had been placed in between the serving dishes and plates. The smell of crusty rolls and loaves of bread combined with those of various stews and spices and steamed puddings.

At one side of the table a large board of creamy, crumbly, sour, sweet and spicy cheeses stood next to a steaming pan of sausage, veal and bacon casserole and beside that stood a large platter of mushroom and onion pasties, oozing with hot gravy. On the opposite side to the stews, casseroles, cheeses, breads, salads, pastries, pies, soups and turnovers stood a bountiful selection of sweet delicacies. Everything from the first mince pies of the season to baked apple pudding, from cinnamon toast and honey buns to blackberry and gingerbread fingers engulfed the table to the point of overflowing.

The two young ladies and the slightly older one gasped in awe at the sight and sheer quantity of the food but none of them were long in seizing a plate and joining the ever-growing queue for the delicious fare.

However much food there had been to begin with, by the time the entire population of Felowspring, plus many others from Talisbrook, Denersdath and Wenerfield, had eaten their fill there was very little left to show for it. The people of Mayhaven certainly knew how to feast.

The musicians, showing no mercy, ruthlessly struck up the first chords of the next dance as soon as the eating had finished, allowing no time for the much-needed digestion after such a feast.

Charlotte and Eleanor had barely finished chewing their food when the sandy-haired, freckled twins Nicholas and Nathan, both farmer's sons and avidly training to be carpenters, bounded up to their table and asked them both to dance. Eleanor they knew of course, and any friend of Eleanor's must be alright - this was their matter-of-fact view.

Eleanor happily accepted, leaping to her feet, and Charlotte, caught up in the moment, followed her lead. She was most surprised at herself when she skipped merrily through to the hall alongside Nathan, Nicholas and Eleanor a few moments later.

Neither Eleanor nor Charlotte had any difficulty in securing partners for nearly every dance that evening. Indeed, Eleanor had to turn down some requests for she found that the evening was not long enough and the dances were too few to fit everybody in. Once the dancing had begun Eleanor saw very little of Charlotte but every now and then Eleanor would catch a glimpse of her new friend from between the dancers. She looked so happy and content surrounded by the pleasant inhabitants of Mayhaven that Eleanor found no reason for concern but chose to instead wholeheartedly enjoy the evening.

She succeeded in doing so until Mr Felton, in the company of Mr Layton, walked up to join her as she was resting briefly between sets. Mr Layton greeted her candidly whereas Mr Felton did not even dine to look at her. It was clear by Mr Layton's expression that he was more than a bit puzzled as to Mr Felton's non-existent reception of the eldest Miss Ashmore, but he knew it was not his business to pry. Making up for his companion's silence, Mr Layton struck up an animated conversation with Eleanor about the food that had been served that night. Eleanor enjoyed making food and Mr Layton enjoyed eating it, so it was always a good topic to converse about. While they were in the middle of discussing when the rich fruit cakes for Christmas had been made and left to mature that year, Mr Layton was beckoned over by his wife.

'Excuse me,' he apologised, bowing courteously to Eleanor before leaving to join his spouse.

Even now that Mr Felton was left alone with Eleanor, he made no attempt at conversation. He stood erect, staring straight ahead, not once letting his gaze waiver to the left or right, his mouth clamped shut.

'I hope you're enjoying our Winter Party,' Eleanor commented politely in a futile attempt to strike up a conversation.

'Yes thank you,' Mr Felton replied curtly, his voice monotonous and lacking any emotion. 'It's very pleasant.'

'And your reading?' Eleanor asked. 'That is also going well I trust?'

'Yes, it is going very well, thank you,' he responded.

Silence relapsed once again between them, Eleanor having exhausted all her questions for the present. After a few minutes Mr Felton turned to her and bowed sharply.

'Thank you for the riveting discourse Madam,' he said with no small amount of sarcasm. Eleanor, stung by the comment, answered somewhat indignantly, her temper and sense of injustice now roused:

'So this is how your behaviour is towards me now! I had expected more from a fully grown and supposedly mature gentleman, but it seems I was mistaken in my expectations.'

Mr Felton sneered at her contemptuously.

'How could you expect me to behave differently when you are the reason for the acute heartache I feel? You cannot know what damage you have done to me and yet your manner is as uncordial as on that hated day of your foolish refusal.'

'I am amazed now that I had the patience and slightest inclination to be in the least bit cordial to you!' Eleanor retorted hotly, trying to keep her voice down so as not to attract attention. 'There was a time when I thought you a gentleman - even an amiable one - but that time has long since passed and will never return. Your behaviour, Mr Felton, is revolting and despicable to me and I beg you now to remain silent, for I fear that every word that comes from your mouth directed at me will only succeed in either deepening my already extensive dislike for you or forcing me to once again repeat my refusal and reasons, which I have already formulated explicitly, in a manner which is unpleasant to both of us. And so please save us both the pain and leave me be.'

Eleanor did not wait for a reply but turned around and pushed her way through the throng of people, confident that Mr Felton would not follow her. Her face was hot with indignation at his sophomoric and entirely disillusioned self-pitying conduct.

'Who does he think he is?' she raged to herself, manoeuvring around tables and clusters of people. 'Speaking to me as if I were no more than an immature child and blaming me unjustly for his own misfortunes!'

'Miss Ashmore? Miss Eleanor? Are you well? You look very flushed. Would you like some fresh air?'

A soft, lisping voice cut through Eleanor's red haze of exasperation and she spun around to see Charlotte standing behind her, concerned blue eyes opened wide at her. Turning her attention from herself to Charlotte immediately succeeded in soothing Eleanor's temper, as was always the way with her. The moment she gave another person her time and attention Eleanor consistently felt more sane and generally sensible than when her focus was entirely on herself; this surely is true of everyone.

Eleanor shook her head lightly as if shaking away the final remnants of her resentment and indignation.

'Yes I am well,' Eleanor answered cheerfully, her cheeks still flushed, no longer from anger but from the oppressive heat in the room. Young Master Whitham had indeed done his job well. 'But I was just on my way to the gardens for some fresh air. Perhaps you would like to accompany me?'

'Yes please,' Charlotte replied, looking equally flushed. 'One does get so hot dancing, does one not?'

Eleanor smiled in agreement and led the way outside through a pair of open doors towards the back of the building, out into the gardens. Eleanor inhaled deeply of the fresh night air and Charlotte followed suit.

***

The young ladies did not linger long outside. The cold air was refreshing, yet sharp and there was still a good deal too much dancing to be done inside.

When they re-entered the hall, bowls of white soup were being served along with glasses of negus. Mrs Ashmore and Mrs Layton hastened to join them, wine glasses clutched in their hands, its contents slopping dangerously as they advanced across the room.

'Hello again!' Mrs Ashmore greeted Charlotte, as enthusiastic as ever. Mrs Ashmore did not believe in hiding her true self in order to make herself 'acceptable' to the normal standards of sophisticated society. If someone found her too overbearing they were welcome to ignore her. This was Mrs Ashmore's general disposition.

Charlotte gave a tentative smile in greeting.

'A pleasure to see you again so soon my dear!' added Mrs Layton, beaming at Charlotte. Mrs Layton leaned in confidentially and would have most certainly commenced a well-meant interrogation if two gentlemen had not appeared at their side that very moment to ask Eleanor and Charlotte for the next dance. As their partners led them to the floor, they passed Miss Bucheron.

'Come dance!' called Eleanor to her.

'I… I don't dance,' responded Miss Bucheron, tight-lipped.

'Now you do,' replied a quiet voice at her shoulder. Mr Ashmore extended a hand towards the French lady. 'Please, it would be a great honour.'

Momentarily speechless Miss Bucheron nodded her consent briefly and Mr Ashmore led her gallantly onto the floor.

But now Mr Ashmore had exposed himself and the moment that dance ended Eleanor seized her father's hand and pulled him back onto the floor.

'Dance the next set with me!' she cried playfully.

'Oh, no. No, absolutely not. No, I am no good at dancing! No Lea, no.'

But Eleanor would not be deterred.

'Oh, alright then,' he conceded with the voice of one who knows when he has met his match and Eleanor flashed him a triumphant grin.

She gleefully pulled him onto the floor and after the set was finished, he had to admit that it had perhaps not been *quite* so bad after all.

'Fustian nonsense!' Eleanor exclaimed hotly. 'You did not stop laughing the entire dance! Not so bad indeed!'

But Mr Ashmore only laughed merrily at his eldest daughter's indignation.

***

A few dances later Charlotte staggered as composedly as possible to the side of the room and propped herself up by clutching the back of a chair. Eleanor, who was inconspicuously keeping her eye on Charlotte, rushed over to her and Charlotte leapt up guiltily. Now it was Eleanor's turn to question Charlotte anxiously:

'Are you alright? Can I get you anything?'

'I am quite well thank you,' Charlotte assured in her impeccable English, but her voice was tense and breathless and her face was pale. 'My… my corset is a little tight,' she confessed.

'Your corset!' exclaimed Eleanor. Her face resolute, Eleanor grasped Charlotte gently but firmly by the hand. 'Come with me,' she instructed.

By the entrance to the hall there were a couple of smaller rooms, which were on this particular night being used as cloakrooms.

'May I remove your corset?' asked Eleanor once they were safely installed in the ladies cloak room, surrounded by silk shawls, fur wraps and colourful spencer jackets.

'Remove… it…?' repeated Charlotte falteringly, unconsciously wrapping her arms protectively around her body.

'Yes,' replied Eleanor firmly. 'You are wearing a bodiced petticoat already, are you not?'

'Yes...but, I always wear it. I have to wear it. I've always had to, in—' Charlotte caught herself hurriedly. 'Where I come from,' she finished in a small voice.

'Well, you don't have to here,' Eleanor answered, now much gentler. 'I don't know where you've come from Charlotte, but here you don't have to. We don't bother with that sort of thing here, no one does.'

'Are you sure?' Charlotte asked nervously. She glanced about her apprehensively, arms still clutched about her body.

'Positive,' said Eleanor firmly. 'I can take it off now if you like? You looked as if you might faint a few moments ago!'

'Well…' Charlotte replied doubtfully. 'I was finding it difficult to breathe, and I suddenly felt so lightheaded, as if I would fall.'

'Exactly!' cried Eleanor and, as Charlotte didn't respond but also didn't disagree, Eleanor took her silence as consent to remove the offending article. She speedily undid the back of Charlotte's dress, unlaced the painfully tight corset, tore it off her and flung it on the ground, before lacing her back up.

'There,' Eleanor pronounced gently. 'Isn't that better?'

Slowly, very slowly, Charlotte felt her petite waist, before caressing her back and waist gingerly, cautiously. Then she spun around, once and twice and thrice. She giggled girlishly.

'*Oui*, it feels lovely,' she whispered. She inhaled deeply, filling her lungs with air. 'And I can breathe again properly!' she added happily.

The young lady's pleasure was infectious and Eleanor felt every bit as pleased for her as Charlotte was pleased herself.

They were about to leave the cloakroom when Charlotte added: 'You can call me Cara. Charlotte is what they all called me in—' she suddenly stopped herself again and hurried on. 'Never mind. But please call me Cara; that's what my brother calls me.'

And with a shy smile, the young lady left.

Eleanor followed her and stood in the doorway of the hall, observing and pondering. The dancers in front of her became a blur as she lost herself momentarily in her thoughts and musings.

She was not left alone for long though, for moments later Mr Ayles came up to her. Eleanor had not seen him yet that evening, indeed she had not seen him at all since they had returned from Southcliffe. Her father had mentioned something about him being kept away from Felowspring on business, but she was no longer sure of the details.

'Miss Ashmore,' Mr Ayles greeted with a bow and a genuinely warm smile. 'I hope I find you well.'

He wished he had the courage to tell her how well she looked. She looked exceedingly well, in her slender, crimson dress which gave her an air of elegance and charm and accentuated the redness of her cheeks and lips.

'Thank you, we are all very well,' Eleanor answered merrily. 'We have missed you these past few weeks though, especially after we saw so much of you in Southcliffe.'

'I was detained on matters of business but, as you can see, I have returned now.'

'And was your business successful?'

'It was.'

'Well then, I hope we shall see more of you again soon,' Eleanor pronounced enthusiastically. 'You must come and call on us, as soon as your availability and desire allow.'

'I have never yet found my desire wanting when it came to calling on you, Miss Ashmore.'

Eleanor smiled softly. The first chords of a new dance sounded, a dance which both of them knew well. The first notes of the melody soared through her ears and transported her in her mind's eyes instantaneously to a warm summer's day some years earlier.

She was in the garden, barefoot, and the grass was at its softest and she was dressed in a light summer gown of primrose yellow, with a ribbon in her hair. Faint strains of music were escaping through the open parlour windows as her father played for her. She was calling to someone, a happy smile on her face. Now she was grabbing someone by the hand and pulling them forward: it was Joshua.

'Come on, dance with me!' she cried.

'I can't!' replied Joshua and scuffed his feet uneasily. 'I don't know how.' But she was not put out for a moment.

'Then I shall show you how!' she laughed. She pulled him closer and showed him how to hold her right hand in his and place his other hand on her waist.

'This is called a waltz,' she explained.

And slowly, patiently, she began to show him the steps. It was a slow, yet beautiful dance and the music encapsulated so many emotions in a few notes.

'Do you remember?' Joshua asked quietly and Eleanor, snatched back into the present, nodded. What she did not know is that, to this day, it remained the only dance Joshua knew; the dance she had taught him that summer's afternoon in the garden.

Joshua offered Eleanor his hand and of course Eleanor accepted, without a moment's hesitation.

CHAPTER TEN

A Time Of Together

A few days later, as Eleanor reflected on the Winter Party and its many occurrences, she was glad that Mr Felton had brought to the surface that unspoken and otherwise entirely unarticulated uneasiness between them, which had hung like heavy storm clouds whenever they were together.

Eleanor could not forget. She could never look at him or talk to him without feeling that pang of memories and emotions she would much rather leave behind and dismiss forever. She could not forget all that had passed between them, but she did move on. In fact, Eleanor did much more than that - she forgave. And she found that she could now look Mr Felton in the eye when they were together in a room or could even initiate a conversation. A proper conversation. The topic of the discourse may be dull and the voices and general demeanour of the conversationalists lacking enthusiasm, but nevertheless a conversation it was. And Eleanor felt that conversation, however limited, is and always will remain better than none in such a circumstance. Whether he ever forgave her, she did not know.

Gradually, the once-existing connection between Mr Felton and the inhabitants of Felowspring, in particular the Ashmores, diminished until no one had spoken with him for countless weeks. He simply buried himself in his books in an attempt to block out the surrounding world.

In a way it was a surprise to no one when the tidings reached their little community that Mr Felton had broken off his studies and returned to his parent's home in the south of England, with no apparent plan of ever returning. A carriage had arrived the week before Christmas, into which two large leather suitcases, numerous crates, pieces of furniture and a great wooden chest had been loaded - the sum total of his worldly belongings. Mr Felton had then left without so much as a farewell to anyone.

Mr Ashmore, as head of the house, highest in the village and closest to Mr Henry Felton, had been the first to be notified of the departure. He had immediately gone and conveyed the news to Mr Layton who, like himself, had invested a good deal of time and resources into that young man's life. The two gentlemen were somewhat disappointed at first - for him to leave without so much as a word of thanks or farewell - seemingly oblivious to their heartfelt efforts, but they were not greatly surprised. Considering life to be far too short to worry about people's opinions, Mr Ashmore and Mr Layton also forgave and forgot.

It was with the tiniest glimmer of regret, but mostly relief and almost exultation, that Eleanor received the news from her mother. Regret that she was still unsure as to whether Mr Felton had truly forgiven her or not. Relief that the unnecessary and unpleasant tension which had, despite all of Eleanor's attempts to clear the air between them, consistently prevailed whenever they were together, was gone. And exultation that she had parted well with him. She had done the right thing and forgiven. And somehow, confidently knowing that, however painful, she had made the correct decision, gave her a triumphant feeling of a job well done.

***

The days grew colder and Christmas drew nearer, bringing with it the sound of sleigh bells, the smell of cinnamon and the deliciously warm and homely sensation of excitement at the festivities, comforts and pleasures to come.

The Ashmores endeavoured to let their Christmas that year be characterised by simplicity and happy harmony with each other and the One to whom they had that special celebration to thank. For the most part they were successful and spent as joyous and peaceful a Christmas as anyone could have hoped or wished for.

Francis had scoured their estate and found a handsome yew tree which had been promptly felled and placed in an immense tub in the parlour. And, as if by magic of the sweetest kind, the next morning they arose to find it covered in yuletide decorations. Sweetmeats, sugared almonds and raisins (each one carefully wrapped in paper) hung from the branches, alongside fruits and toys, all most tastefully arranged. The entire tree was illuminated by little beeswax candles which, from a distance, looked as if the very stars in the heavens had fallen to rest on their tree. Numerous expeditions to harvest holly, ivy and mistletoe were undertaken and hours later the family would return, rosy-cheeked from the cold but with mittened hands clasping big bunches of yuletide greenery.

Elizabelle had deftly woven a kissing-bough using some of the branches garnered on their expeditions. She had then taken a crimson ribbon and a handful of apples to finish it off; hanging from the ceiling in the hallway it looked positively magnificent.

For their Christmas dinner that year the Ashmores had invited Miss Langlois, Miss Bucheron and Mr Ayles to join them, and Francis, Elizabelle and Beatrice were of course also joining them in their celebrations.

The festive table was decked with a tremendous roast turkey, stuffed with sausage and chestnut forcemeat, seasoned with lemon peel, anchovy, nutmeg and thyme, mountains of buttered mashed potatoes, brawn served with mustard, a tureen of bread sauce and one of rich brown gravy, applesauce and a towering platter of pastries.

For dessert there was a Christmas plum pudding which made a spectacular entrance into the room, carried cautiously by Elizabelle, the entire pudding ablaze with brandy. It was satisfyingly oohed and aahed at and, although vast quantities of the main course had only just been consumed, mouths began to water as the pudding was plated up and a big jug of cream was passed around.

Later that evening the family gathered in their second parlour. This room was preferred during the winter for one reason only: the roaring fire which currently burned brightly in the corner, filling the room with welcoming warmth and ambient light. There is something inexpressibly comforting about a good fire crackling in the corner; sometimes one felt as if one could simply sit there and watch it for hours. This room also had the benefit of housing their pianoforte, besides a globe, abacus, painting easel and a stack of French and literature books for the children's studies, all neatly stashed in one corner of the room.

Miss Bucheron, who looked as close to relaxed as any of them had ever seen her, suggested that Charlotte might play for them, if they wished.

'Charlotte plays remarkably well,' added Miss Bucheron, her gaunt cheeks and pencil-thin lips stretching into a small smile. She looked affectionately at Charlotte who blushed immediately. Remonde was now the only one in the neighbourhood who insisted on calling her Charlotte; everyone else had now adopted her preferred name Cara.

'I did not know you played!' exclaimed Eleanor.

'Would you teach me?' interjected Abigail smoothly, flashing Cara a winning smile and batting her eyelashes innocently.

'Let the poor girl play first!' laughed Mr Ashmore, standing up and extending his hand to Miss Langlois. Mr Ashmore then proceeded to help her arrange herself comfortably on the piano stool and gave her some sheets of music, which she flicked through lightly before finding a merry yuletide tune.

It soon became clear that 'remarkably well' was an understatement. Cara played piece after piece and every time her fingers touched the keys of the pianoforte she played as one utterly inspired. It was as if she were transported to another world where she could hear and grasp the most beautiful melody, the melody and magic of that moment, and were then reflecting that sweet sound into our world.

Cara brought great pleasure to her listeners that evening and, if at all possible, even greater pleasure to herself through her playing. Eleanor observed Cara keenly as she played for them and detected, with a happy smile, that Cara's eyes were shining much more than they had been a few weeks before, when she had first come to Mayhaven. And Cara's cheeks were a natural, healthy rosy colour which became her very well; previously her complexion had been cosmetically painted in the French style.

When the Ashmores had first met Miss Charlotte Langlois, only a short time ago, they had thought her very pretty and fair of feature and yet somehow dulled, as if she were in reality a much more vivid and passionate bird which had simply been locked behind bars for so long that it had forgotten how to fly. Eleanor remembered discussing these observations with her parents the evening after their first meeting with Cara, when she and

Remonde had dined with them. They had all detected that same feeling beneath Miss Langlois' light blue eyes, exquisite gowns and fair, golden hair. That feeling of a restless spirit and vivid captive caged behind bars. What these bars, restricting, restraining and draining the very life and colour out of her, could be they knew not. But it seemed to Eleanor that Cara was already breaking out, noticeably since the Winter Party, when Eleanor had torn the encaging corset from her body.

***

Both Miss Langlois and Miss Bucheron and Mr Joshua Ayles called on them numerous times during the twelve days of Christmas. On one of Mr Ayles' calls he arrived at the manor just as Eleanor was preparing to leave for her almost daily walk, donning her coat, scarf and mittens, all of which were very necessary with the weather as it was. Though the sun shone brightly, the cold air was bitter enough to take your breath away. He asked if he may not join her and so the two of them left the house together and conversed pleasantly as they passed snow-laden branches and holly bushes.

'Oh Joshua, I have such a strong desire to *live* life!' Eleanor suddenly exclaimed, flinging one arm out and brushing her right hand across the top of a snow-laden bush, sending powder-fine snow flying through the air in front of them. A startled bird took flight, bursting forth from the comparative warmth of the hedgerow with a surprised chirrup.

'I don't want to just stumble through from day to day and reach the end without having *lived!*' Eleanor continued. 'I don't want greyness and gloom, I desire colour! Even if that means I must romanticise my life: Smell the roses like they are the sweetest scent on earth, taste summer berries like I've never sampled them before, dream of places I have not yet seen as if I had already been there, dress every morning like a queen preparing for a ball! I shall really *live,* to such an extreme that the most everyday things become exciting. I am sure that is the way it is meant to be. I cannot believe we were made for less than fullness of life, and I am determined to rise higher than the mundaneness of tasks and chores and customs to greater things!'

Eleanor suddenly gave a self-conscious little laugh and looked down at her feet, the edges of which were encrusted in snow.

'And I unfortunately do not know in the slightest whether what I just attempted to articulate made any sense to you at all, or whether I have merely succeeded in confusing or alarming you! If the latter, then please forgive me for that was not my intention in any way. I'm not entirely sure what I was trying to say.'

But Joshua smiled.

'But I do,' he replied. 'I do know. You have not alarmed me. Please do not think that my silence spoke of disapproval or confusion. It is simply that I was failing to find any words sufficient to describe my agreement with you on that matter. And I confess I was also rejoicing in the fact that you feel able to talk of such matters in such an unguarded and open way with me; that you trust me to such an extent.'

'I do trust you Joshua,' replied Eleanor and the young man's smile grew even wider.

***

After Christmas had passed and the New Year had dawned, the spirits of all the inhabitants of their little community were somewhat dampened. The festivities had ended, the leftovers had been eaten, decorations were being packed away. The weather was cold, the trees were naked, and spring seemed to be a thousand years away. It was the normal, post-yuletide blues which passed after a few days and soon everyone began to set their hopes on the first precious signs of spring. Every single new bud of life that was discovered on the pitifully bare branches of a tree was celebrated with joyous exclamations.

Eleanor, on one of her walks through the village and their estate, some weeks now after the start of the new year, began to wish that spring would simply hurry up and arrive, even though she usually tried so hard to be optimistic and patient. And sometimes, it is when we are just about to give up hope that the night will ever turn into day, that we find a bright star to remind us that the night also has a unique beauty of its own. So it was with Eleanor. Hidden in the snow she discovered a solitary snowdrop, perfect in all its innocent beauty, covered in tiny dew drops which had frozen on the petals, creating delicate pearls. Eleanor marvelled that the flower had managed to burst through the thick crust of snow and ice surrounding it. Surely such a delicate thing of beauty shouldn't be able to flourish in such a hostile climate. But it is often the way that a beautiful thing springs up, not despite the hostile and challenging surroundings, but because of them; it is the challenging surroundings which purify and bless it with strength.

Eleanor then rushed home, full of happiness. A seemingly over-exaggerated happiness considering she had only discovered a secret snowdrop, not a secret world, yet it was the simple, pure things which often provided Eleanor with the most joy.

Her news was received with great exultation. Every day after that she would bring back news of more snowdrops appearing and a week later Eleanor heard for the first time that year the sweet simple song of a bird and it thrilled her as if she had never heard a bird sing before that day.

Spring then properly sprang. Every last trace of snow

melted and the puddles that remained were soon dried up by the sun which increased in warmth with every day that passed. Soon the cows could be heard calling impatiently to be let out. Even behind closed barn doors they could sense everything waking up and they too awoke with it. It was a joyous sight to behold - the day the animals were first let out into the meadows and fields after the long months of winter confinement. Gambolling and frolicking and leaping and dancing, even the very oldest animals among them rejoiced as though they were new-born.

***

Charlotte and Remonde were just walking up the path to their front door after returning from a turn around the village, when they heard a shout from behind them. They turned to see Abigail, with hair flying and face flushed, draped over the low stone wall which enclosed their garden. She waved enthusiastically at them.

'Mama and Papa ask if you won't come and join us for a picnic in the garden!' she called cheerily. 'The weather is so glorious today and the flowers and trees are practically beckoning us to be outside! Will you come?

You will, won't you? I'll go and tell them! Elizabelle has prepared a proper feast. You must come. I shall see you soon!'

And with that she dashed away, her skirts hitched up in her one hand, auburn hair streaming out behind her. A few yards down the road she stumbled into Mr Layton's butler Gibbs, who was just about to go to the market. The basket of fresh radishes he was carrying was sent flying to the ground.

'Oh, I'm so sorry!' Abigail exclaimed remorsefully, blushing bright red, and she dropped onto her knees to help him gather the vegetables together again. 'I'm so, so sorry!' she repeated.

'That's alright Miss Abigail,' laughed Gibbs light-heartedly.

Straightening up he pressed a big bunch of radishes into the girl's hands. Then, with a smile and a wave he went off down the road. Abigail watched him leave before resuming her journey home, at a slightly more sedate pace, just occasionally breaking into a little run and gleeful skip.

Charlotte and Remonde did as they had been instructed and appeared a short time later, armed with parasols (for their complexion) and a sweet bunch of pansies, picked not over an hour ago from their own little flower bed. A very heart-warming sight met their eyes as they skirted around the outside of the house, towards the back of the garden.

The rugs and blankets, which had not had a decent airing since the tea party nigh on nine months ago, had been spread out and all the Ashmores were merrily scuttling back and forth through the open parlour doors, carrying plates, cushions, drinks and food. With consideration to the more delicate female members of the family a few shawls and tasteful blankets had been brought out, lest anyone should catch a chill. Francis and Mr Ashmore had found a great many old garden chairs in storage above the stables which they had hauled down, cleaned and positioned in the dappled sunlight beneath the oak, a little way removed from the food and blankets; these were primarily for Miss Bucheron's use.

Mr Ashmore had just broached a bottle of champagne when he saw the two ladies walking up, faces alight at the cheerful sight in front of them. Miss Bucheron's pencil-thin lips were now more and more becoming accustomed to smiling instead of being perpetually pursed; it gave her face such a different appearance - the change was startling in the best way. Mr Ashmore abandoned the wine bottle with Francis and escorted Miss Bucheron to a seat in the shade. Cara however was more than happy to arrange herself on the blankets and when Mrs Ashmore appeared with Eleanor, Charles, Abigail and Ethan in tow, each laden with a plate or basket of some good thing, they found Cara looking quite at home, face upturned to the warm spring sun, parasol held gracefully above her head.

They all waved cheerily to her and Abigail and Ethan ran the final steps, hurriedly placing their burdens down and flinging themselves next to Cara. Glasses of the chilled champagne were poured and distributed and the children were given equally refreshing glasses of lemonade. Elizabelle decided to join Miss Remonde in the shade and Eleanor and Mrs Ashmore began to uncover and unpack all of the delicious fare. A large meat pie, a bright platter of cold, chopped vegetables (with the radishes in pride of place), sliced meat and cheese sandwiches wrapped in damp tea towels, bunches of grapes (a gift from the Layton's hot house), apple turnovers, jam tartlets and a little jam jar of cream, wrapped in green leaves to keep it cool, were unveiled in turn.

'A toast!' cried Mr Ashmore, raising his glass, its bubbling contents glistening in the light. 'To family and friends and *life*!'

'To life!' they all chorused. A sudden stillness lingered as their voices faded into silence and a brief wave of something washed over each of them. They all felt it, a feeling of delight, a sudden thrill. How beautiful life was to be sure.

***

'Do you think the birds understand us?' mused Abigail lazily sometime later. She was lying flat on her back, arms stretched above her head, gazing up at a swallow swooping above her. Many swallows nested every year in the eaves of their house.

'I doubt it,' replied Charles, who was lying on his stomach, head resting on a cushion. He propped himself up on his elbows.

'May I have the last jam tart Mama?'

His mother nodded and Charles lunged forward gleefully. He brushed a few stray crumbs off his shirt as he swallowed the last mouthful. A swallow plummeted, snatched the crumbs and soared off again.

'I wish I could live in a palace, like a princess,' remarked Abigail as she watched the swallow circle around above them.

'How did you get from birds to that?' exclaimed Charles, but Abigail hushed him.

'Perhaps you might not wish for that,' murmured Cara in her gentle French accent. Several heads whipped around to look at her; Mrs Ashmore's moved so quickly that the crack in her neck was audible.

'Why do you say that?' asked Eleanor curiously.

Cara blushed. Her eyes swept over the questioning faces of these kind people in front of her and she sighed heavily. She glanced back at Remonde, who looked equally resigned.

'I say that because, in France, I sat with the princesses, duchesses and countesses of the land, at court, in the presence of the King,' she explained.

'You what!?' squealed Abigail, sitting bolt upright. 'Oh Cara!'

A dreamy look entered Abigail's eyes. Cara smiled, but it was a sad smile.

'Be careful what you wish for,' she responded. 'It was not as perfect or romantic as you envision.'

'But… but why not?' queried Abigail. 'And… and why were you there anyway?' Suddenly a thought came to her and she gasped, her whole face alight with awe. 'Are you a princess Cara? A French princess? Is that why you sat in court?'

Abigail leaned forward eagerly.

'No,' Cara replied slowly. 'I sat in court because my brother is a prince. At least he is a *prince étranger* - a foreign prince.'

No one spoke, but silently everyone leaned in with bated breath, awaiting the rest of the tale.

'My mother was French, a noblewoman, a *comtesse,* and she married an Englishman, my father; I don't remember either of them. My father was a soldier and he died when I was very young, while fighting for the

French crown. My mother died shortly after, while my brother was in England; it had always been my father's wish for him to be educated there. My brother returned immediately and inherited my mother's property, which was very grand, with many peasants working in and around it. My brother worked the land well and he found favour with the King and, partly because of the military success my father had, was given command of a regiment of his own. My brother's men soon became strong, skilled and well-trained and served the King well, and in this way my brother again distinguished himself in the eyes of the King; he was given the title *noblesse d'épée,* a Noble of the Sword. Soon people began to call him *prince de soleil*; everyone thought he was a *prince étranger,* a foreign prince. In France, the title *prince étranger* is very… ambiguous; many have misused this title. The King likes adornments to his kingdom,' and here Cara's voice was very bitter. 'The other foreign princes normally act as living ornaments to his majesty by remaining in attendance at court. For this reason the King welcomed my brother as such an ornament and willingly bestowed upon him the official title of *prince étranger,* as well as Noble of the Sword. But my brother had not sought such distinction and, unlike the other foreign princes who seek fortunes and influence in the court of the King, he would not move to Versailles. I however was offered a *tabouret,* a stool in the presence of the King, on account of my brother being a *prince étranger.* Overjoyed, I accepted. I was dressed in the finest robes and adorned with jewels and I was surrounded by some of the most influential men and women in France.'

Abigail let a little sigh of longing escape her lips. Cara shook her head vigorously.

'*Non* Abigail, do not envy me. The pettiness of some of the men and women's conduct and the unyielding rigidity of the expected conduct was little more than slavery; I was caught in the bondage of social conventions and I did not know how to escape.'

A long silence followed this tale.

'But how did you come to be here?' pressed Mrs Ashmore gently.

'My brother,' Cara replied simply. 'After a short time at court I became ill, the doctors called me frail and sickly, and they sent for my brother who abandoned his regiment immediately and came to my side.'

Cara's voice broke slightly and her eyes were unusually bright.

'Some of the sweet fruits that were prepared for the royal family and their hangers-on were exported from here - from Mayhaven. And the strengthening quality of Mayhaven's water, combined with the pure air which seems to blow only here so richly, is widely spoken of. It was decided that I should be sent to Mayhaven, to regain my strength. My brother prepared everything and sent his friend to accompany me and my companion Remonde,' here Cara glanced over her shoulder at Remonde, whose eyes were also glistening more brightly than usual. The lady's hands were clasped very tightly in her lap.

'Remonde was my governess when I lived on my late mother's estate with my brother and aunt. It was decided that she should accompany me to Mayhaven as my chaperone and companion; I don't know what I would have done without her.'

Behind them a small sob escaped Remonde's mouth and she clasped her hand to her lips, horrified. How rude, how ill-bred and unmannerly of her! Her whole body trembled with apprehension. But then she remembered - she was not in court, she was here. She stopped trembling, the terrified look vanished from her eyes and, as Elizabelle placed a comforting hand over the lady's own bony ones, Remonde allowed the tears to trickle down her face. Cara leapt up and threw her arms around Remonde and the two ladies embraced affectionately, Cara's tears now also flowing freely. And for once, Abigail did not know what to say.

CHAPTER ELEVEN

Celebrations And Surprises

'John, it is your mother's 70th birthday in a few weeks!' declared Mrs Ashmore over breakfast one morning. She always saved her declarations for mealtimes. It made the whole experience more enjoyable and dramatic and *loud.*

'Ooh isn't she old,' giggled Abigail mischievously to her brother and partner-in-crime Ethan.

'Practically ancient,' chuckled Ethan in well-meant amusement.

A reproving look, which would have silenced a dragon, shot from Mrs Ashmore's eyes and the two young would-be rascals fell silent. Mrs Ashmore looked expectantly at her husband, awaiting his response, but he showed no sign of reciprocating. Never one known to be overly patient, Mrs Ashmore repeated herself in no uncertain terms.

'*John!* It is your mother's 70th birthday in a few weeks!'

Snapped out of his peaceful reverie, John started forward and blinked owlishly at his spouse.

'Hmmm, what was that dear?'

A grunt of derision sounded from the cheap seats at the other end of the dining table, where Abigail and Ethan were sitting. However, when their mother turned exasperatedly towards them, both of the culprits sat demurely, trying their best to look like innocence itself.

Mr Ashmore winked at his eldest daughter. John Ashmore found great pleasure in teasing his wife, for she was so easily taken in time and time again; but he also knew he was treading on thin ice now.

'Thank you dear for the reminder,' Mr Ashmore answered. 'But I am my mother's son and therefore I am aware that it is her birthday this year just as it was last year and has been for, as you say, 70 years. I shall not forget.'

Now it was Olivia's turn to snort in derision. Mr Ashmore tried to look hurt, just for the fun of further teasing his wife, but he failed.

'My dear John, I was not suggesting that you would *forget*. I merely wished to remind you and venture to suggest that, since it is her 70th birthday, we might *try* and make an effort.'

'I have never neglected my mother's birthday!' replied Mr Ashmore indignantly. 'I always make an effort!'

'I was not suggesting you did not!' exclaimed Mrs Ashmore, her eyes opening wide. 'My, how touchy you are this morning!'

Mr Ashmore's eyes now also opened wide and he looked at Eleanor with a face the very picture of righteous indignation and hurt innocence.

'I— ' he began, but his spouse was not yet finished.

'It is therefore my humble suggestion,' she interjected, with practised ease. 'That we give her a really special, memorable gift by paying her a surprise visit. And anyway, I'm sure it would be good for all of us to have a change of scenery for a few days.'

'I'm sure it will be a surprise, but whether us turning up will be considered pleasant…?' Abigail whispered maliciously to Ethan. Alas for Abigail, her parents' ears were remarkably sharp.

'Thank you Abigail, for volunteering to assist Elizabelle with the washing up,' said Mr Ashmore calmly to his daughter without bothering to look at her, and the tone of his voice brooked no argument. Abigail opened her mouth to protest but, upon seeing the warning look from her mother, thought better of it and received her consequence meekly.

'I'll help,' whispered Ethan consolingly to his sister and Abigail smiled at him with a smile that would have charmed the very birds out of the trees. The two of them slipped away from the table and the sound of their laughter and chatter could be heard echoing up the corridor as they made their way to the kitchen.

'As long as I can bring a book,' muttered Charles from the other end of the table, although he was not wholly in earnest; he was very fond of his grandmother. Mrs Ashmore pretended not to hear him.

'I think it is a very good suggestion,' said Mr Ashmore approvingly, in response to his spouse's proposal.

Eleanor was glad and nodded her head happily in agreement with her father's sentiments but then, as her parents discussed the time frame for the intended surprise birthday visit, she remembered an already existing engagement of hers with Hailey.

'I really can't excuse myself now,' Eleanor explained apologetically to her parents. 'I see so little of Hailey as it is, and we have had this arranged for so many weeks now.'

'Of course, you cannot possibly cancel,' said Mr Ashmore understandingly. 'You can manage quite well here with Elizabelle and Francis, I should think, so long as you don't mind the quiet and solitude for a few days.'

'On the contrary, I shall embrace it,' replied Eleanor with a smile.

But her time alone at Felowspring Manor would perhaps not be quite so quiet as she expected.

***

Fortunately for Eleanor her personal departure to visit

Hailey was a day before her family's and, in that way, she was able to avoid the frantic, last-minute packing and preparations. Eleanor left early in the morning, having said her goodbyes the night before. She also left her newest piece of artwork, a sweeping seascape, on the parlour table, prettily wrapped, as a birthday gift for her grandmother. Francis was waiting for her with the buggy and, carrying only a small reticule and valise, she leapt up beside him.

Talisbrook, although on the far side of Mayhaven, was no great distance from Felowspring and by late afternoon the buggy was turning off the road and up the very narrow drive which led to the Williams' little house. The horse's hooves and the crunch of the buggy wheels on the gravel announced their arrival and Hailey flew out of the front door, carrying in her arms a bundle. Eleanor leapt down lightly and rushed to embrace her friend. Hailey pressed the bundle into her arms and Eleanor's eyes opened wide in astonishment.

'Meet Alice,' Hailey laughed. Eleanor stared down at the darling baby girl in her arms and back at Hailey, her mouth open in disbelief. Eleanor had not had the slightest idea that Hailey was expecting; they had not seen each other for over half a year and Hailey had never mentioned any such thing in her letters. In her last letter Hailey had simply expressed a wish to see Eleanor again as soon as possible, and so the two women had agreed on the beginning of May.

'Her confinement would of course explain her absence at the Winter Party,' thought Eleanor fleetingly as she held the bundle out to Francis who had now joined them.

Despite his frantically alarmed mutterings of 'No, no, no I can't!' Eleanor pressed the newest member of the Williams family into his strong arms. At first, he held Alice as though she were a tiny cannon that might detonate at any moment, a humorous expression of painful alarm and gentle delight on his face. But after a couple of moments his shoulders lowered away from his ears and he felt it was safe to breathe; he laughed nervously.

Francis refused Hailey's offer of tea and, after kissing and congratulating the new mother, whose eyes were shining, he tickled Alice lightly on the cheek, took his leave of Eleanor, leapt into the buggy and, with a quick pull of the reins, disappeared back down the narrow drive.

***

'What news from Felowspring?' inquired Hailey as she watched Eleanor make them both a cup of tea. They were sitting in the kitchen at an old scarred oak table which Richard had not yet had a chance to refurbish. Alice had just fallen asleep in her mother's arms and Hailey was subconsciously rocking to and fro, the wooden chair she was seated on creaking slightly with every movement. Eleanor poured their tea into two cups.

'The milk is in the larder,' Hailey said and nodded her head in the right direction. Eleanor nipped off and returned immediately, clutching a stone jug of cool milk. She added a splash to their cups before carefully setting one in front of Hailey and settling herself in a chair beside her.

'Not much,' Eleanor said in response to Hailey's question. She took a careful sip of her hot tea.

'What's not much?' pressed Hailey. 'How are the two new gentlemen settling in? Mr Edwards and Mr Felton, wasn't it?'

'They are not settling at all!' replied Eleanor. 'They have both left.'

'Left?' repeated Hailey incredulously. It was very uncommon for people to leave Mayhaven. 'But why on earth would they want to leave?' She said this more rhetorically than anything else and Eleanor merely shrugged her shoulders in response.

'Oh, but how was the Winter Party?' Hailey cried, suddenly remembering what she had wanted to ask. 'I told Richard he ought to go, but he refused; he didn't want to leave me alone in case something should happen. I was being strong when I said he could go, but I confess I was secretly relieved when he said he wouldn't.'

Eleanor readily told Hailey about the Winter Party and about their new neighbours, the two ladies from France.

'My, we are becoming famous!' exclaimed Hailey and laughed. 'I had no idea Mayhaven was talked about so. And even *abroad*! I wonder what it's like in France?'

'So do I!' said Eleanor wistfully. France had a certain romance to it somehow. Just then Alice stirred in her sleep and Hailey resumed her rhythmic rocking as the little baby opened her eyes blurrily and then slowly closed them again.

'I can make dinner,' whispered Eleanor softly, anxious to not wake Alice.

'Oh, would you?' asked Hailey gratefully.

'Of course,' said Eleanor brightly, slowly pushing her chair away from the table and standing up. The wooden feet of the chair scraped ever so slightly on the stone floor of the kitchen and Eleanor winced painfully; but Alice slept on oblivious.

From her sedentary position Hailey gave commands and Eleanor set to with a will. By the time Richard returned from Talisbrook where he had been completing his day's work as the village carpenter, toothsome smells were emerging from the kitchen, causing his weary feet to suddenly tread lightly again. He fairly pranced into the kitchen and swung the now wide awake Alice into his arms.

Later, as Eleanor served the food, Richard, who had Alice tucked snugly into the crook of his arm, said: 'You know, you can come and stay more often if you like. You can bring your recipe book next time too.'

Hailey made as if to swipe at him reprovingly, on the arm which wasn't holding Alice, but Richard speedily picked up his wine glass with that hand and gave his spouse a triumphant grin. Hailey tried to maintain her disapproving look but failed and she and Eleanor both broke out into fits of laughter. Moments later they suddenly became aware of a curious little noise. They stopped and were still, straining their ears to identify its source.

'It's Alice!' cried Richard laughingly, looking down at her, and indeed it was. The little baby was gurgling merrily, mouth wide open in a toothless grin, big eyes open wide at her father. And despite the copious amounts of drool dripping down her tiny chin, Eleanor thought it was one of the sweetest sights she had ever seen.

***

Eleanor stayed a week with Hailey and was, in that time, able to assist Hailey in every way she could. Primarily by cooking, holding and lavishing love upon baby Alice and also by becoming better acquainted with her husband Richard. This was an opportunity Eleanor embraced most gratefully. She knew really very little about the man her best friend had married. She had seen him only as the person who had taken her companion away from her but now, as Eleanor watched the way Richard cared for his wife and child, working with abounding initiative and helpfulness, she saw just how unjust and mistaken she had been in her prejudiced judgement of him. He was in reality kind, patient, hardworking, loyal and most importantly, loving.

Altogether Eleanor enjoyed her trip to the Williams

immensely, even if it was only a short and quite emotionally intense visit. Eleanor hoped that she, in her turn, had also been able to bless and encourage the young family.

'You must bring all the others to visit very soon,' urged Hailey as they bid one another farewell.

'I shall,' Eleanor promised.

She kissed them all goodbye and, as Francis drove the buggy off down the drive, Eleanor waved tirelessly to the happy couple and their baby until they were lost from sight around the bend in the road.

The Ashmore house was deserted when Eleanor arrived home and, weary yet happy, she laid aside her shawl and carried her bag to her room. Everything was as she had left it and for the remainder of the day she occupied herself with unpacking, tidying and other such small yet necessary household tasks.

Elizabelle had been out shopping and had then stopped by at her sister Marguerite's house on her way back from the village. She returned late in the afternoon and on her arrival back at the manor she found the house tidied and Eleanor standing by the kitchen table which was laid with a delicious dinner. Tears leapt unbidden into Elizabelle's eyes.

'Bless you,' Elizabelle whispered after she had laid aside her bonnet on the kitchen chair in a slightly dazed state. She kissed Eleanor on the cheek and squeezed her hand tightly: 'Bless you.'

Eleanor wrapped her arms around the lady's waist and gave her an affectionate squeeze. They then lit some candles, more for the atmospheric quality than out of necessity, and settled down to enjoy their meal.

***

The two women were assisting each other in the kitchen the next morning. Elizabelle was zealously starching and ironing while Eleanor baked some buttery shortbread biscuits which she planned on taking to Cara and Remonde later that day. Up until then the two hard-working women had not talked much, preferring to enjoy each other's company in companionable silence, which was a rare opportunity for them both in that household. Elizabelle was the first to break the silence.

'I heard some rather surprising news from Mrs Layton yesterday when I was in the village,' she mentioned cautiously, trying to appear casual, as if she had only just remembered this fact.

'Mrs Layton and Felicity were just coming out of the post office when they saw me and immediately hurried over. She, Mrs Layton that is, asked me if I would pass on some news to your mother as soon as she returns.'

'Hmm,' was Eleanor's non-committal response. Eleanor was not quite so excited about the prospect of news, as she did not share Mrs Layton's passion for knowing everything - or at least her ambition for striving to know everything. Elizabelle furtively glanced sideways at Eleanor, who was washing her baking utensils in the sink; the older lady was now distinctly uneasy.

She continued. 'It would seem that Mr Edwards has returned to Mayhaven.'

Eleanor dropped the dish she had been wiping and it fell with a clatter to the kitchen side. She had certainly not been expecting this.

'Mr Edwards,' Eleanor repeated, turning to look at Elizabelle. 'Mr *Aiden* Edwards? Are you quite sure?'

'Yes. Well, fairly sure. Mrs Layton is convinced she saw him just this morning. It would seem he has returned as suddenly as he left.'

Elizabelle returned to her starching. A look of intent concentration entered her wrinkled face as she spread out an item of clothing made of fine muslin and proceeded to starch it fastidiously.

'But… Mr Edwards *here,* in Mayhaven?' Eleanor repeated again, still disbelieving. She left the kitchen sink and came to stand next to Elizabelle.

'Yes,' Elizabelle reiterated, this time more emphatically, nodding her head to accompany her statement, however not removing her eyes from the task at hand. 'At least, Mrs Layton was almost certain she saw him. As she so rightly pointed out, there is no mistaking his handsome appearance. He certainly stands out among the men around here in my opinion, with the possible exception of Mr Ayles. He is also mighty good-looking; a regular out and outer. It came as a surprise to me as well, dear! But I thought I should tell you… I hope I was right in doing so…'

'You were right, thank you for telling me Elizabelle,' said Eleanor, swiftly leaving the room, drying her hands on her apron as she did so.

Eleanor hurried out into the fresh air where she always found she could think more clearly. Aiden here in Mayhaven? It somehow seemed unreal. Eleanor had, by now, started to accept the fact that he had left, that he was gone forever, that he was not coming back, that she would not see him again. And now, he was here. Why had he come? Would he call? No, surely not. But what if he did? How should she act? Would she be able to hide her true feelings behind veiled eyes or would her eyes betray her heart?

She paced around in the rose garden for quite some time before returning to the house and entering the parlour where she tried to apply her mind to reading. She thought it may calm her thoughts, but she found that her thoughts were too stormy to be calmed by mere words on a page.

***

At that very same moment, Aiden was marching purposefully towards the Ashmore's estate - a walk which he knew well. He too was trying to calm his thoughts, but to no avail. If anyone had seen him that day they would have most certainly wondered where he could be going or what could have caused him to behave so, for he was practically shivering with an uncontrollable passion and apprehension and his feet where pounding into the ground, as if to make sure he did not lose his footing and fall. But no one saw him.

The gentleman walked beneath the emerald covering which canopied the driveway, the trees of which were now brimming with new leaves. It was then that he first saw the house again. Running the last few steps to the building he leapt up the stairs and knocked forcefully on the front door. The sound of footsteps could be heard from the other side, hurrying towards the door, and seconds later Elizabelle opened it a little. She gave a start when she saw Aiden standing there, breathless from his walk, his eyes filled with zeal.

'It's you!' she exclaimed, a more appropriate greeting failing her.

'I'm here to see Miss Ashmore. Is she in?'

'She is, but the rest of the family are away visiting relatives.'

Elizabelle hesitated and then opened the door a little wider. 'I will take you to her if you wish.'

'Thank you,' replied Aiden breathlessly. 'That is what I wish.'

Elizabelle led him down the various passages and entreated Aiden to wait in the corridor while she scuttled off and knocked on the parlour door where she knew Eleanor had been for the past few hours.

'Eleanor?' she called. 'Eleanor dear? Mr Edwards is

here. May I show him in?'

Eleanor, who had finally managed to read a few pages of her book, sat up as suddenly as if someone had tipped ice cold water down her back.

'Mr Edwards here? Now?' she cried, her voice unusually high-pitched.

'Yes, dear. May I show him in?' came Elizabelle's faintly anxious voice from the other side of the door.

'Yes, yes,' replied Eleanor distractedly. She abandoned her book and rushed to the window, gripping the sill, her knuckles and cheeks white. She knew not what to expect, she knew only what she hoped for. But she feared her dream may be too perfect to come true.

CHAPTER TWELVE

In The Rose Garden

As Aiden rounded the doorway, he saw Eleanor standing by the window, her hair hanging loose down her back, shining in the sunlight. She turned around upon hearing him enter the room, but immediately lowered her head so as not to make eye contact. Aiden fiercely tried to compose his thoughts, but he found he was scarcely able to. Absence had done nothing to weaken his already passionate feelings for her. Seeing her afresh, he realised with a rush that she was even more beautiful than he had remembered.

Aiden bowed and an unsettling silence descended upon the room until Eleanor timidly ventured to raise her head to look at Aiden. She found she did not know what to expect. Would he be altered? What were his feelings towards her? So much could have changed during their time of separation. These and so many other questions raced through Eleanor's head at such an alarming speed that she felt she must sit down for her bewildered feelings and thoughts were threatening to overwhelm her.

Eleanor gestured to an armchair where Aiden had seated himself many times before. She then went and perched herself opposite him, on a seat by the French windows. As Eleanor looked at him now, she perceived that he had changed, but only slightly; only noticeable to her because she had seen his face in her mind so many times these past months. His hair had grown a little longer and his face was no longer clean shaven but stubbly; it pronounced his strong jaw line even more. It also seemed to Eleanor that he had grown taller somehow. And yet it was still the same Aiden. The same endearing, gentle smile. The same piercing eyes and soft, deep voice. The same tousled, wild hair.

Not trusting herself to speak, Eleanor remained silent, hoping against hope that the reason for Aiden's coming had not been mere politeness, but that he still harboured feelings for her; that the reason for his painfully sudden and unanticipated departure had had nothing to do with her conduct; that she had not in any way destroyed forever the soul tie which she was sure had once existed between them.

Aiden sat on the edge of his chair. He cleared his voice in preparation to speak but fell silent again. The carefully prepared speech which he had practised and memorised in his mind for the past months had evaporated the moment he saw her again. Aiden had thought he knew what she looked like - he thought he knew what to expect - but somehow his memory, or maybe his imagination, had deceived him for, sitting in front of her now, everything he had planned to say seemed unfitting; he found he could form not one single comprehensible sentence, let alone a declaration of that which he wished to express to her now. They sat like that for some time, neither one daring to speak.

Eleanor justified her silence with her sex. 'Surely,' she reasoned with herself. 'It is fitting for the man to begin and not the lady.'

Aiden could find no such justification and he knew that he must speak soon, for their time alone might be interrupted at any moment. He stood up suddenly with such a resolute firmness that Eleanor felt sure he had taken offence and was about to leave - she also hurriedly stood up. But he did not leave. Instead, he strode purposefully over to her and stopped directly in front of her, his breath coming thick and fast but with an unmistakable certainty and conviction in his eyes.

'Forgive me for remaining silent so long, for I am struggling to find the words.'

He paused for the briefest of moments, studying her face. Eleanor felt a panic and breathless trepidation rise up in her.

'I...must heartily apologise for my conduct and beg your forgiveness. I should not have left you as I did that evening in the garden, without any explanation. And I should have written long before now.'

'I confess that, although I did not understand your sudden departure, I assumed there must have been an important reason,' Eleanor answered. 'In fact, I wondered if I had offended you in some way.'

'No no,' Aiden responded quickly. 'It was not your doing.' He sighed heavily.

'Before my mother died she brought her younger sister, who was with child, to live in her own home. She, that is, my aunt, was weakened by childbirth and never fully recovered. My mother cared for her sister and child but fell ill and passed away soon after. I was not able to be with my mother when she died; the news reached me too late.'

The pain in Aiden's voice made it sound as though she had died only yesterday. Eleanor's heart ached for him.

'I took on my mother's responsibilities, as I knew she would have wanted me to, and cared for my aunt and her child. Another issue arose which brought me to Mayhaven. I promised those closest and most dependent upon me at home that my absence would be no longer than absolutely required. I completed my business quickly. But I had found you and I could not bear the thought of leaving you, so I lingered here a little longer.'

'I had a premonition the night before we last met. I

saw my aunt, she was dying, and her child was weeping by her side, alone and comfortless. The image pierced me; I had already stayed away too long. That very next day I called upon you, I wanted to explain, but it was so difficult. I wanted you to understand why I must leave, why I might never be able to come back, but when I saw you, such a conflict arose within me. I wanted to abandon all responsibilities and stay with you, but of course I could not. I could not find the words, and my conscience was screaming at me to flee. So I left you without a word of explanation that night in the garden. I cannot convey to you how it pained me to leave you like that. It grieves me even now to think of the pain I must have caused you. Let me say it again: I am truly sorry.'

'I returned home. My aunt, although still alive, was much weaker than when I had left her; nine months later she died. Her daughter was adopted by close friends of mine, who were in a much better position to care for her than I. Suddenly I was free to return to Mayhaven, which I did without delay.'

'I see,' said Eleanor quietly. Outwardly she appeared composed, but inside she was rejoicing; it had not been her fault! She had not said or done anything to make him leave, on the contrary, it had pained him to leave her!

Silence relapsed, though this time it was a settled one, for both of them now felt a great burden lifted and hope rekindled. After a little while Aiden suggested they take a walk in the garden. Eleanor heartily agreed and after strolling they chose to sit on a bench overlooking one of the small fountains at the front of the house.

'What has happened in my absence?' Aiden asked, watching a bird perch on the edge of the fountain to take a sip of water. 'What have I missed?'

'Not much,' Eleanor laughed.

'And what of your family?' he prompted. 'I trust they

are well.'

'They are,' she replied and began to tell him about their seaside holiday, finishing with recounting Rumpus' excitement at their return from Southcliffe: 'He barked and licked us as if we had been gone a year!'

She smiled at the recollection. Aiden smiled too, his eyes still fixed on the little bird, which was now bathing in the water, fluttering its wings lightly.

'Eleanor,' Aiden said quietly and he turned to face her. Eleanor felt a tremor run through her; never before had he called her by her first name. She felt as if he had called to her very soul, for something leapt within her chest as he said her name, an urge to respond to his calling.

Hesitantly Aiden reached forward and took her thin, cold hands in his.

'You Eleanor have ravished me, you have undone me in a way I had not thought possible. And to be with you is both torture and delight; torture only because I cannot call you my own. Please, let me now call you my own... I need you… Do you need me?'

Eleanor nodded slightly. 'I do,' she murmured, her voice barely audible. 'I do need you.'

Aiden dropped down onto one knee without taking his eyes off her.

'May a humble shepherd dare ask for the princess' love?'

Behind them the splashing bird fell silent.

'I hope he does dare,' she replied quietly. 'For he is not merely a shepherd in my eyes, but also a king. And if he does not ask,' she added. 'She cannot say yes.'

'Would you?' he whispered, a smile beginning to curl his upper lip.

'I would,' Eleanor answered, and she laughed. A smile like the sun spread across Aiden's face, and, leaping to his feet, he caught Eleanor up in his arms and pulled her in tightly; he laughed joyously and so did she.

Releasing her from his strong embrace Aiden tenderly stroked her cheek with his fingertips. And finally their lips found each other in a passionate, inarticulate confession of love.

***

That afternoon was one of bliss; Eleanor had not known that the human heart was capable of containing so much joy and love at once. The two of them stood for some time in front of the fountain where the little bird had now resumed its gay splashing, Eleanor's head resting on Aiden's chest and his arms surrounding her protectively. Merely to be so close and to allow the heartache of separation and unknowingness to heal was for them both the most beautiful experience.

After a while Aiden took Eleanor by the hand and led her towards the rose garden. When they reached the arbour, which provided the entrance to the exquisite little flower garden, Aiden sank down once again onto one knee. There, under the climbing blooms, amidst the sweet smell of roses intermingling with the poignant scent of lavender, he produced a tiny box from his pocket. Within lay a delicately flawless ring, shaped like a sickle moon and studded with the tiniest creamy white pearls. Aiden gently took Eleanor's left hand in his own and slipped the ring on. It was a perfect fit, not only in size but also in shape and colour. It seemed to mould itself into Eleanor's hand and moments later, as Eleanor lifted it up into the sunlight to admire it, the pearls glistening as they caught the rays of the sun, it seemed as if it had always belonged on her finger.

Aiden laughed again and felt as though he could scarce contain his happiness a moment longer. He lifted Eleanor up in his arms and spun her around and around until they both collapsed, dizzy and laughing to the ground. Then, oblivious and indifferent to everything and everyone around them, Aiden bent down and kissed her under the rose arbour, the sweet smell of the flowers wafting up, surrounding them in a cocoon of luscious fragrance and love.

Joshua Ayles, who came up the driveway leading to the house at that very moment, witnessed this happy scene and heard that sound of pure laughter and love. The beautiful bunch of crimson roses and lilies which he held in his hand fell to the ground and with them fell his heart. The flowers, in falling, lost many of their petals and now lay crumpled and broken on the gravel path. Joshua tore his eyes away from the rose garden and looked down at the fallen bouquet. Through the red haze of angry and impassioned tears that welled up in his eyes, he thought he could see the broken shards of his own heart amongst the dust and dirt, once again broken, torn apart and discarded. Joshua clenched his fists tightly, the veins protruding along the surface of his hands, his knuckles painfully white, then he turned and fled.

***

A little later, as Aiden and Eleanor walked together, they came across Francis who was working by the stables. Upon seeing them come over he immediately dropped his rake to vigorously shake Aiden's hand.

'So good to see you Sir,' he said, brushing his grey ponytail behind his back with a shake of his head; Aiden echoed the sentiment. A beautiful white mare poked her head out of her stall at that moment, butting against Aiden's shoulder.

Francis laughed and rubbed the horse affectionately on the neck.

'She's not shy is our Fay!' he said. 'Why don't you take her out?' he added.

'Do you want a ride, 'ey girl?' murmured Aiden,

stroking the mare's silky soft nose. She whinnied lightly in answer and nibbled the end of his hair. Aiden shed his jacket, waistcoat and sword and flung them across Fay's stall. He disappeared into her stall and reappeared a moment later, leading a saddled Fay by her bridle. He passed the reins to Eleanor and was about to assist her in mounting, but she leapt lightly into the saddle with practised ease.

'You're used to this, aren't you?' commented Aiden, pleasantly surprised at Eleanor's proficiency on horseback. Eleanor grinned.

'Yes, Josh - that is Mr Ayles - taught me.'

'Ah,' replied Aiden and said nothing more. He disappeared again into the stall next to Fay's and returned leading a chestnut horse by the reins. He too mounted his horse, a fine thoroughbred named Jo, and the two riders grinned down at Francis, who just chuckled and gently slapped Fay's flank. The mare reared lightly and galloped off, taking the wooden fence to the meadow in one effortless leap; Jo followed suit. The fresh air felt cool against Eleanor's flushed skin and she breathed deeply. The breeze whipped through their hair and across their faces as they cantered across the meadow and into the field beyond, scattering sheep as they went. The horses' hooves pounded into the soft grass beneath them, arousing a kaleidoscope of butterflies, which circled around them once, before flitting off. Eleanor threw her head back and laughed out loud. To her, this is what flying felt like.

***

Aiden and Eleanor steered the two horses towards the brook where they dropped their heads and drank greedily before cantering back to the stables. Francis was waiting for them and skilfully caught the reins which Aiden tossed to him.

'The sun's just settin' over the woods Eleanor,' Francis pointed out as he led Fay and Jo to their stalls and a fresh supper of hay. 'Why don't you walk that way for a bit?'

'I think I ought to—,' Eleanor began, but she did not get any further.

'Elizabelle's gone to see 'er sister in the village; she's taken some of those biscuits you baked t'gether this mornin'. I took the liberty of helping meself to one just before, just to check the quality you understand.'

Francis grinned at her, eyes twinkling. 'Anyhow, she's eating with 'er sister. Don't waste an evenin' like this by bein' inside!'

Francis would have slept every night under the stars if he had thought he could get away with it. Sleeping with the horses was the closest he could manage.

'We shall take your advice,' declared Aiden as he retrieved his jacket, sword and waistcoat, and he extended his hand to Eleanor, who interlaced her fingers through his.

As Francis suggested, they chose to walk up through the garden and into the woods of the Ashmore estate. Had they perhaps been more aware of their surroundings they might have noticed the bent figure, concealed in the shadows, which immediately scuttled off along the road as soon as they left the stables and began to head for the woods. But they did not notice.

Francis had been most assuredly correct in his recommendation. The sun had just set below the horizon and the soft, diffused light caused by the reflections of the sun's lingering rays welcomed the twilight. All around them the trees and bluebells were bathed in the radiance of twilight, where the two lights - the fiery sun and the gentle moon - blissfully collide.

'It feels like I have stumbled into a dream and I almost dare not breathe lest it all vanishes, like a delicate morning mist hanging over the dewy fields,' Eleanor confided.

'But I will not disappear, like the mist,' replied Aiden. 'And should I ever leave you, just know that I will always return. For though the moon kisses the sun goodbye every evening, yet the sun always rises again in the morning. So know this - I will always return.'

'I confess that, during your prolonged absence, I assumed you must have forgotten me,' said Eleanor. 'At least, that you must have forgotten any feelings you may have once harboured for me.'

'I could never forget you,' Aiden answered sincerely. 'For every time I looked up at the night sky, I saw you shining down from the moon and dancing with the stars.' This made Eleanor smile.

The light encompassing them was now fading and all around the shadows were lengthening. Dusk had gradually been creeping up on them and, all of a sudden, or so it seemed, it was night. The moon was bright that evening, although only in its sickle form, slender and haloed in a fragile lustre of beauty. The stars were now also springing forth, each one individually beautiful and splendid, yet all bowing to the superior light of the fair princess and gentle ruler of the night sky, the moon.

It remains a mystery how, what seemed such a perfect moment, where everything was as it should be, could be shattered into so many tiny pieces, as though a glass ball had been thrown from the sky onto a stone floor, its broken shards, too sharp and painful to pick up, leaving wounds so deep and delicate that only love and time will heal.

For suddenly, out of the darkness, a voice called out to Eleanor and Aiden, halting them abruptly in their tracks.

It was a voice Eleanor knew well.

CHAPTER THIRTEEN

Moonless Violence

'Wait,' the voice called with such cold authority that they obeyed unthinkingly. Unnoticed by Eleanor, Aiden's hand flew to his sword. The evening had turned cold and with that voice came a gust of wind which was as chilling as only fear can be. Eleanor however thought she caught a touch of fire behind that ice cold voice.

Forth from the shadows of concealing darkness stepped Joshua Ayles, accompanied by two men whom Eleanor had never seen before. All three were cloaked in mantles of grey cloth, proof of the fact that they had been waiting and watching in the cooling night for some time. Clouds, in what had moments ago been a cloudless sky, concealed the comforting light of the moon and Eleanor, despite herself, trembled. Aiden felt the tremor and, although the three men had not yet indicated in any way that they meant them harm, he gently positioned her slightly behind his back so that he may protect her. Aiden would, he knew, do anything to keep Eleanor safe.

Eleanor felt again a tremor run through her, yet this time one of affection for this man who had, with a simple gesture, shown his willingness to place himself in a vulnerable position in the interest of protecting her. She would, however, not be pushed behind, regardless of the incentive for doing so.

'Joshua! What are you doing here?' Eleanor cried, stepping out from behind Aiden. Joshua's eyes were of steel, as hard and unflinching as diamond and as cold as the northern side of the seas. But upon hearing her voice, full of concern and innocent warmth, his icy facade melted just a little and he looked at Eleanor with the great depth of affection he still felt for her. Then, like an ice bolt blasting through him, he remembered with a sickening shudder. Remembered the laughter he had heard only a few hours ago. Remembered seeing the two of them together. And the ice once again enclosed around his heart, this time clinging on with a vice-like grip, not to be so easily removed. He turned his gaze away from Eleanor to Aiden.

'You,' Joshua said, trembling. 'You. You thief! You would come and steal her away from me. I have watched her these many years and I have waited. Oh, I have waited. And she was always worth the wait. And then you,' he fairly spat the words out through clenched teeth, his eyes flashing dangerously. Joshua took a step closer. 'You come along and steal her from me. You have no right to her heart. You have no right, do you hear me? She belongs to me.'

His voice broke and a sense of desperation and hopelessness crept in, quite uninvited. 'I have to have her. You don't understand; she's all I've got.' This last sentence he murmured under his breath through gritted teeth.

Here Aiden broke his silence, releasing his hold of Eleanor and stepping forward, his anger now also roused.

'She belongs to you?' he repeated in a low voice, which was gentler than Joshua's, not quite so harsh; and yet it contained just as much warning and danger. 'No I think not; she never has, and she never will.'

Stung by these words spoken with such conviction, Joshua took an enraged step towards Aiden, his left hand falling to rest on the hilt of a sword fastened around his waist. Slowly his fingers clasped the hilt and tightened. Both men now stood facing each other, the anger and unspoken threats between them causing the air to virtually crackle with undisguised apprehension.

'You think you love her?' Joshua challenged, his voice low but dangerously clear. 'Are you ready to fight for her?'

Faster than anyone could think, let alone react, Joshua had drawn his sword and swung it viciously at Aiden who was only saved by his own agile reflexes. Aiden leapt back, narrowly missing the sharp point of his opponent's blade and quickly drew his own weapon. The two combatants circled each other, each one eyeing the other warily, every muscle of their bodies tense, watching and waiting for an opportunity to pounce. Joshua gradually began to advance on Aiden, gaining quite some ground until Aiden found himself with his back against a tree. It was apparent who the stronger and more experienced fighter was. Aiden had both strength and agility, yet he lacked the general skill and expertise of his opponent.

Joshua flicked his weapon this way and that, the blade light and lethal in its master's undeniably seasoned hand, seeking an entrance - a weak spot in Aiden's defence. He found it and, like an adder striking its prey, thrust towards Aiden's exposed left side. Aiden quickly spun to the right, just avoiding the tip of Joshua's blade once more, and ducked behind the thick, protecting trunk of a tree, appearing again from the other side to strike Joshua's arm with the flat of his own blade. Joshua cried out in pain and, with the added speed and ferocity of this injury, equalled his opponent's strike by swinging his sword under that of Aiden's and thrusting upwards, missing Aiden's heart yet piercing deeply the flesh of his right shoulder. Aiden leapt back, his left hand flying to his injured shoulder, his face twisted in agony. He staggered backwards a few more steps, the point of his blade still held up in the defensive, ready and expecting another attack.

Eleanor, who had until then stood as one in a trance, awoke with a cry of anguish and ran towards them, placing herself between the two men who fought so viciously for her heart.

'Please,' she begged, turning first to the one and then the other. Her eyes beseeched theirs as Aiden and Joshua stood there, shoulders slumped, eyes flashing, faces twisted in pain and yet still with their mouths set in a grim line of stubborn, dangerous determination.

'Please,' she repeated. 'Please, stop it. Put an end to this… violence and anger. Look at yourselves now, look at yourselves, not as adversaries and enemies, but as men. Look at yourselves. And *see* each other. *Please.* Don't fight.'

For a moment it seemed as if some of the hostility which encircled them like an army of archers with bows drawn, waiting the command to fire, subsided. Joshua looked at Eleanor and, once again, his affection momentarily overwhelmed his anger, enabling him to see and think clearly. But then that light of love was once more strangled in the darkness of fear. And the need for control, which so often comes hand in hand with violence, overcame him.

Signalling discreetly to his fellow men who had temporarily withdrawn themselves from sight, Joshua advanced once more upon Aiden. As he passed Eleanor she reached out and grasped his arm.

'Please, Joshua,' she pleaded. Her touch startled him, but only succeeded in confirming his assurance that she was worth fighting for. He dragged himself away from her and swung his blade towards Aiden.

Eleanor made to run forward and once again place herself between the combatants, but the two cloaked men, who had crept up on her like shadows, seized her from behind, grabbing her arms tightly. Shocked by this unexpected assault she screamed and Aiden and Joshua, who were locked in their battle, whipped their heads around. One of the men endeavoured to silence Eleanor, roughly placing a hand across her mouth and, with the other hand, locking her arms behind her back and so restricting all movement. Eleanor, in the face of such strength, was not capable of resisting or fighting back in any way.

The sight of Eleanor, helpless and in danger, pierced Aiden like a sword being driven through him and, with a sudden burst of energy and speed, he whipped his sword out from where Joshua had held it pinned, slicing Joshua's hand open as he did so. Wrenching his other arm away, Aiden leapt towards Eleanor, winding the one man with a well-aimed kick, while seizing her out of his grasp. The other man backed away from Aiden's threatening blade and Aiden, seizing the opportunity, ran with Eleanor to the trees from where the two men had emerged. From those trees Aiden had heard the tell-tale sounds of hooves and the swish of a horse's tail and his senses had not deceived him. There, in a thicket of protecting bushes, stood three horses. One of these Eleanor recognized to be Joshua's own steed, a magnificent stallion of jet black.

Aiden seized the halters of a chestnut brown horse which stood closest to them and the horse immediately whinnied in alarm, rearing up. But Aiden stood his ground and began to make such noises which he knew to be soothing and comforting to most horses. In seconds the steed had calmed itself sufficiently for Aiden to swing Eleanor up into the saddle. The sound of muffled words and then heavy steps running sounded from just outside the thicket and Aiden looked tensely behind his shoulder and then back at Eleanor.

'Ride,' he commanded. 'Get away from here.'

Eleanor shook her head stubbornly.

'I'm not leaving you here!' Eleanor cried indignantly.

'Yes, you are,' replied Aiden, 'hold on!' and he firmly slapped the horse's flank as he spoke. The horse reared, alarmed out of its senses, and then bolted, charging from the thick cluster of bushes and overhanging branches and galloping across the forest glade. A branch cut her cheek sharply and Eleanor barely had the presence of mind to cling on tightly. She fumbled with the reins for a moment before managing to wrap her fingers round them tightly and yank back, halting the horse so that Eleanor could look over her shoulder. She saw that Aiden had now also emerged from the thicket. But then something stirred in the shadows. Joshua, coming upon him from behind, sword held high, slashed down mercilessly upon Aiden's unprotected back. Aiden fell heavily to the ground and lay unmoving. Eleanor cried out in anguish, as if she too had felt the stroke of that blade, and the horse, at the sound of her cry, reared up once again and bolted. Fortunately, Eleanor was this time mounted astride the horse and better able to keep from falling.

As the horse careered off at breakneck speed, Eleanor dashed her head against the metal of the horse's bridle and was temporarily stunned, capable only of clinging onto the reins. Branches scratched both horse and rider and loose sticks fractured beneath them like gunshots as they hurtled through the trees.

How long the horse galloped through the woods Eleanor knew not. After a while, seconds merged into minutes and minutes merged into hours and still she clung tightly to the reins, her hands now numb, but her heart mercilessly not so. Tears streamed unceasing down her face and it seemed that all she could see was Joshua leering over Aiden with his sword drawn and Aiden's face, full of shock and pain, as the blow fell.

The horse slowed from a gallop to a canter, then to a steady trot and finally to a slow walk. Eleanor, who had fallen into a kind of stupefied daze on the horse's back, awoke when the horse came to a halt. The darkness was already beginning to fade and dawn was creeping over the hills and through the trees. With a start Eleanor realised that she had been out in the woods all night, but thankfully the horse, confused and being ridden by a stranger, had not ventured so very far away, despite his frightened gallop through the woods, and Eleanor was now not too far from her own home. Slowly turning the horse back the way they had come, she urged him into a trot and they reached the estate within the half hour.

Heartsore and weary Eleanor descended from the horse's back and fell to the ground, her tired limbs giving way after her wild midnight ride and the prolonged tension and pressure of holding on. The horse immediately cantered off, undoubtedly returning home to its master, in search of a warm stable and hay.

Bewildered and not knowing what to do Eleanor entered the house and fled upstairs, making no more noise than the shadow of the moon. Locked in her room she paced the floor for many hours, too anxious and restless to sleep.

CHAPTER FOURTEEN

Relief Of Return

It was not until mid-morning that Eleanor was awoken by Elizabelle knocking on her door.

'Are you there Eleanor?' Elizabelle called out anxiously. Then, looking over her shoulder at Francis who was standing a little way down the corridor, clutching in his hands a fresh cup of tea, she murmured. 'Perhaps I didn't hear her after all? Oh, but where is she?'

'I'm here,' answered Eleanor faintly.

Elizabelle had just been about to leave but she hurriedly turned back and joyfully pressed her hands against the door, crushing her ear very tightly against it.

'Oh, you're back!' Elizabelle exclaimed joyfully and behind her Francis loosened his overly tight grip on the tea cup.

Elizabelle heard the creaking of the bed and that of the floorboards as Eleanor rolled over and stood up. A moment later the key was turned in the lock and the door opened to reveal Eleanor, very tired, but very there.

Elizabelle threw herself forward and embraced Eleanor tightly.

'I've been so worried,' she cried and broke down sobbing. Eleanor rested her chin on Elizabelle's shoulder and comfortingly rubbed her hand in circles on her back.

'I'm here now, and I'm well,' reassured Eleanor. 'I'm sorry Elizabelle, I did not mean to alarm you.'

The frizz of white hair, which normally surrounded Elizabelle's hairline like a snowy mist, was pressed flat from all the times she had clasped her head in her hands over the last few hours. She had tortured herself considerably; Francis had needed to make her many cups of strong tea. He had also strategically forgotten to mention the generous dashes of fortifying brandy he had added to her cups. How could she have left Eleanor with a guest in the house *alone*? Even if it was Mr Edwards. How could she have stayed so long at her sister's? What would she have done if something had happened to Eleanor? These and many more accusations had been Elizabelle's constant companions throughout the early hours of the morning, filling her head incessantly with imaginings, each one worse than the previous.

It took a little while but soon Elizabelle had composed herself enough to hold Eleanor at arm's length so that she might better make her own assessment of Eleanor's wellbeing.

'I am fine,' repeated Eleanor, seeking to make her voice alert and cheerful so as to disperse any worry in Elizabelle's mind. But either Eleanor's acting skills had lessened or Elizabelle simply knew her too well, for the good lady was far from convinced. But she refused to pry.

'Well,' Elizabelle continued, the doubtful tone in her voice undisguisable. 'I received a note just this morning from Mrs Ashmore saying that they return this evening and will want sustenance when they arrive.'

'Oh good! I am glad they are coming home today.'

'I'm sure we all are,' agreed Elizabelle wholeheartedly. 'Anyway,' she continued. 'Is there any specific meal you would like me to prepare for their dinner this evening?'

'No Elizabelle,' replied Eleanor, shaking her head. I am sure whatever you deem appropriate will be far better than anything I could suggest. You are the expert in the matter.'

Eleanor stepped back and slowly began to close the

door. Elizabelle sighed, still considerably unsatisfied by her conversation with the eldest Miss Ashmore.

'Very well Eleanor. I'll be downstairs if you need anything.'

'Thank you,' Eleanor answered, her face now barely visible through the crack of the nearly closed door. She then shut it firmly and turned the key in the lock once more. Moving to the window Eleanor thrust aside the pale lilac curtains, unlatched the clasp on the window and, with one big tug, opened it fully. She stuck her head out as far as she safely could. Inhaling and exhaling very deliberately Eleanor tried to steady her breath and calm her heart which thrashed painfully in her chest. Although Eleanor's mind was full of restless, clamorous thoughts, one concern was foremost, eclipsing every other wondering: Aiden. How was he? *Where* was he?

Her concern grew with every passing moment; her unease increased in leaps and bounds as the evening drew nigh and still no one called. No horses' hooves clattered up the drive. No messenger came bursting through the gate with a letter. She stood by her window overlooking the tree-arched drive and watched and waited. Eleanor's gaze fell to her left hand where the pearls of the ring glistened, as if a moonbeam from the previous night were still caught in them. Tears welled up in Eleanor's eyes as the memories of yesterday flooded her heart and mind. She remembered the overwhelming feeling of supreme happiness with Aiden, out there in the rose garden, riding across the fields and then walking through the woods. Then her mind came back to reality with a jolt as she remembered the moonless violence that had taken place. She was sick at heart to think of it and yet think of it she found she must. The image of Joshua fighting Aiden loomed in her mind's eye, threatening and menacing her until she thought she could bear it no longer.

Just then the Ashmore carriage drove up and Eleanor saw her mother, father and all her siblings waving cheerily to her from the carriage windows, all in high spirits after a few jolly days of birthday celebrations. The sight was a healing balm to her soul, rescuing her in the nick of time from sinking into a gloom of despond. Eleanor waved back vigorously and dashed down the stairs to welcome them. She swung the front door open just as the carriage wheels stopped.

Her greeting was one of heartfelt sincerity and affection and, as she hugged her siblings and kissed her parents, Eleanor felt her sanity returning, like that single bright morning star which heralds the dawn when all hope of light is lost. Her family were indeed to her an anchor in fierce storms, this Eleanor now realised.

Francis came to help with the bags, and everyone entered the house boisterously, excitedly shouting to Eleanor.

'We brought you back a slice of birthday cake!'

'Grandmother loved the picture! She has already sent off to have it framed.'

'You look tired Eleanor dear.'

This last remark came from her mother. Eleanor hastily dismissed the comment.

'Disturbed night,' she said with a smile and allowed Abigail and Ethan to pull her into the dining room where Elizabelle was waiting with dinner. Francis was about to slink off when Mr Ashmore caught him firmly by the shoulders and steered him into the dining room.

'Oh no you don't! The horses will have to do without your company this evening Francis.' Mr Ashmore's voice was kind but firm and Francis relented and willingly took up a place at the table next to Eleanor.

Dinner was a conglomeration of every food that everyone liked best which meant it was, to say the least, a peculiar combination. But this did not lessen the enjoyment and general deliciousness of the meal in any way. Homemade peach preserve, plum cake, veal and mushroom pasties fresh from the oven, clotted cream, fruit salad, Elizabelle's special herb and bacon loaf, toasted cheese and gingerbread had never tasted so good together. Elizabelle allowed the family to eat their fill, which they did with great exuberance, before telling Mrs Ashmore, and anyone who cared to listen, the tidings Mrs Layton had bidden her to pass on as soon as possible.

Mrs Ashmore almost spat out her mouthful of tea when Elizabelle told her of Mr Edward's return. She hastily swallowed what remained in her mouth and then turned to her husband and began prodding him enthusiastically on the arm.

'Did you hear that John!' Mrs Ashmore goaded. Mr Ashmore winced; his spouse had a very strident voice when she chose, and her mouth had been alarmingly close to his ear. Mrs Ashmore noted his pained expression and lowered her voice to a whisper before continuing.

'Did you hear that? Mr Edwards has come back!'

Mr Ashmore massaged his ear with his fingertip and gingerly retrieved his arm from Mrs Ashmore's zealous prodding.

'Yes, I heard,' he replied.

'But… don't you think it's good news?' pressed Mrs Ashmore. She turned to Elizabelle. 'We must invite him round at once.'

'*If* he has returned,' interjected Mr Ashmore.

'Yes, yes, *if* he has returned,' agreed Mrs Ashmore impatiently. 'But I am quite sure there is nothing wrong with Mrs Layton's eyesight.'

Unnoticed by anyone else Francis glanced at Elizabelle and they both turned quietly to look at Eleanor who in turn beseeched them with her eyes. Without a second thought they answered the young lady's unspoken plea: neither would mention anything of the occurrences yesterday. Eleanor smiled gratefully and her uptight shoulders relaxed briefly. Francis, who was sitting beside her, reached for her hand under the table and gave it a gentle squeeze.

Eleanor had carefully removed her ring before coming down to join the others. She desired Aiden to talk to her father in private first, before openly announcing their engagement, as was only proper. And she wanted to have him standing next to her when they told people; she didn't want to do it alone.

Despite her ignorance as to Aiden's current health and whereabouts, and the turmoil this wrought in her, Eleanor still felt a spark of excitement when she thought of that: she was engaged to *Mr Aiden Edwards*! Sitting at the table with her family it all seemed so unreal, like a dream, and she felt that she was still in the middle of the dream, unsure of what the ending would be. But Eleanor had great faith in the power of love, for, as her mother had instilled into all of them: love never fails. This belief had proven itself true time and time again in her family's life and so she rested in the confidence that, no matter how circumstances seemed in the present moment, all could still somehow end well.

'Why are you so excited Mama?' asked Abigail. 'It is only Mr Edwards.'

'Because, my dear,' Mrs Ashmore answered as patiently as she could, which was not very, 'because I am not even halfway through getting to know him and I am therefore still less than half-acquainted with him, which is a state I cannot abide. I must know him fully and then I shall be satisfied.'

'And why must you know him fully?' persisted

Abigail.

'Because I cannot abide half-finished things,' her mother replied.

Mr Ashmore raised his eyebrows questioningly at his wife.

'I shall remember that,' he chuckled. 'You do not like unfinished things?'

He chuckled again. Mrs Ashmore narrowed her eyes at him.

'I may not have attained perfection yet, but perfection is my goal and therefore I am ambitiously striving towards it. I may not always finish a job… '

A derisive snort issued from Mr Ashmore. 'Not always' was a gross understatement. In his eyes, 'almost never' would be more appropriate. Mrs Ashmore haughtily ignored the interruption.

'...and I may not stick to one task at a time very well, but it is my aim to improve and therefore I can and will say, with an easy conscience, that I cannot abide half-finished things. And that,' she concluded, turning pointedly back to Abigail, 'is why I am quite determined to get to know Mr Edwards. I do not desire to know everyone, but he is one of the rare cases and therefore I am quite determined to have satisfaction in this matter.'

With that she drained her tea and arose from the table, issuing commands as she did so. 'The hour is late. It is time for bed for you and you and you. Please wash and lay out your clothes, you can unpack properly tomorrow. Oh, and Eleanor, how are you, my dear? How have you managed here? Has anything much happened in our absence?'

Eleanor, who had once again positioned herself by the dining room window, which also conveniently looked out onto the driveway, turned her head towards her mother, not quite meeting her eyes.

'No, Mama. No… nothing much has happened here.'

CHAPTER FIFTEEN

Eleanor's Vigil

The next day brought still no news of any sort and Eleanor's patience was sorely tested. And the next day and the next and the next were just the same, bringing no relief to Eleanor's anxious vigil. So far, she had walked into the village every day, but knew better than to blatantly enquire after Mr Edwards. Most of the villagers did not even know he had returned. Even news of Joshua would have been some comfort, but no information was offered and Eleanor was forced to endure the wait alone. No one else knew she was even waiting and that somehow made the entire situation worse. And yet Eleanor still did not wish to inform her family of all that had occurred in their absence between her and Mr Edwards. She had waited for so many months with little to no hope - she could wait a little longer now.

Finally, as the end of the second week since Mr Edwards had come to the house drew to a close, Mr Ayles called on the Ashmores. Eleanor, from the window in her bedroom, saw him approach and suddenly found that she could not face the thought of seeing him. How could she look him in the face and greet him as if nothing had occurred? No, she could not. She would not. Eleanor therefore threw on her shawl, flew down the stairs and out of the kitchen door, and, hurrying along the outskirts of the building, she fled to the home of Cara and Remonde. They were surprised to see her but welcomed her in graciously. It was another fine day and so they sat together outside, drinking tea daintily, surrounded by the pleasant sounds of bees busily going about their business. Cara and Remonde were far too well-bred to ask why Eleanor had come to call on them and Eleanor was grateful that they did not pry.

She did not venture to return to the house until nightfall, when she felt sure that Joshua would have long since departed. She had however underestimated Joshua's determination to see her, for Eleanor had been the sole reason for his visit to the Ashmores. When Eleanor returned, her mother informed her that she had only just missed him. He had stayed for almost the entirety of that afternoon and evening and had left with much regret at not having seen her.

'He really was very reluctant to leave without seeing you Eleanor,' pressed Mrs Ashmore. 'He thinks very highly of you, you know.'

'I am sure he will get over it,' was Eleanor's dismissive response and Mrs Ashmore was quite at a loss as to what could have brought about this sudden change in Eleanor. Being deeply puzzled, she voiced her thoughts to her husband.

'You know, it's most unlike Eleanor,' Mrs Ashmore said to her husband the next afternoon as he was sorting through some old files and books which had begun to flow off the shelves in his study.

'She and Joshua have been such good friends as long as they have known each other. They have always cherished their time spent together, in increasing measure, especially over the last months. And now she seems to have rejected him! It is most unlike her. I really cannot fathom it. I have asked her about it though you know, but she gave me no proper answer and I'm still none the wiser. I do hope nothing is wrong. Do you think we ought to do something about it John?'

'Hmm, what was that dear?' her husband asked,

turning to face her with a pile of books in his arms and a blissfully ignorant look on his face.

Mrs Ashmore harrumphed.

'Nothing!' she exclaimed indignantly. 'Absolutely nothing! Honestly, sometimes I don't know why I bother.'

And she swung around and began to leave the room, muttering darkly to herself. Her spouse abandoned the books on his desk and hurried after her, feeling a slight twinge of guilt at his lack of concentration. He seized her by the arm before she could storm away.

'Forgive me, forgive me, I repent in sackcloth and ashes! It won't happen again,' Mr Ashmore declared humbly, but his wife merely snorted disbelievingly.

'And I did hear what you said, at least part of it,' continued Mr Ashmore. 'I'm sure I deciphered the general gist of it anyway - the important bits.' He smiled disarmingly.

Mrs Ashmore scowled slightly and raised her eyebrows sceptically to the ceiling, creating magnificently symmetrical arches Mr Ashmore noticed, but he thought he had better not mention it. He didn't think his wife would welcome a comment about her eyebrows just at that moment. He hurried on with what he was going to say.

'I really don't think you need to worry about Eleanor, or Joshua. Eleanor knows what she is doing.' On this occasion he trusted his eldest daughter's judgement better than his wife's speculative observations.

'I know she does John, but still, do you not think it a little odd?'

'No, I do not. I am certain all your questionings will have been for nothing. It will all come out in the wash, you'll see,' he concluded confidently.

Mrs Ashmore, although still slightly dubious, was somewhat appeased and she nodded in agreement.

***

But alas, Mr Ashmore was a little too optimistic, for the rain refused to come and wash away the complication and resolve the uncertainties. Mr Ayles called every day that following week and every time Eleanor successfully made some valid excuse as to why she was required to be out of the house - all day. Eleanor had still heard nothing of Aiden and neither it would seem had anyone in the village and she found herself growing increasingly desperate. Where was he? Her mind, with hostility, continually suggested to her that he was dead, but her heart would not agree. In her heart she was utterly convinced that he was still alive.

She was not the only one to feel a great and ever escalating desperation. Joshua had spent the majority of every hour of daylight that week waiting for Eleanor and being entertained by Abigail, Ethan and Mrs Ashmore, and even on occasion by Charles, which showed how dire the situation was. Charles was not really one for entertaining, except in situations of absolute necessity, and even then he did so with bad grace. It was therefore really no wonder that Joshua was feeling desperate.

Eventually he could bear it no longer. He came once again to the manor in the afternoon, this time however gaining entrance through the back door, and was then informed by Elizabelle that Eleanor was in the library. Joshua knew the house well and immediately set off for the library. On his way he stopped at Mr Ashmore's study, briefly entering and talking with him, but Mr Ayles emerged a very short time later, leaving Mr Ashmore much graver than he had found him. Finally, he reached the library and knocked gently on the door, breathless now, trembling with pent-up passion and trepidation.

'Come in!' called Eleanor who had been, until one

moment ago, engrossed in a new novel which had been lent to her by Cara. She stood up as the doors opened, fully expecting to see her father standing there, and her expression changed to one of shock when she saw Joshua.

'Joshua!' she cried.

He entered the room, greeting her with a curt bow.

'You have been avoiding me this entire week, have you not,' Joshua stated, eyebrows even more furrowed than usual.

Eleanor had now sufficiently recovered from her initial shock. She straightened her neck and stood tall in front of him.

'Yes, I have been avoiding you. And you can surely be in no doubt as to why,' Eleanor responded.

Joshua clenched his fists and lowered his voice. 'No, I know exactly why.'

Eleanor's voice shook as she crossed the room towards him. 'How could you Joshua? How could you? Why did you do it? *Why*?'

Eleanor had, ever since that fateful evening, been subduing any thought and reflection about Joshua – Aiden had been the utmost thought in her mind. But now she realised just how hurt she felt by Joshua; just how betrayed she felt by him. She had trusted him, more than she had first realised, and he had betrayed that trust; deep are the wounds wrought by betrayal.

Joshua was silent, striving in his mind to find a way to continue. Eleanor observed him as he stood there in uneasy, restless silence, his dark head bowed, his fists still clenched by his sides. Even in this current state of agitation he looked handsome, yet it was not a beauty of the day but rather of the night. A dark, mysterious beauty, full of moonless secrets and starless whispers.

'Who were the men?' Eleanor asked sharply, suddenly

remembering Joshua's two accomplices who had hidden themselves with him in the wood that night. She had not heard them speak once.

'They are old friends of mine,' replied Joshua in a defeated voice and Eleanor's eyebrows raised questioningly, unsatisfied with his answer to her inquiry.

Joshua slowly fixed his flashing eyes on her steady ones and held her gaze. It seemed that from her he drew the strength he needed, somewhere hidden in that gaze.

He spoke again: 'They were men from the forest people. I lived with them for several years, before coming to Felowspring. That's why I call them old friends.

They're more like brothers.'

Eleanor frowned slightly.

'But, who are they? The forest people?' she repeated, even more bewildered by this information.

'They're a group of people who live in the forests in Wenerfield. They keep themselves to themselves mostly, nobody hears or sees them much. It was there that I learnt to ride and to fight; I have met none more skilled with a sword than the forest people of Wenerfield.'

'I've never heard of them,' replied Eleanor wonderingly. 'How long were you with them?' She was very quickly realising just how little she actually knew about Mr Joshua Ayles.

'Just under three years. They adopted me into their group and soon I was as much one of them as anyone else, though my skin betrayed me; the forest people are all dark, not pale-skinned like I.'

'But what about your parents? Why were you not with them? How did you come to be adopted by the forest people?'

Joshua swallowed uneasily. Eleanor did not notice and pressed on regardless: 'And how did you come to leave them if you were so well settled?' By now Eleanor's fierce anger was subsiding and a compassion for this young man was starting to rise up in her; she wanted to know his story, to try and begin to understand his conduct that fateful night.

'I won the estate on which I now live in a fight, a duel. We sometimes had other people, travelling in large groups, stay with us for a while. They would pitch their tents alongside ours and we would exchange goods and news and in the evening there would be singing and challenges. One such group had a renowned fighter among them who challenged us to a duel, offering his own estate as a prize. He had only just inherited this estate from his deceased mother. I was put forward to represent the forest people of Wenerfield and before I knew it I was fighting for my life. I won and suddenly I owned an estate in Felowspring. But I was not interested in leaving Wenerfield and some weeks later I travelled with a few of my brothers to Felowspring to see if I could not sell the estate. And then I met you.' Here Joshua finished abruptly.

'Pardon…?' Eleanor stammered. This was a twist she had not at all anticipated.

'You were out with your mother, buying fruit from the market stalls.'

Joshua spoke softly and he seemed lost in thought for a moment; he could remember the sight as vividly, as if it had only happened yesterday. Eleanor nodded, eager for him to continue his narrative.

'You did not see me, but I saw you. I watched you as you moved around the market and after you left, I enquired of a stall owner as to who you were and where you lived. He told me that I had seen Mrs Ashmore and her eldest daughter, who lived here, in Felowspring. And so my fate was sealed; I had no choice in the matter. I left Wenerfield and came here.'

'I had no idea,' replied Eleanor.

'But your parents...,' she began, remembering her previous question which still remained unanswered. Then, with a burning jolt, she remembered Aiden and she speedily withdrew her questioning. A coldness spread across her entire body; she did not want to know anything about this man. She did not care, for he who had once been her friend had betrayed her, shattering all her dreams. Joshua watched the coldness cover her like a blanket and she suddenly seemed unreachable to him, a thousand miles away - certainly not in the same room. He sighed heavily, his eyes now downcast.

'I have written you a letter,' Joshua muttered. He looked up again. 'Miss Ashmore, may I endeavour to justify my actions that night, however unjustifiable they may seem to you? I do not even ask for your concentration while you listen to me. This letter, I hope, explains all - at least everything I was able to capture and contain on paper.'

Eleanor stood in stony silence, the features of her face rigid and emotionless and yet her eyes screaming. She briefly nodded her head in acceptance of his request and Joshua placed a letter on the window seat beside her. His hands shuddered as he did so, as if they were trying to bear up the weight of his heavy heart. He moved to the doorway and turned around to look at Eleanor again.

'Miss Ashmore,' he said, bowing in farewell. She did not return the goodbye, but turned her head away, her own heart so overwhelmed that she did not dare look him in the eyes, lest he see the tears which glistened there. If only she had faced him once more, she might have seen the tears which stung in Joshua's eyes too. The gentleman exited the room and, just as he was about to close the door on her, whispered in a barely audible murmur:

'Goodbye, Eleanor.'

Eleanor maintained her aloof stance of defiance, but moments later, when horses' hooves informed her of Joshua's departure, she let out a desperate sob and flew to the table, seizing the letter and feverishly tearing open its seal.

'Dear Miss Ashmore,

I am in no doubt as to the lack of regard you must currently harbour for me and can fully imagine how distressed and resentful your sentiments must be. I can also envision how my conduct that evening may have caused many feelings of confusion and unclarity to arise within you. If I am correct in my assumption, allow me to enlighten you to the best of my ability as to why I behaved thus in the woods that night.

First however I must inform you a little of situations and occurrences which took place many years ago that marked me terribly.

I was born into a relatively wealthy family and as a child I wanted for nothing in material things. I was provided with a suitable education and was therefore adequately prepared for life, or so it was supposed. As I grew up, I learnt to fear my father. I do, and I think you share my belief in this matter, believe that a healthy fear can and does exist, for example that reverent fear which exists between man and God. Regrettably, the fear I had of my father was not of this kind. Every single task I completed or every word which came out of my mouth was judged and criticised by my father, to the extent that he rarely spoke to me if it was not to rebuke or chasten, or simply force my spirits down until I was subdued to a mere harmless, passionless, enchained being of toil and harsh words. This was the way my father liked me. Of nature I was much like my mother - passionate and vivid, adventurous and seeking knowledge. To be told from an early age and indeed all through my childhood that everything I did or said was little more than worthless and would never amount to anything or be nearly good enough when judged by the world's standards was torture to such a heart as mine. It drained me of life and hope. However, my childhood was not entirely without light. My mother was quite the opposite of my father. She raised me to the very best of her abilities and I am certain that, without her, I would not be able to function at all, for she brought some stability into my life. There were days, and on seldom occasions even weeks, where my father would be away from home on business and during these days my mother would endeavour to undo everything my father had made of me. We would laugh and talk about genuine matters and we would take walks together and discover new places and sometimes she would even teach me how to play the piano. But the blow of my father's return would simply sting yet more unbearably after such times of exquisite freedom and happiness in his absence. One of the most bitter realities of this situation remains that, on the surface, it looked like my father was raising me as any responsible parent ought to raise their child. The ugly truth was always concealed carefully. When I was but ten years old my mother disappeared. I never found out where she went and to this day, I do not even know whether she still lives. I only know that my father drove her away. I awoke one morning and she was gone. I felt as if the only light in my life had been extinguished - that I had been robbed of the only thing dear and precious to me. After she left I lived and breathed only for the day I also could leave the house and escape from the encaging shadow of my father. When I was fourteen, I ran away in the night, just as my mother had done, and I have never returned since. I searched for her at first but, as every day passed with not a single trace or hint as to where she might be, I gradually gave up hope. I stumbled across Mayhaven and remembered my mother telling me tales of it. Had she been allowed a holiday, she would have travelled here, she had often said. I was set upon in the forest by a group of boys no older than me, I noted enviously that each one carried a weapon. They took me back with them, to the camp which they called home and there I lived for three years. They called themselves the forest people of Wenerfield. They taught me to ride and fight. To trade and work the earth for food. One day I won a piece of land in a duel with a wealthy landowner. My newly acquired property was in Felowspring. I came to Felowspring with the intention of selling the property but at the market I saw a gentle young lady unlike anyone I had met before; she had the same hair as my mother. The locals told me her name was Miss Eleanor Ashmore. I did not sell the estate that day, instead I moved permanently to Felowspring. Here I have lived ever since.

We became acquainted soon after and you brought hope back into my life, shining into the dark corners which I had thought would never see the light again. In the forest I learnt how to fight and how to protect myself and that which was my own. But in Felowspring I learnt how to feel again, how to express myself; but the past haunted me.

You recently were made aware, in less than pleasurable circumstances, of my feelings towards you. Perhaps now you can attempt to understand why I reacted in such a way when learning that my affections for you could never be returned. A fear and dreadful certainty came over me that you too were to be taken away from me and an anger which I had not known I was capable of came over me. All those years ago when my mother left, an angry flame was kindled inside me. That flame has continued to increase in size and danger over the years, though I have fought it with tears, and was finally released that night in the woods.

Although I know that nothing can justify attacking a fellow man, I hope that you can now at least endeavour to understand my desperate motives. I was terrified of again losing the light and the only thing dear to my heart.

As to all that occurred since your flight on horseback: as soon as my blow had fallen on Mr Edwards, it was as if a veil of rage fell away from me. Overcome with remorse at my actions I immediately carried him to the nearest doctor. That very same night I obtained the knowledge that his closest friend had just returned to England from France. Writing with all urgency and sincerity I begged him to come as soon as possible so that he could best decide what the next course of action ought to be. He arrived the next day. Mr Edwards had to be transferred to a larger hospital and from there he could travel to France with his friend, to be treated by doctors more experienced in treating such wounds. The hospital he was headed for is the Val-de-Grâce. The last I heard he was to set sail two days ago. I will not trifle with you as to his condition. The doctors had little hope of his survival. The wound was deep and inflamed and they had insufficient expertise to treat him in a way necessary to secure his survival.

I was fully prepared to bear the consequences for my actions, but before I left him, Mr Edwards revived sufficiently to cancel any debt I owed him and entirely forgive all past misdeeds - I shall never forget it and I weep bitter tears as I write these words.

This letter has been lengthy, but it is heartfelt and sincere. Please know, I never wanted to hurt you.

Yours faithfully, Joshua Ayles.'

***

'Eleanor... *Eleanor*!' cried Mrs Ashmore, rushing from one room to another, growing increasingly agitated, her voice getting louder and louder. 'ELEANOR! Elizabelle, have you seen Eleanor?'

A few moments later she burst unceremoniously into the library.

'There you are!' Mrs Ashmore gasped, rushing over to Eleanor, ignoring her daughter's dazed look, and seizing her by the arm.

'What do you think Mr Ayles just told your father?'

Without waiting for a response, the feverish mother hurried on with her news: 'That he is leaving Felowspring! And not just Felowspring, but Mayhaven altogether! He is simply leaving! And while we are on the abominable topic of leaving, Mr Edwards would appear to have left again, without so much as calling on us or even greeting us in the street! No one has seen him for weeks and no light has burned out of the windows of his house for quite some time. I do wonder why he even bothered coming back. He must have been here no more than a few days. Ah well, we shall see if he ever returns. Oh, and I did so want to become better acquainted with him! It is all so very vexing.'

She paused for a breath and then, with a start, recollected her original reason for seeking Eleanor out.

'Yes indeed, can you believe it Eleanor? Mr Ayles leaving us! He leaves this very day I do believe. He called very briefly on your father this afternoon I am told and then left! Will you miss him very much?'

Eleanor suddenly whipped her head up to look at her mother, as if finally awaking.

'Today? He leaves today?' she questioned hastily, frantically turning and shuffling the papers of the letter together and stashing them back in the torn envelope.

'Oh Eleanor! Whatever is the matter?' said Mrs Ashmore, suddenly observing her daughter's tear stained face. She peered over Eleanor's shoulder at the letter, but Eleanor clutched it firmly to her chest. Now was definitely not the time for lengthy explanations required to satisfy her mother's maternal worries.

'Mama! Does he leave today?' repeated Eleanor urgently.

'Yes, yes I believe so.' She raised her eyebrows. 'If he has not already left!' She sighed despairingly.

Eleanor fled the house and ran through the streets of Felowspring to the marketplace, her skirts hitched up in one hand, still clutching the letter in her hand. Surely, surely, he could not have gone yet. He must wait, just one minute was all she needed. But she had to speak with him. She had to.

A lump formed in her throat as she hastened through the village, impeding her already ragged breathing and finally she came to a trembling halt at the corner of the marketplace, her limbs shaking from the unexpected exertion and her breath coming in rapid bursts. While recovering her composure as best she could, Eleanor scanned the little square and the neighbouring streets. Late afternoon was now greeting early evening and people were making last minute purchases and preparing to return home for their evening meal and a well-earned rest. Frantic now, Eleanor rushed forwards, her eyes running this way and that.

'Eleanor! What is the matter? Can we help?'

A gentle voice startled Eleanor and she quickly turned around to see Cara and Remonde, arm in arm, with a parcel of fruit and a basket of vegetables and bread clutched in their hands.

'Have you seen Josh... Mr Ayles?' Eleanor asked anxiously, rushing towards them.

Sensing the urgency in her voice, Cara wisely skipped any idle words.

'Yes, we saw him just now speaking with a gentleman whom I did not know, over by the bridge. He had his horse with him.'

'Thank you,' Eleanor cried and ran in the direction of the bridge. Behind her Cara clasped her dainty hands anxiously and exchanged concerned looks with Remonde.

Eleanor crossed the marketplace swiftly. Just as she was about to turn to the left, she heard the unmistakable clatter of horse's hooves on stone, away to her right. And sure enough there was he, riding away from her at that very moment. Had she been but a second later she would most surely have missed him.

'Joshua!' Eleanor cried desperately. 'Joshua!'

Whether he actually heard her voice or whether his soul caught the plea of her soul, he never knew. Sometimes there exists but a thin line between the two.

Quickly swinging his horse around, Joshua looked and saw Eleanor, standing there apprehensively, shivering. She began to run towards him, but he covered the distance in seconds. Leaping down from the saddle he swept off his own cloak and hung it around her shoulders.

'Miss Ashmore! What are you doing here? The evenings are still too cold to be out with no coat.'

He did not want to talk to her of weather and coats, but he found that no other words would come. Eleanor was still too breathless to answer and so she simply looked at him, and her gaze spoke more to his heart than mere words ever could.

'Joshua,' Eleanor gasped at last. 'I read your letter.' And her eyes spoke sufficiently for Joshua to discern that she had forgiven him and that his openness towards her concerning his past had in no way been in vain.

'Are you really leaving?' Eleanor asked softly, her chest still heaving.

'I must,' he replied. Eleanor knew that what he spoke was the truth but that in no way eased the pain.

'I am to join the army,' the young man explained. 'I travel back to the area of my birth. A regiment is leaving in two days and I am to accompany them. It was settled only this morning.'

'You shall make a fine soldier Joshua,' Eleanor found herself saying.

He knew why he had to leave. She was not his to have and never would be, never could be. He had accepted that now. Mayhaven held too many bittersweet memories for him to stay any longer, but he felt sure that leaving now would enable him to someday look back and remember the sweet without feeling the bitter quite so terribly.

'I should go,' sighed Joshua, pulling on the halters of his horse.

'Yes of course,' agreed Eleanor and took a step back. Tears welled up in her eyes.

'Must you leave,' she whispered quietly, her head downcast so that he might not see the tears in her eyes. But she knew the answer. Eleanor looked up at him one last time. Reaching for his hand, she gently rubbed the surface with her fingers and pressed it gently to her lips. Then she slowly reached up and lightly kissed Joshua on the cheek, her lips as gentle as a butterfly's wing.

'Goodbye, Joshua. I won't ever forget you.'

Joshua placed his forehead against hers and so they stood for a few moments. Then, tearing himself away, Joshua swung himself into the saddle and Eleanor was sure she saw tears streaming down his face as he rode over the bridge and out of sight.

CHAPTER SIXTEEN

A Fateful Article

As Eleanor awoke the next morning her mind immediately went to plans for getting to France and to what she would tell her family. In the meantime, the Ashmores' monthly magazines and weekly newspapers had arrived and after breakfast they were eagerly pounced upon, whisked away to the parlour, and promptly devoured and criticised. Eleanor's family felt it their obligation to complain about the lack of useful or interesting content in some of the magazines and the shameful waste of paper and ink which was dedicated to unnecessary advertisements. After these minor criticisms were out of the way, they felt far more at liberty to enjoy the magazines. There was something for everyone it seemed. Abigail siphoned off one of the most colourful magazines for her own personal consumption; she needed the fashionable dresses for inspiration. Mrs Ashmore found a shortened biography of an artist which she proceeded to peruse. Charles discovered a meteorological table at the back of one magazine; it examined all the weather since the snow had melted that year. And Ethan, well, he was content to watch.

Mr Ashmore on the other hand, picked up the thick, dull-looking wad of newspapers, which the rest of his family had entirely neglected, leaned back in his favourite armchair, positioned the cushions more comfortably, and began to browse through them in the hope of finding some snippets of political information. As he was doing so a fateful, bold headline caught his eye and, as is invariably the way with news, the announcement was tragic, relating to an appalling accident out at sea. A passenger ship, which had departed a few weeks ago from England, had sunk in a dreadful storm. Many lives had been lost and the list of deaths which followed the article was horribly long, each name representing so much untold grief. Mr Ashmore's eyes slowly flicked through the list, his face full of sorrow and silent reverence for the lost lives. Suddenly his hands clutched the paper, and an involuntary gasp escaped his lips. Both Mrs Ashmore and Eleanor heard the gasp and quickly looked up.

'What is it dear?' asked Mrs Ashmore. Mr Ashmore didn't answer for some time and when he finally spoke it was in a quiet grave voice.

'I am afraid Mrs Layton must have been mistaken dear,' and he pointed to one name in that list.

Mrs Ashmore leant over, following her husband's finger and read the name which had evidently perturbed him so. She also now gasped, bringing her hand to her mouth. Eleanor, turning pale, snatched the paper from her father, smoothed out the crumpled pages and read the article, her face softening with sympathy.

Eleanor suddenly felt a jolt of excruciating pain, the newspaper slipping out of her numb hands and falling to the floor. She clutched the sides of her chair and bent forward in an attempt to breathe through the leaden lump which had formed in her throat. Her head spun dizzily and throbbed with a sudden intense ache. She was dimly aware of voices, her parents' vague faces leaning in anxiously towards her, her siblings behind them, highly distressed to see their sister like this, but all of Eleanor's senses seemed to be drastically impeded with the painful shock. Her eyes stung with tears, though no drop trickled down her cheek. Her face froze, incapable of any movement and she stared unseeingly ahead of her, rigid with distress. Eleanor longed to shout and scream, to weep and lament, to somehow release the burning torment inside her and express her grief, but no words would form in her dry mouth. She sat there immobile, only just remembering to breathe, all else insignificant and entirely forgotten. She wished to stubbornly deny what she had read, to eliminate the picture from her memory, but it was engraved there, as painfully as if someone had taken a sharp knife and carved it into the very bones of her body. Among '*Balfour, Mr Joseph*' '*Beverly, Miss Emma*' '*Cawdell, Mrs Ingrid*' and '*Fawcett, Mr Alexander*' was a name, the name which was forbidden to stand in such a list of despair: '*Edwards, Mr Aiden.*'

There could be no mistake. No relief from the harrowing pain of the reality. The reality of the death of the man she had only recently, but too late, realised her tender affections for. Too late. Those words carried so much hopelessness. So much pain. So much grief: Too late. Too late to say and do and wish and dream everything that now filled her being, longing to be released into the one person she would never see again in this lifetime. Too late. Those dreaded words carried a certain amount of decisiveness. Of finality. Of something that cannot and will never be changed, however much one wished or wept. He would never come back. He was gone forever. The tide had left, never to return. It was too late. Too late.

And then, finally, the hot tears which had refused to come earlier poured out of her and coursed down her cheeks, each one containing a bittersweet memory of him. Eleanor clamped her hand across her mouth to suppress the agonised scream which threatened to rip from her throat to express the fiery anguish inside her.

She rocked to and fro, her body shaking with violent sobs as she grasped her face in her hands, unknowingly digging her nails deep into the soft flesh of her cheeks. How long she sat there in a dazed stupor she knew not. Her parents, thoroughly alarmed at this response, called for Elizabelle and together the three of them tried to bring Eleanor from her grieving trance. Finally she did respond to their desperate efforts and the dim faces around her came into focus once more.

'Breathe,' Eleanor told herself repeatedly. 'Just breathe.'

Elizabelle lifted a glass of cool water to Eleanor's lips and her mother clutched her daughter's hand. No one spoke; breathing was the only sound that could be heard in the room. Eleanor's eyes were downcast and she kept repeating those words like a mantra in her head: 'Breathe. Just breathe. Just breathe.' Slowly awareness came back to her limbs and her breathing became more stable. When her head had stopped spinning Eleanor stood up, shaking off the shawl which had been hung around her shoulders. She began to move through the silent figures which stood watching her. Eleanor was now desperate to be on her own. She obtained the doorway and, snatching her hand away from her father who had reached out to grasp her, she fled the room, ignoring the anxious calls which followed her, focusing only on escape - she had to be on her own.

***

The orchard was pleasantly silent and the boughs of the tall fruit trees provided cool shade from the sun. Under one of these trees, in a convenient dry and grassy gap between the thick roots, she flung herself unceremoniously, letting the hot tears burn a course of heartache down her face. It may have been biologically unthinkable, but Eleanor was convinced now that it was all too possible for a heart to break. For it to be so impacted by the loss of a loved one that it finally tears open.

Eleanor curled up between the roots and cried bitterly until no more tears would come. She wished she could fall asleep, her heart was weary enough, but sleep and the moon were faraway, banished by the sun which stubbornly refused to relieve her from her torment.

After some hours had passed Eleanor made her way indoors, preferring to return of her own accord instead of being sought out. She had hardly pushed the front door open when her mother, who had clearly been waiting for her, pounced on her with a motherly concern. Not waiting for permission Olivia wrapped her eldest daughter into her arms and embraced her. She then held her at arm's length and felt her forehead, which had now gone from clammy to cold. Eleanor's face was pale and drawn.

'You could have caught a chill outside. Here's a shawl.' She wrapped it around her daughter's shoulders. 'Come into the kitchen, Elizabelle has prepared some food for you.'

'I'm not hungry.'

'Nevertheless, you must eat,' replied her mother firmly. She did not mention Aiden and neither did Eleanor.

'Very well Mama,' she replied, allowing herself to be steered into the comforting warmth of the kitchen, where she ate a little of the bread, cheese and fruit which had been prepared for her, and drank some wine. This brought some colour to Eleanor's cheeks and Mrs Ashmore, temporarily comforted, left her daughter alone for a time.

As soon as her mother had departed Eleanor threw herself on the stone floor next to Rumpus, who had been whining quietly by her side ever since she entered the kitchen. Rumpus' big eyes stared forlornly up at her and he rested his soft head on her knee; something was wrong, he knew that. Eleanor buried her fingers in his soft fur and hugged the dog tightly, who responded by licking her repeatedly.

***

The younger children had been informed by their father of Mr Edwards' death and, though neither of them were especially distressed by the loss, they were very distressed by the effect it was having on their sister. Charles, who had hardly spoken more than five words together to Aiden, was surprisingly agitated about his death, but he had always been rather soft hearted and easily distressed at the thought of anyone or anything dying. Truth be told, he was, like his siblings, most agitated about Eleanor, for he loved her deeply.

Mr and Mrs Ashmore were shocked and saddened by the news of Mr Edward's death. It was so rare to actually be personally acquainted with someone whose name is written on such a list. As Mrs Ashmore so aptly put it: 'It is a shame and always painful when anyone dies but such is life, we will all die of old age some time. But when young people die, that is a great deal more tragic, for their lives were still to a certain extent unlived and not ready to be ended so. The death of young people is never meant to be.'

Mr Ashmore nodded slowly in agreement, his mind deep in reflection, so acutely reminded of the frailty of human life.

***

Eleanor paced her bedroom restlessly that first night, only to perch on her bed moments later, rocking herself to and fro, her arms wrapped tightly around her shoulders. And through her rantings and ravings and cries of anguish she heard a small voice which whispered soothing words into her soul and quieted all her desperate questions.

In the early hours of the morning, before the sun began its ascent and the birds heralded the dawn, Eleanor took a quill and endeavoured to release the pent up words in her soul onto a sheet of plain, empty paper. Tears smudged the ink but Eleanor carried on regardless, knowing that the words she wished to say to his soft, welcoming eyes she would only ever be able to say to a lifeless sheet of paper. She continued to write and cry until her lids became too heavy and her head dropped wearily onto the smooth wooden surface of the desk, just as the rays of morning sun broke through the parted curtains of her bedroom.

***

'Come in!' called Mr Ashmore, as a quiet knock sounded on his study door. His eldest daughter entered, the weariness in her body unmistakable. She walked over to her father's desk. He immediately stood up and wrapped his arms around her. Her tears flowed freely now, soaking her father's shirt and waistcoat and trickling down into her own mouth, tasting as salty and bitter as her heart felt. After a while Mr Ashmore held his daughter at arm's length and gazed at her with fatherly concern and love.

'What is it Lea?' he asked. He tucked a stray strand of hair behind his daughter's ear, his brow creased with concern. 'What is it? Why has Mr Edward's death distressed you to such an extreme?'

Eleanor rubbed a hand against her eyes in an attempt to stem her tears.

'He was my happiest thought,' she whispered.

Eleanor then related to her father all that had passed between herself and Aiden. That is to say, she told her father of their increasing mutual affection for each other which, just before Aiden's departure, had blossomed into the unmistakable rose of love, and then of their intended engagement that perfect afternoon. Eleanor related to him also the events of that night in the woods, but was careful to also reveal to her father the reason for Joshua's conduct.

Mrs Ashmore joined them in the study soon after and the narrative was repeated once more for her singular benefit. After she finished her account, Eleanor was startled to find tears in her mother's eyes and to see her father sitting with his head bowed and his face sunk in his hands. Her parents felt keenly their daughter's pain and they grieved greatly with and for her.

Later, Olivia Ashmore reflected that this was undoubtedly the reason for her own unaccountable eagerness to become better acquainted with Aiden Edwards - he was to have been her son-in-law. A sudden sob escaped the mother's mouth as she sank into an armchair. The thought that he might have been her son - the envisioning of her own son dying out there at sea - shook her deeply and she rested her auburn head on the arm of the chair and wept bitterly, as a mother might grieve for her own son.

CHAPTER SEVENTEEN

On The Third Day

It was now the third day since the news of Aiden's death had been received, and a truly exquisite specimen of a morning it was. The sun rose in a glorious splendour of delicate shades of blush, ochre and lilac, and a fragile mist hung over Mayhaven.

Eleanor awoke much refreshed, to her great surprise, and walking to the windows, she drew back the curtains and thrust them wide. She was just in time to witness the beauty of that charmingly ethereal dawn and it brought her heart comfort. She inhaled deeply of the fresh, uniquely beautiful smell of the new morning, full of hope and flowers and birdsong, with just a trace of the moon still lingering. Exhaling gradually Eleanor felt some of the weight lift from her which had clung on like a great boulder these past two days. Washing her face in the bowl of clean water standing on her dressing table she succeeded in cleansing her face of the dried layers of tears which had accumulated. Eleanor dressed herself in a lilac muslin gown and slowly made her way downstairs into the dining room from whence the most pleasing aroma of coffee was ensuing. The dark mahogany dining table was laden with bacon, warm rolls, soft-boiled eggs, honey cake, buttered crumpets, peach preserve, a jug of fresh milk and a pot of coffee, prepared with coffee beans which had been ground that very morning. This pleasant sight and smell also served to refresh Eleanor somewhat and she ate breakfast that morning with an appetite she had not possessed these past days.

Her parents were greatly encouraged to see the improvement in their daughter's countenance; the past days had been torturous for them. Both had felt helpless, forced to watch their child suffer, and that is a punishment no parent can or should have to bear or endure. The worst, they hoped, was now over and the longer process of grieving could now begin. Their daughter had braved that first tempest of shock. All would be well.

***

Cara called in on them briefly that morning, as they were finishing breakfast , and suggested that they might all take a walk into the village together. There was a special market being held in the square and she and Remonde were eager to go. The proposition was warmly received and in very little time a company could be seen strolling through the arch of trees, out of the gate and along the lane. Charles and Ethan ran on ahead, each one brandishing a stick with which they hoped to beat up any bandits they may meet. Their dangerous journey down the country path was bordered by flourishing fields and flowers that day.

Abigail had accosted Cara and the two young ladies now walked together, arm in arm, conversing pleasantly with one another. That is to say, Abigail talked and Cara listened, for on that day what Abigail really wanted was simply someone to listen and agree with her every word and, although Cara would never agree with anything obviously wrong, she did indulge Abigail a great deal. Most probably more than she ought, but that was tolerable for it was a rare enough occurrence. Mr and Mrs Ashmore strolled arm in arm, embracing the chance to spend unhurried time together and soak in the atmosphere of that beautiful morning.

Eleanor trailed behind, preferring her own company.

Although her heart was heavy and she felt as fragile as a snowflake that might crumble at the slightest breath of wind, she was not entirely incapable of smiling. Indeed, that morning was such a morning that somehow demanded a little lightness of spirit.

They reached the main road of the village, but no sooner had they taken a few steps along it, when they were joyfully hailed by a disembodied voice from behind the hedgerow to their left.

'I say! Mrs Ashmore, Mr Ashmore! Is that you?'

A head, presumably belonging to the voice, popped up from behind the hedge and it was Mr Layton.

'Why, this is good! Tremendous, tremendous! And Miss Ashmore and Miss Langlois! And all the rest of your children! Why, Mrs Layton and I were just this very minute planning on walking to the square. You know today they have a special market on and we thought we might, after viewing what the stalls have to offer, go sit by the stream awhile. The magnolias are now in full bloom and are breath-taking to behold. Won't you wait a moment? We shall join you directly!'

And with that he disappeared once more. A happy shriek, which sounded suspiciously like it may have emanated from Mrs Layton, issued and moments later the couple appeared from where they had been harvesting early peaches from their private hot house.

'Keep up the good work Gibbs!' called Mr Layton to his butler, who was also harvesting the peaches. A cheerful 'Right you are sir!' came in response.

'Oh, and could you look in on Felicity in a while?' added Mrs Layton. A slightly less enthusiastic 'Right you are ma'am' came back. And so, the little gathering of friends and family set off once more.

***

The marketplace was awash with people, noises,

smells, colours and festivity. There were stalls of every kind, each item on display unique and oozing with homemade love. One lady was selling sugar plums and crystallised ginger in little pouches, a stall next to hers was emitting mouth-watering aromas of iced buns and another stall beyond that was selling great baskets of cherries, oranges, and even a couple of pineapples. A small group of children, dressed in frocks as bright as the vibrant fruit, had gathered around the pineapples to marvel at them. Most of them had never seen such a curious and exciting looking fruit. Down by the stream there was an old wooden cart which had been filled to overflowing with flowers of many kinds. Such a glorious amassment of colours and fragrance on display.

Mrs Ashmore found a second-hand stall which she promptly raided, much to the exasperation of Mr Ashmore. She returned shortly with Abigail and Ethan in tow and proceeded to excitedly show Eleanor her purchases. She spread out a few items on an obliging bench: a reticule, a scarf and something which looked like it might be a bonnet.

'The owner said they were pre-loved,' Mrs Ashmore explained proudly.

Mr Ashmore, who had also come to take a closer look, picked the bonnet up between finger and thumb, peered at it with a mixed look of amusement and exasperation, before dropping it again.

'I think it was pre-abused actually,' he remarked drily and Eleanor stifled a giggle.

'I found a ring!' exclaimed Ethan shoving his hand as close to his father's face as he could. A gold ring which was rather too big for him gleamed on his thumb.

'Hhhmmm!' was his father's non-committal response and he and Eleanor exchanged glances.

'Men don't wear rings,' said Abigail with a sniff. She

was trying to tie the garish scarf into her hair.

'Aiden does,' retorted Ethan hotly. Abigail gasped sharply and glared meaningfully at Eleanor and then back at Ethan. A look of realisation came over Ethan's little face.

'Oh!' he whispered. 'Sorry!'

But Eleanor had not heard. She was now watching Cara, who was passionately trying to persuade her companion Remonde to pick a flower for her hair from the overflowing cart.

'Oh go on! *Please*!' implored Cara.

'No! I will not wear flowers in my hair!' replied Remonde firmly, pursing her lips and sticking her chin out resolutely. But the stall owner plucked out a beautiful bloom and held it towards her.

'Here Miss,' he urged. 'This one matches your eyes perfectly.'

Remonde hesitated but finally conceded, accepting the flower with a courteous bow of her head. Cara gleefully tucked the flower into Remonde's tight bun and gave her a kiss on her bony cheek.

'There, you look beautiful,' declared Cara happily and Remonde smiled, a rare commodity which became her very well.

After strolling around for some time and viewing everything to their heart's content, the party moved off to the magnolia trees where benches had been set up. A number of people had already moved away from the market to enjoy the peace and beauty around the stream. The sweet scent of the magnolia beautifully complemented the sound of the gurgling merry stream. A weeping willow, which must surely have been growing for decades longer than anyone could remember, stood by the edge of the water, its branches hanging so low that they rested in heaps on the ground, creating an entirely enclosed, secret hiding place.

The boys ran off to dam the stream (or at least try to) whilst their parents sat together on benches and talked as parents will, and Cara and Abigail went in search of fallen magnolia blossoms to adorn their fair heads with. Remonde decided to go for a little constitutional on her own. Mr and Mrs Layton were nowhere to be found. Eleanor meanwhile slipped away to the weeping willow and gently parted the branches, making an entrance for herself so that she may pass through into that beautiful hiding place. Despite the density of the branches and multitude of leaves, much sunlight still managed to penetrate the layers of foliage and fall down in sundrops of splendour. The dappled light played all across her face and she slowly exhaled.

'Just breathe,' Eleanor whispered, as she had reminded herself often those past three days. 'Just breathe.'

A gentle rustling hardly more than a whisper aroused her from her reverie and she turned around to see where the sound had come from. Standing there was a figure, a very familiar figure and yet she looked upon him as if he were a stranger, so great was her shock at seeing him. The figure slowly - cautiously - moved towards her until he, for it was a man, stood right in front of her, so close that she could feel his breath on her forehead. Still Eleanor made no sound, no movement. Only her eyes moved. They looked up in innocent astonishment and questioning hope.

'Can it be?' Eleanor whispered, gradually lifting her hand and reaching out to touch his face. She gently tucked a strand of his hair behind his ear. She dared not breathe for fear this was merely a dream - how could it be real?

'Do you know me Eleanor?' he said in his deep soft voice, and the moment he said her name, Eleanor knew there could be no mistake. The man leant forward and rested his forehead against hers.

'It is I,' he whispered. 'I have returned; I have come back to you.'

Eleanor's eyes filled with tears as she suddenly realised it was true. This was no illusion. Here stood Aiden in front of her. With a joyful gasp of laughter Eleanor threw her arms around his neck and he too laughed aloud and swung her up into his arms and around and above his head; and the sound of their laughter echoed the very spirit of that glorious day.

Outside Mr and Mrs Ashmore and all the others heard that sound and rejoiced with them. They knew its source and the cause, for they had directed Aiden to Eleanor's retreat.

All around them the birds sang sweeter and everything was perfect once more.

As Eleanor and Aiden emerged from under the willow tree Mr Ashmore hurried forward to shake the gentleman's hand firmly. In the background Eleanor could see her mother beaming, clutching Ethan's hand ecstatically. Then she noticed a man she did not know standing behind her mother – it was Raymond. He too came forward and clapped Aiden on the back.

'At long last, we meet!' the man exclaimed, greeting Eleanor with a roguish grin. He bowed gallantly, taking her outstretched hand and kissing it.

Aiden laughed at Eleanor's slightly bewildered look. He was about to explain who this man was when Cara returned with Abigail. Cara glanced at Raymond, then did a spectacular double take.

'Ray!' she cried out in surprise. 'What are you doing here?'

Raymond continued grinning and inclined his head a little to the left. Cara shifted her gaze from him to the person standing next to him, who was partially concealed by Eleanor. She screamed, flung aside the petals in her hands and launched herself forwards, throwing herself into the man's arms. Aiden laughed and embraced her tightly.

Everyone around them, with the exception of Raymond, gawped, jaws slack and eyes wide. Abigail was the first to manage a comprehensible utterance.

'*You*,' she cried indignantly, stepping forwards and prodding Cara viciously. 'Know *him*?' She turned and prodded Aiden. '*And you didn't tell me?*' she finished heatedly. She stopped, words failing her.

'What...?' Eleanor stammered, looking first from Cara to Aiden and then back to Cara. 'How…?'

Just then Remonde returned from her walk. With a sharp intake of breath she recognised Aiden and Raymond, but speedily composed herself and, with great dignity, she curtsied deeply.

'Your Lordship,' she greeted.

'*What?*' Abigail cried again, rounding on Remonde. 'What did you just say to him?'

Cara suddenly giggled. All heads now whipped around to look at her.

'Sorry,' she apologised, clapping a hand to her mouth, but from behind her slender fingers she giggled again. 'It's your faces!'

'I think we had better explain,' decided Aiden, taking compassion on the Ashmore family, who were looking more befogged by the minute.

'Yes please,' replied Eleanor firmly, a dazed look still very much present on her face. But Cara couldn't wait.

'Aiden is my *brother*!' Cara burst out, as if that explained everything.

'Your… your *brother*?' repeated Eleanor uncertainly.

Cara nodded happily.

'But… but he can't be!' exclaimed Abigail in a deeply shocked voice.

'Why not?' asked Cara with a laugh.

'You don't have the same surname,' pointed out Charles reasonably from the back.

'True,' chorused Abigail, Eleanor and Mrs Ashmore.

'You know me as 'Langlois'. Langlois means 'English man' in French,' explained Cara. 'It's the name which was given to me at court in France. 'Edwards' was not French enough for them, so they called me Charlotte Langlois, instead of Charlotte Edwards.'

'Ah,' said Charles, nodding his head sagely.

Slowly Eleanor turned to Aiden.

'But,' she began hesitantly. Her mind was still trying to take in and process all of this startling information. Primarily how Aiden came to be alive and well after the papers had pronounced him dead!

'But that means that you are the brother which Cara, I mean Charlotte, has told us about. The brother who lives in France and was given a title by *the King of France*? You are the *prince*?'

Aiden nodded.

'I would have told you,' he said sincerely. 'And in any case, I'm not a *real* prince. Just a *prince étranger,* whatever that counts for. I'm not a prince by birth, only because the King willed it.'

'And what would you be here, in England?' inquired Charles curiously. 'I mean, what would we call you? We don't really have foreign princes here. And I can't even pronounce what you just said.'

Aiden shrugged indifferently. 'Maybe a Lord or an Earl. It doesn't really matter; it's of no great consequence now.'

'It doesn't matter?' repeated Abigail incredulously. She and Ethan were both looking at Aiden with an entirely new reverence. He was a *prince.* They were in the presence of a *prince.* Even Mrs Ashmore looked deeply impressed. The subject of their admiration did not notice it; his attention was elsewhere. Aiden looked intently at Eleanor, who was gazing out across the stream. The wind rustled the willow tree lightly and the longest branches which hung over the surface of the water brushed against it lazily, causing ripples to spread and dance into each other. That same breeze rustled through Eleanor's hair and scattered it lightly across her face. She pushed it back over her shoulder absentmindedly and turned to face everyone again.

'Do you know what?' declared Raymond grandly. 'I think what we need is food - and wine. We need to celebrate. I don't know my way around here though, so I shall need someone to accompany me. And at least one other man to help me carry,' he added quickly, when three eager but rather small hands shot up.

***

A little while later Remonde had seated herself with Mrs Ashmore on a bench, they were conversing in low, excited tones, and everyone else but Aiden and Eleanor had dispersed in various directions to procure what Abigail liked to call 'survivals.' Aiden caught Eleanor gazing at him, a look of disbelief on her face.

'Do you doubt I'm real?' Aiden asked with a small smile. He stepped forward and held the palms of his hands towards her.

'Is this not real?' He grasped her hands in his own.

'Yes but… you're a prince,' said Eleanor uncertainly. 'Should I be calling you 'Your Highness' or 'Your Lordship?'

'Only if you let me call you "My Lady," 'Aiden replied, his top lip curling into a smile.

'I always thought you were too good for me,' said

Eleanor. 'Now I know why.'

'You're too good for me,' she repeated with a small shake of her head. 'I don't know Aiden the prince, a Noble of France. I only know Aiden, the gentleman, who I thought was just a humble shepherd.'

Aiden squeezed her hands.

'I have passed through fire and storms to be with you,' he said in a deep voice which trembled with feeling. 'Don't distance yourself from me now.'

Eleanor nodded in response. Aiden pulled her into his chest and held her tightly, his heart pounding in his chest like a hammer.

'Food!' came a gleeful voice from behind them. It was Raymond, who had returned victorious with his entourage of assistants, each one armed with enough food to feed the masses.

'And wine!' he added, raising the bottles high in the air.

They had managed to acquire a rug and basket, as well as plates, glasses and a big bunch of flowers which had been arranged in a donated jam jar which was subsequently placed in pride of position on the rug.

'Were the flowers really necessary?' inquired Charles.

'Oh yes,' replied Raymond in a deeply serious tone of voice, while beginning to pour everyone glasses of wine. 'A feast table *must* be decorated with flowers.'

Charles was about to correct him - 'technically it isn't a table' - but Mrs Ashmore nudged him gently but firmly and shook her head. Ethan was just about to eagerly accept the proffered glass of wine Raymond was holding out to him when Mrs Ashmore speedily intercepted it, ignoring the young boy's deeply disappointed face.

'No,' said Mrs Ashmore firmly. 'Definitely not.'

Ethan, who had opened his mouth to protest, shut it again grudgingly, but brightened up a few minutes later when Raymond surreptitiously passed him his own glass so that he might try it.

'No wine for me thank you,' said Abigail in her best bay-windowed accent.

'Don't worry,' remarked her father in passing. 'You have to be at least ten years older before I let you drink wine.'

Abigail glared at him as he passed, but she was smiling again before long.

'How long have you both been here?' asked Cara eagerly, taking the plate of sandwiches which Mrs Ashmore offered her.

Raymond answered first. 'Just over a day. We docked in the South, in Folkestone, last night. I only just managed to persuade Aiden to spend the night in an inn. He would have ridden until dawn to get here if I had let him.'

He looked despairingly at his friend who shrugged off the comment lightly.

'I would have had the doctors after me!' Raymond exclaimed with a laugh.

'Doctors?' repeated Cara anxiously, turning her golden head to face her brother, her blue eyes open wide with ill-concealed concern.

'Don't worry,' said Aiden reassuringly to his sister, clasping her hand affectionately. 'I am in perfect health - Ray can vouch for that.'

Cara looked dubiously at Raymond who was nodding his head vigorously whilst reprimanding himself for not being more guarded.

'Oh, but where have you been?' Cara continued, pacified for the moment. 'And how did you get leave from your regiment to come and see us?' She took a sip of wine and awaited his answer eagerly.

'I won't be going back,' responded Aiden slowly. He

fixed his eyes on Eleanor and his gaze was soft but intent. 'I'm giving the ownership and responsibility of my estate and regiment to another. The one I desire is here, not in France.'

Eleanor's eyes opened wide as the full realisation of that statement sunk in. Cara's mind meanwhile immediately went from A to Z in a matter of moments.

'Oh, but then I can live here forever! Can I not live with you and Eleanor? And Remonde would have to come and live with us. And you must stay here too!' she added to Raymond. He blinked owlishly, at a loss as to what to say.

'Charlotte!' said Remonde reprovingly. 'You cannot invite people to *live* with you on other people's behalf!'

But Cara was too much elated to take any notice. She simply seized the lady's hand and squeezed it joyfully.

'But why?' asked Eleanor disbelievingly. 'Why would you do that for me? I didn't ask you to give up anything. You don't have to throw all that away for me.' She said this because she was completely overawed.

'I would do so much more, for the love of a princess,' Aiden responded. And he spoke with such heartfelt sincerity that she had no doubt whatsoever as to the truth of his words. Eleanor was rendered speechless; she did not even notice Cara and Abigail's little wistful sighs.

***

Aiden and Ray accompanied the Ashmores back to Felowspring Manor and it was with great reluctance that Eleanor saw Aiden leave.

'I will come again tomorrow, as soon as I can,' the gentleman promised and then, with one last wave, he left, leaving Eleanor in a blissful ecstasy.

CHAPTER EIGHTEEN

Ever After

Just when it seemed that surely the highest level of joy had been obtained, more joyous tidings were disclosed to the occupants of that home. On this particular afternoon, not a full two days since Aiden's return, Mr and Mrs Ashmore gathered their offspring together in the garden, under the shade of the oak tree by the gurgling brook and informed them that they were soon to have a sister. Eleanor immediately received and processed the news in the blink of an eye, faster than a fairy could beat its wings, but her siblings were somewhat slower. For a good few moments Charles, Abigail and Ethan stared blankly at their parents, their innocent faces wearing a rather gormless expression. What could their parents mean? Another sister?

'But I already have two!' thought Charles.

Abigail was the next to understand and she expressed her excitement at this revelation in no quiet way. With exuberantly joyful shrieks she leapt to her feet and for a few minutes, simply jumped up and down, hardly knowing how to express her surprise. Then she began to skip around the lawn, calling to her brothers as she did so.

'Don't you see? Oh, don't you see? We are to have a sister. A baby sister! Mama is to have a baby!' the girl cried.

'She is *pregnant*!' Abigail added, just in case they were still in any doubt. A look of realisation came over little Ethan's face and sparks practically shot out of Charles' eyes as the two boys finally grasped what their parents had meant.

Ethan joined his sister in leaping around before rushing to his parents and treating them each to what he imagined to be a great big bear hug.

Charles sat where he was, clenched his fists and wriggled in his skin, his face the very picture of delight. Then he ran indoors to recover and process this information alone, in the safety of his room. Very shortly he returned, beaming.

'That's really exciting,' he said to his parents. 'Really exciting.' And then he left again.

Eleanor waited until Ethan and Abigail had twirled far enough away and then walked over to her parents, her eyes shining and her steps practically floating above the ground. She kissed first her mother and then her father and then stood before them and released a sigh of supreme satisfaction.

'Oh, I am so unbelievably happy!' was all she could say and it was all that was necessary, for that was the truth.

'You're positively glowing at the moment, do you know that Lea?' her father remarked.

'That's because he has sun-shined my being,' she replied simply.

'Anyone home?' called a voice from behind them and Raymond and Aiden strolled around the corner of the house and into view.

'Ah, there you all are!' exclaimed Raymond, waving cheerily.

Cara and Remonde also made their appearance shortly after, walking through the open parlour doors. Cara, seeing her brother, affectionately greeted him. He embraced her before wrapping his arm around her shoulders and leading her and Remonde over to the corner of the garden where they had set up camp for the day. Raymond was sprawled on the grass and Ethan was seated very close to him, eyeing his sword enviously. Abigail rushed forward and grasped Cara and Remonde's hands, pulling them away from Aiden energetically.

'Guess what? *Guess what?'* she cried gleefully and pulled the two women round in circles. '*We're going to have a baby sister*!'

Cara and Remonde both gasped and turned to look at Mrs Ashmore with eyes and mouths wide open. Mrs Ashmore laughed.

'It is quite true!' she assured.

'*Oh, c'est merveilleux!* How *wonderful*!' cried Remonde, raising her bony hands into the air in celebration, and she rushed forward to congratulate Mrs Ashmore, wrapping her arms around her neck. Everyone around them, Cara included, looked on in astonishment and one by one they fell about laughing.

***

A little later Aiden quietly led Eleanor to one side.

'I'm going away again in a couple of days, to France,' he said to her in a low voice and Eleanor's eyes flew to meet his, wide with anxiety.

'Why?' she questioned, trying to sound composed and calm, but her voice betrayed the panic which her heart felt.

'I must settle everything in Cardieu. I must explain to my men why I am leaving them and I must confer with the new owner; there are still many details to discuss.'

'Oh,' Eleanor replied and nodded. 'I see.'

'Aiden!' Raymond interrupted as he strode over. He clapped his friend on the arm. 'Let us have a duel.' He was already tearing off his jacket and cravat, both of which he tossed to the ground unceremoniously. Remonde tutted and hurried forward to pick them up but

Cara beat her to it. The young lady speedily lifted the garments from the grass and neatly folded them.

Aiden grinned at his friend. 'Very well,' he answered and he too proceeded to remove his jacket and cravat. He passed them to Eleanor who, after arranging them neatly, clutched them in her arms as Cara had done. Charles and Ethan both rushed into the house to tell Elizabelle to come and watch. Soon their audience settled themselves around the open lawn which was to be their field.

Aiden and Raymond drew their weapons and assumed their starting positions, swords clasped firmly in front of them, knees slightly bent.

'That's called *en garde,*' Cara whispered informatively to Eleanor and Eleanor nodded wordlessly. With a joint cry both men sprung forward, steel clashed upon steel, and the fight began. The men ducked and swerved, first facing this way, then the other. They fought energetically, baiting each other, playing to each other's strengths and weaknesses; they were both skilled swordsmen and had trained together often. Swiftly they parried and swerved, striking with the flat and then retreating. Charles and Ethan sat cross-legged on the ground, not more than a metre away from Raymond and Aiden's feet, entirely engrossed in the duel. The adults were sitting on garden chairs a little further away and Mrs Ashmore, Remonde, Abigail and Elizabelle had to keep looking away and stifling screams as the lethal blades spun, whirled and clashed speedily in front of them, often barely missing the men's faces. Mr Ashmore and Francis (who had quietly walked up to join them) were, on the other hand, immensely enjoying the contest. With a sudden burst of speed and energy Aiden, as Raymond lunged toward him, parried the stroke, brought his sword up vertically and deftly wrapped it around Raymond's blade, jerking it towards himself suddenly. Raymond's sword flew out of his hand and landed, quivering, point down in the grass a few metres away.

'Disarmed!' cried Charles exuberantly and he sprang forward, picked the sword up and carried it reverently to Raymond, presenting it to him as the bishop might present the crown to the king. Raymond laughed.

'Well fought!' he praised.

'You too,' replied Aiden with a grin to match his friend's.

Aiden grabbed Raymond's outstretched hand and they embraced before stepping back to face each other, swords now returned to the sheaths around their waist. They bowed respectfully - thus ended their fight - and the onlooking spectators crowded around them with shouts of admiration and excitement. Cara and Eleanor brought cold beverages to the two men who gratefully accepted them, downing them in one long drink, their faces still gleaming with sweat, their breath ragged.

After dinner that evening the men departed. Raymond and Aiden first escorted Cara and Remonde back to their house and then proceeded to pack what little they needed, saddle their horses and ride through the night so that they might take the ship to Cardieu the next day.

***

'Why are you forsaking us?' cried one French soldier indignantly, after Aiden had gathered his men together in the courtyard of his estate to inform them of his permanent departure. All the men murmured and grumbled in agreement.

'No woman is worth that!' the man cried out again.

'This one is,' replied Aiden with a small smile, answering in perfect French. Aiden always chose to speak to his men in their native tongue, even though his education and upbringing had been in England. Upon his return to Cardieu after his mother's death he had immediately adopted the native language, choosing to speak English only to Raymond, who could speak very little French, and to Cara, who at the time could speak only French.

Aiden assured his men that they were not being abandoned; that they would be looked after.

'We know you'd never abandon us!' called one young man, pushing his way to the front. 'I'm happy for you! You deserve all the happiness in the world. If you ever need anything Lord, I would be glad to serve you.' And the young man bowed down on one knee.

And one by one, like a wave, every man present joined the young soldier in dropping down onto one knee and respectfully bowing their heads, adding their pledges to his.

Raymond, who was observing everything from a distance, shook his head wonderingly.

'How do you do it?' he asked Aiden a little later. 'I can barely get my butler to willingly make me a cup of tea!' But the question was a rhetorical one.

Aiden had also guaranteed that the household staff, who were currently, and had been for many years, responsible for upholding his estate, were cared for. He had spoken kindly but very firmly with the new owner, a French marquess, and impressed upon him that the staff were under no circumstances to be dismissed, unless they should wish it.

'Yes, *Seigneur*,' the man had replied obediently and Aiden had nodded, satisfied. He then visited his young cousin, who greeted him with a cry of delight, throwing aside her parasol and flinging her arms around his neck.

The two friends were in France a fortnight and only when everything had been entirely settled did they return to Mayhaven.

***

A day after his return from France Aiden rode out on Jo with Eleanor on Fay, first galloping around the fields where the sheep were being pastured, before branching out and setting off in the direction of the village.

As they rode past the neighbouring fields, awash with golden wheat, they saw a man struggling along the road side with a heavy load on his back. His feet were shoeless and he had nothing but an oversized shirt draped over his thin body and a pair of baggy trousers hitched around his waist. The clothes had undoubtedly fit him at one time, but lack of food had wasted him away until he appeared not much more than a skeleton whose bones were mercifully covered with skin.

Eleanor looked down at him pityingly but Aiden halted Jo, flung the reins to Eleanor and leapt lightly off the horse. Walking up to the man they conversed for a long time while Eleanor watched and waited, holding the two horses steady. Fay impatiently pawed the ground and Eleanor reached forward to pat the mare's silky neck soothingly. Leaning her head against Fay's mane Eleanor strained her ears to catch any part of the conversation but they conversed in tones too low to be understood from a distance. Eleanor's eyes opened wide in surprise as she saw Aiden remove, not only his waistcoat, but also the gold signet ring he wore on his finger, which had been bestowed upon him by the King of France.

Eleanor looked at him questioningly as he finally strode up and swung himself into his saddle, his face grim and set. Aiden did not speak but took the reins from her wordlessly and they proceeded to swiftly ride into the village. Here Aiden bade Eleanor to wait with Fay and Jo while he made several enquiries and purchases. Many of the people who saw Aiden as he purposefully strode in and out of the various shops bowed respectfully as he passed, before muttering excitedly behind their hands to each other; everyone in Felowspring now knew that he was a French prince.

A little while later Aiden emerged from the bakery with numerous packages tucked under his arms, just as the man, now wearing Aiden's waistcoat, trudged into the village square. The haggard man's eyes scanned over the numerous people who were walking, milling and shopping around the square. Upon seeing Aiden he hurried forward. As he drew closer Eleanor could see that his condition was even more pitiful than she had first observed from afar. The man's hair was as dry as straw, and matted and tangled beyond belief. Originally golden, the colour of his hair was now indistinguishable under the grime which caked, not only his face, but his entire body. The man's feet were calloused, torn, bruised and congealed in blood. But despite his appearance he firmly held out his hand to Aiden with all the manners of a gentleman. Aiden grasped it tightly and shook it.

The man clasped his other hand over Aiden's and his Highland voice broke as he spoke: 'I cannot repay you, you know that? At least not right now. But if ever I can, I will.' And the man spoke earnestly, his voice trembling with feeling.

'I don't desire any repayment,' replied Aiden and handed the man the first package.

Slowly, gingerly, the man unwrapped the contents and held up first a crisp, clean pair of shirts, then several cravats, a pair of breeches, a navy waistcoat and finally a fine coat complete with a top hat. The next package contained a pair of shoes and the next was a brown bag full of freshly baked buns, still warm. The man had not stopped shaking his head since he received the first package from Aiden and even now, as he took out a bun and bit into it, his head still shook.

'If you should desire to stay here after all, I'm sure Mr

Ashmore would be able to find you a position,' Aiden offered and Eleanor nodded her head vigorously in agreement, not knowing what to say as she watched the man ravenously devour the warm roll.

'No Sir,' replied the man through a mouthful of bread. 'I have to go back, it's all I've wanted these past three years.'

'Very well then,' said Aiden and he passed an envelope to the man. 'This contains the money for your fare, besides a little extra. You can give it as a gift to your wife and child when you find them.'

The man accepted it with a trembling hand, and just stared at it for a moment. Then he stood up very tall and straight before Aiden. He bowed courteously and Aiden nodded his head in acknowledgement. The man then turned to leave, his head held high and shoulders pulled back; and he now appeared to be a full head taller than when they had first encountered him trudging along the roadside only a few short hours ago. The bag he carried with him was now slung almost carelessly across his shoulder.

'What's your name?' called out Eleanor and the man turned his head.

'Phillip!' he called back, his voice clear and strong. 'Phillip Camden.'

Eleanor rushed forward, hurriedly untwisting the string of pearls from around her neck, and she pressed them, with her shawl, into the man's hands. After some protests he reluctantly accepted them.

'For your wife,' Eleanor explained.

Phillip bowed his head gratefully. 'Goodbye Lady,' and with a final bow to Aiden the man left and was soon out of their sight, lost amongst a crowd of people entering the square.

Fay and Jo were waiting patiently where they had left

them and at first neither Aiden nor Eleanor spoke as they rode home.

'Why was that man in such a terrible state?' inquired Eleanor as they slowly rode past the Layton's estate.

'He was offered a position in the North - work with food and lodgings provided. He had no money with which to care for his wife and young child. They were on the brink of destitution.'

Eleanor nodded. Aiden continued, his voice grave:

'Their dire situation forced him to accept the work and so he left his family. He travelled across the country to the North but when he arrived, with many other men who had also been driven there by desperation, their lodgings were a single room in which they were forced to sleep, with barely enough room to turn over; and their food was such meagre rations, hardly sufficient to provide them with the energy for their hard labour.'

'But that's terrible!' Eleanor cried, utterly appalled and scandalised at what she was hearing. 'Did no one do anything about the situation? Did they not protest against the injustice of it?'

'Phillip told me that some did,' replied Aiden, his mouth set in a grim line. 'But no one dared to again.'

'How did he escape?' asked Eleanor, horrified. Her eyes were wide with consternation, but she nodded for him to continue. They had now reached the estate, but neither was ready to return to the house yet, so they entered the sheep fields again. A few sheep looked up and bleated a welcome, while the remainder of the herd continued their resolute grazing.

They rode in silence for a moment, gently rising and falling as the horses interchangeably trotted briefly, before falling back into a slow walk. Then Aiden answered: 'He broke out one night with a group of other men. But they had no money. What little they had been paid over the past months and years they had been forced to use to buy food so that they might not faint from hunger while working. Penniless but free the men departed, each one in a different direction. Phillip had been walking for five days with no food but what he could scavenge when we encountered him.'

A solitary oak tree stood in the centre of the field. A majestic specimen, the reddish bark of its trunk was deeply gnarled and furrowed, and its far-reaching, leaf-adorned branches encompassed a large area, casting a tremendous shadow in its circumference. They dismounted and the horses galloped a short distance away from them before lowering their heads and beginning to graze contentedly. Eleanor reverently touched the bark of the oak tree and threw back her head; the tree seemed to go on forever, stretching way up into the sky. As the sun shone on the leaves of the tree, it gave them the appearance of being two-toned and the overall effect was beautifully grand. Aiden and Eleanor sank down onto the dusty earth at the foot of the tree and leant their backs against its uneven surface.

'One thing that puzzles me,' she said. 'Why, being a prince, did you take such humble accommodation when you came to Mayhaven?'

'I had no desire to be bowed to or treated as someone of great importance. To live humbly for a while, to embrace the common assumption that I was little more than a shepherd, was a delight.'

'And you still haven't told me,' Eleanor said. 'About what happened.'

Aiden looked down at the earth between his feet and sighed heavily.

'No I have not. But I will, if you really desire to know.'

'I do,' said Eleanor decisively.

'Don't tell Cara,' Aiden added quickly. 'About any of

it. I don't want her to know.'

Eleanor merely nodded. Aiden looked out across the swaying meadow in front of him, the blades of grass rustling like waves, a few bright bursts of colour - wild flowers which were the delight of the butterflies and bees - hidden amongst the green lushness. Aiden watched as a stronger breath of wind sent a dandelion clock flying into a hundred tiny pieces, each seed dancing lazily away on the wind.

'When I awoke, I was in a hospital I did not know. Joshua was by my side; later the nurses informed me he had scarcely left my bed for a week. As soon as I was conscious and able to speak, he apologized fervently. He told me he was fully prepared to take the consequences for his actions, however grim they may be. But it was not in my heart to condemn him. I had no desire to see him suffer any more than he already had, so I forgave him. I think he had already considered his fate sealed, so that, when I told him I would not press charges, that he would not be brought before the magistrates, a heaviness visibly lifted from him.'

'I'm so glad you forgave Joshua,' Eleanor whispered. 'He is not a bad man.'

'No,' replied Aiden with a small laugh, looking down at his feet again. 'The worst thing he ever did was try to take you away from me.'

Eleanor smiled.

'But that,' Aiden continued in a low voice. 'Is something I will allow *no one* to do.' And the tone of his voice sent a glorious tremor down Eleanor's spine.

Aiden gazed across the field a while longer before continuing his tale; Eleanor did not rush him.

'But the pain grew worse instead of better and the doctors told me they could do no more. Joshua had written to Ray while I was unconscious and shortly after he received a reply, requesting that Joshua, with all urgency, see to it that I was transferred to a specialist hospital in France. Ray told him that he would personally be awaiting my arrival at the harbour in Cardieu, a stone's throw from my estate, on the day after tomorrow.

But our ship never arrived in Cardieu. It had sailed unknowingly into the very eye of a storm which had been brewing for some hours and, in the dark moonless night, we struck an outcrop of rock, just as land was in sight. The crew immediately sent out distress signals and we were close enough to the mainland to be seen, but only a few fishing boats were able to respond. In the panicked rush to board the boats I was separated from the doctor who accompanied me. I never saw him again; I was one of the few who made it onto a fishing boat. As soon as the keel of the boat scraped the sand I was whisked away to the nearest town where Ray and two of my men sought and found me. I awoke again several days later in my own bed, where I was being treated by my own doctor and a friend of his, a physician, one who specialised in war wounds. They later told me my wound had become inflamed and infected, but after only a couple of days in their care I felt my energy return and the pain subside.'

'My recovery was somewhat hastened by a newspaper article Ray reluctantly showed me, which told the tale of the storm and the pitiful few survivors; most of the passengers onboard had perished in the wreck. Upon seeing my name among those listed dead I was seized with an urgency and relentless desperation to return to you. I assume, as I was nowhere to be found among the survivors on the beach, they supposed me dead. Ray tells me the paper has this week printed a subsequent correction to the list, though I doubt anyone will read it; such an article is hard enough to stomach once. I would have travelled that very day if Ray and the two doctors had not bodily constrained me. I remained in bed only under the condition that Ray secured us both passage to England as soon as obtainable. A few days later we sailed, stopping only one night in Folkestone before coming here. We arrived at the house and Elizabelle informed us you were in the village. Many people pointed us in the right direction until I found you.'

A long silence followed Aiden's tale. The two of them looked out across the meadow for some time. As the wind shook through the mighty branches of the oak tree above them, the shadows cast by its leaves trembled slightly, dancing on the ground in front of them. Then Eleanor spoke:

'You went through all of that pain because of *me*. You risked yourself for me, that night in the woods. It was my fault. And after everything you had been through,' here Eleanor shuddered. 'Shipwrecks and storms and… and *horror*, still your first thought was how you could return to me. You could have stayed in France with fortune and power, but you didn't.'

Aiden turned his gaze from the swaying meadow and looked steadily into her eyes, his gaze unwaveringly fierce, and yet still so gentle, a beautiful contradiction. And he repeated to her the same words he had spoken that day by the willow, when he had returned to her: 'I would do so much more, for the love of a princess.'

Eleanor was once more silenced by his words. Then a sudden thought came to her.

'But you said you were a shepherd!' she exclaimed indignantly. Aiden shrugged his shoulders offhandedly.

'I am, at heart,' he replied.

'That's not the same,' retorted Eleanor, narrowing her eyes at him, but he just laughed.

'Forgive me, My Lady, for not being entirely explicit with you,' he responded in a serious voice, his head bowed slightly, but there was laughter all over his face.

'I might,' Eleanor replied haughtily, but here she broke into fits of laughter.

'And *do not* call me My Lady!' she firmly commanded, seizing a handful of grass and flinging it at him. But the wind snatched the blades away before they could reach their target. Aiden too seized a handful of grass but Eleanor sprang up and leapt away playfully, skipping through the grass like a young doe. Aiden gave chase. With a little scream and many giggles Eleanor ran off and they chased each other around the field. Aiden had almost succeeded in wrapping his fingers around her waist when Fay trotted up and came to a whinnying halt in front of them. She pawed the ground and shook her mane enthusiastically.

'I think she wants to join in!' cried Eleanor delightedly and she leapt onto her back. 'We'll race you,' she said mischievously, leaning forward to pat the mare's neck as she urged Fay forwards. Aiden cried out indignantly in

protest but then laughed and swiftly leapt onto Jo's back and galloped after the escaping horse and rider.

***

Charles had thought two sisters rather a lot and had just about come to terms with the addition of a third when, a few short weeks later, Mr Ashmore threw out a rather revolutionary statement at breakfast.

'You know Olivia,' he began, addressing Mrs Ashmore but knowing very well that, in reality, he was addressing his entire family, who had all stopped chewing and were waiting for him to continue.

'You know, I really don't see why Cara, and Remonde naturally, do not come and live with us - here. They are already such regular visitors to the house and, although they are too well-bred to confess it, I am sure they must feel, on occasion, lonely in that house. Quite frankly it seems to me simply the most reasonable, logical, sensible and pleasant thing to do. Wouldn't you agree?'

Mrs Ashmore put her coffee cup down slowly.

'Well, Cara certainly fits into the family. Why, ever since I first met her at the Winter Party I have treated her as my own daughter. And she has truly blossomed since she came to Mayhaven and, although I would never want to sound arrogant, I cannot help thinking that we as a family may have played some part in achieving that improvement in her.'

'I am sure no one would blame you for stating that my dear,' agreed Mr Ashmore.

'And Remonde is also most agreeable, especially now that she has relaxed into Mayhaven life,' added Mrs Ashmore, and her husband nodded his agreement.

So far everyone else had remained silent, unusually so, for they were very eager to see how their mother would react to the suggestion. But now Mr Ashmore turned to his offspring and asked them for their opinion, which they readily gave, with much enthusiasm and excited shouts.

'Cara will be my sister, won't she Papa? And Remonde… she can be my aunt!' cried Abigail.

'Elizabelle, will you be able to quite cope with the addition of two more people to the household?' asked Mrs Ashmore as Elizabelle made her way around the table, gathering empty plates and cups together.

'Two or twenty, makes no difference to me,' she replied cheerily. 'I'm happy to cook for whoever you would like me to and I shan't feel overwhelmed, I assure you. It's my pleasure.'

Mrs Ashmore stood up and kissed Elizabelle fondly on the cheek and Abigail hurried around the table to wrap her arms around the older lady's waist.

'You're so lovely!' exclaimed Abigail affectionately.

This sent Elizabelle into a fluster and she bustled out of the room, clutching her tray tightly.

In short, the suggestion was exceedingly approved of and unanimously voted a good one and so it was settled. Miss Cara Langlois, or perhaps she should now be referred to as Miss Cara Edwards, and Miss Remonde Bucheron would, if they were agreeable to the suggestion, come and live with them.

The proposal was proposed without further ado and, after Remonde's instinctive '*Oh non*, we could not possibly!' had been violently hushed by all, the two ladies gladly accepted the offer and immediately began to make plans. And so it was that Charles gained yet another sister.

Raymond continued on in Aiden's house 'just for the meantime' he said, but nobody believed him or expected him to ever leave Mayhaven.

***

A couple of days later, before they had even breakfasted, Eleanor opened the front door to find two young men standing on the doorstep, both ashen-faced. They were dressed in mottled colours of the forest and their skin was tanned darkest brown from the sun; they introduced themselves as Joshua Ayles' brothers. They handed her a note, not much more than a scrap of paper, on which was written the news that Joshua Ayles, soldier and volunteer in the militia, had died in combat during an uprising last week. The men explained that Joshua, before he left Mayhaven, had bade them to immediately inform an 'Eleanor Ashmore who lived in Felowspring', if anything should happen to him.

Eleanor wept bitterly and grieved for many days.

***

Aiden and Eleanor were married on Midsummer's Eve, in the garden of the Ashmore home; all of

Felowspring were invited to the feast to celebrate with them. Together Elizabelle, and Maurice, whom the Laytons gladly spared, oversaw the culinary preparations. Abigail and Felicity took great joy in selecting and arranging flowers for the tables whilst Francis transformed the garden into a veritable paradise of blooms, adding his own special touch by clipping the yew trees into the shape of two horses rearing. Aiden had entreated Raymond to be his best man and bestowed upon Charles and Ethan, his two new brothers who were already dearer to his heart than any blood brother could be, the great honour of drawing swords to create an arch for the bride and groom to walk under. On the wedding day Mrs Ashmore was in her element, conversing with so many of the guests that by evening she was quite hoarse. Mr Ashmore, in giving his daughter away, discovered that he was even more attached to her than he had realised. Cara and Hailey were maids of honour, Remonde smiled more on this day than in the past ten years put together and Mr and Mrs Layton brought enough gifts for every single wedding guest. In the interests of avoiding a rumpus, the dog Rumpus was confined to Mr Ashmore's study with a large new bone to compensate him.

In short, it was the most beautiful wedding Mayhaven had ever known.

***

'Can't we just run away?' Eleanor asked Aiden one day.

'And where would we go?'

'Anywhere - it doesn't matter as long as I'm with you. Just… let's run away. Please, come away with me.' And so they did. It was not that they wished to leave their family, nor that they were unhappy in Mayhaven, it was simply a deeper yearning. A longing to run - not away from something - but to something more.

They were of course terribly missed. But soon the people of Mayhaven began to describe them as the sun prince and the moon princess, who had ridden away over the faraway fields one night, into the setting sun - just like in the stories - and the thought was such a happy one and conjured up so many pleasant imaginings that people rejoiced for them and forgot to be sad.

A little over a year later the two of them returned to Mayhaven, bringing with them Philip Camden and his family, and together they founded a school for boys *and* girls. The French prince Aiden and his bride Eleanor finally settled in a modest cottage in Felowspring, where they entertained the highest and lowest in society, their open hearts and noble manner inspiring those around them to love and to dream, and to live beautiful lives.

THE END

If you would like to connect or find out more about me, my book and what inspires me, please feel free to visit my website: https://moveswithgrace.net

www.blossomspringpublishing.com

Made in the USA
Middletown, DE
15 February 2021

33072390R00163